TRAM ANGEL

by

WALTER SIEWERT

TRAM ANGEL

Published by HeartBeat Productions
Box 633
Abbotsford, BC
Canada V2T 6Z8
email: heartbeatproductions@gmail.com
604.852.3761

Printed in Canada

CONTENTS

THANKS

I would like to thank all the guys at work for letting me use their names and pictures to complete my bucket list book. It's great to be able to work and live half my life with such a great group of guys like you. Thanks so much.

I also want to thank Anita and Stefani for your contributions to the book, they really blessed me.

I would also like to thank you Ty for your sketch of Sam and the scroll that you created for the book.

And lastly I would like to thank my family for their encouragement and help in getting my first bucket list book written.

PROLOGUE

Every little boy has a dream of being a superhero of some kind, whether it be Batman, Superman, Spiderman, 007, or Jason Bourne. Every boy lets his mind wander and daydream to another time, to another place, where he becomes the hero of his own imagination... a place where he gets to stand up in front of a cheering crowd of people who appreciate and adore him. Unfortunately ninety-nine percent of the hopes and dreams of young men eventually come crashing down around them.

Soon they are smothered by the life of the mundane with the duties and the expectations of others. Their dreams of heroism turn into the nightmare of paying the bills and working a six day week. Life becomes a repetitive ritual of the same old things day after day and boredom finally sets in.

Every man needs a dream in his life. Every man needs a purpose. Every man needs an adventure, something different from the ordinary.

Yes, that's how I would describe the seven men in this story; ordinary, yes very ordinary. As a matter of fact so ordinary that each one of them through different circumstances found themselves flying to northern Alberta in search of something different, something to get them out of the mundane that surrounded them. Something to help pay the bills a little more easily. Something different was better than no change at all.

First, let me introduce Kevin Conrad.

Status: Married with a wife and two children.

Former Occupation: restaurant and pub owner and is currently one of the Saskatchewan Rough Riders' biggest fans.

Kevin is also the foreman on Team B of the Tram Operators. For those of you who don't know what a tram is, it has been described as a giant green-headed snake slithering through a maze of steel pipes and tanks. This green headed snake makes sure the two thousand construction workers get to work on time and back to their places of residence in the evenings. The head of the snake is a diesel-propelled, four-wheel-drive John Deere tractor, followed by the body of the snake which is made up of three nine-meter-long trailers built to haul people. It's almost like a subway on wheels weaving and slithering its way through the ever-expanding work plant.

Then we have Edmond D'eon.

Status: Married with a nine-year-old daughter.

Former Occupation: Lobster buyer and fish cutter.

Edmond's hobbies and pastimes centre around horses, swords, and knife-making. He is the Tram Operator of Tractor # 7.

Then we have Mike Street.

Status: Married with one daughter.

Former Occupations: Hunting Guide and Rodeo Clown.

Mike still loves to do farrier work on the side and tries to fit in gold panning, fishing, and boating whenever he's not on his iPhone. Mike is the Tram Operator of Tractor # 5.

Then we have Rob Reimer.

Status: Married with two daughters.

Former Occupation: Auto body man and mill worker.

Rob loves to make people laugh and make work enjoyable. When at home, Rob's passions seem to be home renovations and flying his F-16 Fighter Jet (it's a remote control F-16). Rob is the Tram Operator of Tractor # 6.

Then we have Cory Mott.

Status: Single but living with his girlfriend. They have no children.

Former Occupation: Forest Fire Fighter and Crew Leader.

Cory loves anything to do with the outdoors. Hunting, fishing, hiking, and camping, just to name a few. I guess that's why he was nicknamed "Nature Boy." Cory is the Tram Operator of Tractor # 2.

Then we have Raymond Marten.

Status: Currently single with two children.

Former Occupations: Youth worker and Oil Fields Worker.

Raymond's passions are golf, playing his drum, and singing at as many Round Dances as he can get to. Raymond is the Tram Operator of Tractor # 1.

Then there's me, the writer of this book, Walter Siewert.

Status: Married to Lisa with four children, two in university and two still at home.

Former Occupation: Health Care Worker for twenty years.

I love anything to do with the outdoors and totally enjoy doing "fun and exciting things with the family." I have been given the nickname Wally Bear. I am the Tram Operator of Tractor # 3.

In the eyes of most people here at work, I guess I would be defined as "fairly religious" and I suppose that would be the case. But in order to move forward into the story of this book, I need to go back in to my own history just a little bit to pave the way for you the reader. Yes I would confirm that I am "fairly religious." From the first Sunday after my birth I started attending church regularly with my parents. I grew up in a home where faith was commonplace and church attendance was a must.

During those early years I was one of those boys in the neighbourhood that seemed obsessed with adventure stories and also with being the hero of those stories. Not a day would go by during the spring, summer, and fall, without living out some kind of adventure in or around the lakes, orchards and mountains where we lived.

My bike's name was 'Lightning Bolt' and it carried me over hundreds of miles of incredible journeys every summer. Shoes were only worn on Sundays, public events, or at school. We built rafts, swam, hiked, biked, hunted, fished, built forts, climbed mountains and spent endless days exploring caves with gas-soaked rag torches.

Those were the good old days for me, when mom's only words after breakfast were, "Make sure you're home before supper." I loved those words because I was free and the rest of the day was mine, to do anything that my heart desired.

In my teens, my adventures slowly began to take on different shapes, forms, and ideas. My two-wheeled bicycle got traded in for a four-wheeled chariot called a truck. It didn't take me long to figure out that a person could have many new and exciting adventures with high speed travel at their fingertips. I won't go into the details of my escapades, but I'm sure anyone reading these pages could easily fill in the blanks.

In my graduation year I was determined to send myself on what I thought would be the adventure of a lifetime. The year was 1977 and my sole purpose in life was focused on moving up to Northern Alberta to strike it rich in the oil fields. To this day I'm not sure why I made that decision but in my mind I was on my way there already.

Here is a direct quote out of my 1977 grad yearbook which I penned when I was seventeen years old, "Going up North and making some money are in Walter's plans but he hopes he doesn't have to stay in Osoyoos to earn it". I had a get-rich-quick scheme in my mind but it was not to be. For whatever reason that I can't even remember, my Fort McMurray dream turned into a nine-to-five job pulling boards off of a greenchain and working in different sawmills to make ends meet.

After several years of the mundane, my spirit of adventure

seemed to somehow survive. I decided to travel and see the world and do some volunteer work while I was at it. My journeys took me to the Dominican Republic to help rebuild houses that had been destroyed in a hurricane.

Next, I found myself in the mountains of Guatemala helping to build a church in an obscure village at the end of a dirt road. Then I moved on to Mexico where I worked in an orphanage and helped build houses for poverty-stricken families. Over the next few years I continued to combine my love of adventure with a helping hand for those less fortunate. I loved my new field of work but that was about to change drastically.

On my last trip out of Mexico in 1988 I met and fell in love with my soon-to-be wife, Lisa. We were married in May of 1989 and little did I know at the time that an adventure of a lifetime awaited me after I said those two little words, "I Do."

But of course as anyone who is married knows, everything changes after you say those two small words "I Do" and everything did change. During the first eight years of marriage we had four children in our tiny house, lots of diapers, and lots of bills.

After eighteen years of marriage, working at the same job, and with a busy growing family, I was looking for a change of pace. In my mind just about anything would do so long as we could pay the bills. A friend of mine had been talking to me about coming up north and driving a tram. I didn't even know what a tram was at the time but I was certainly ready to give it a try. I was willing to try anything. Yes, a new adventure and I was definitely ready for one.

So almost exactly twenty years to the day, I left my health care career behind and stepped onto a plane headed for Ft. McMurray. I was headed into a world I had only dreamed and written about almost thirty five years ago when I was seventeen years old. With this brief telling of my life's history, let's move on - into the story.

CHAPTER ONE

ELEVENS

The alarm clock shattered the silence, its screech jarring me awake as it ended a dream that I couldn't really remember anyway. Another short night had come to an end as I pushed the switch of my battery powered alarm clock. I had six minutes to collect my thoughts and get out of bed or try to slip back into unconsciousness and let my second alarm clock wake me up. I chose the former and threw the blanket from my body, swinging my feet over the edge of the single bed and onto the carpeted floor.

I waited for a moment with my eyes still closed and then headed over and turned off the alarm on the second clock that was about to go off in two minutes. "Just two days left" I thought to myself, before my fourteen day rotation ended in the oil sands of northern Alberta. Then I would be back on a plane heading home to see my family. Two weeks in and two weeks out was not a bad shift to work at all. It gave me six months at home every year and a decent pay cheque on top of that.

After getting dressed in my three by four meter room, I stepped towards the door and reached out to open it. The second my hand came in contact with the door handle, my digital alarm clock went off again flashing out the numbers 4:11. Hitting the off button once again I said to myself, "What's up with that?" It wasn't the first time strange things like that had happened to me.

Actually, many strange occurrences of this nature had started happening to me as long as eight or nine years ago. I'm not exactly sure when they started or why they started but all I know is that they did start happening. At some point during 2004 it finally dawned on me that the number 11 was popping up randomly during the course of my day. Maybe my subconscious mind was taking me back to those terrible events when the twin towers in New York City came crashing down on 9/11/2001. Maybe it was because I used to get my coffee at 7 11 before Tim Horton's came into town.

I don't know how or why it started to happen but all I know is that it did that morning. I was about to turn around and leave my room when the hair on the back of my neck seemed to stand up straight. Instantly I felt like there was another presence in my tiny room. As I turned towards the door I was slammed by a blinding light which seemed to drain all of the energy out of my body. I immediately found myself on my knees, then face down on the floor and flat on my stomach. How long I remained there I wasn't sure, but it seemed like an eternity.

My mind began to clear and I started pulling myself to my knees and then pushed myself up onto the bed. I stood upright on my feet and looked around the room in disbelief at what had just happened.

What did just happen? No idea. Had I just passed out? I remembered something similar happened to me in 1992. I had just put my newborn baby Julianne down to sleep in her crib. I walked into the bathroom and BOOM; it was like someone had just turned the light switch off in my body.

I woke up on the floor flat on my face calling out my wife Lisa's name. As she helped me up, I remember having no strength and my body and mind were buzzing like I was plugged into an electrical outlet.

This somehow seemed different. This felt like some kind of an encounter with a living force or something just unexplainable. I turned and looked around the room and I noticed my digital alarm clock was still flashing "four eleven."

Had all of this just happened in the span of one minute or was my alarm clock just malfunctioning? I started pressing the stop button to see if I could get the flashing to stop, but nothing helped. The number 4:11 continued to blink like it was trying to say something to me. I had to leave and get to work but this clock was starting to get under my skin, so I reached for the cord and yanked it out of the wall socket.

Nothing changed. BLINK! BLINK! BLINK went the numbers. I flipped the clock over, opened up the battery compartment and disconnected the battery. "Well that should do it" I thought to myself as I turned the clock upright to set it back on the table. I was in the process of setting it on the table when I looked at it then promptly jumped back in disbelief and tossed it on the table. Without any power source the clock was still flashing 4:11. I locked and closed the door behind me and headed down the long narrow hallway, my mind and my thoughts reeling at the events that had just taken place in my bedroom.

The normal workday crept slowly by, and I began to regain my strength with each passing hour. Returning to my room that evening my eyes immediately searched the table where I had thrown the alarm clock. All was silent and nothing in my room seemed out of the ordinary. Maybe it had just been a bad dream and maybe I should just forget about the whole thing. I had just enough time to get changed and make it to the 7:30 PM church service that happened every Sunday night.

Since I was the speaker that evening, I wasn't sure whether I should mention the events of the day or not. While walking to the meeting I decided I wouldn't tell anyone or say anything because I wasn't sure what had happened anyway. Was it just a random act of coincidence or was there some kind of spiritual significance to it? I had no idea.

The church service went well and everyone seemed to enjoy it. Five of the people who came were regular attendees. One fellow named Matt had come for the first time. After the service ended Matt and I chatted for a while, shook hands and said our goodbyes. Just as he was leaving to go outside and close the door behind him, I called to him and said, "Hey! Sorry I forgot your name already! What is it again?"

"Oh, it's Matt" he responded. "Actually, my full name is Matthew King and I am staying in trailer four, room eleven. See you around!" he said.

As the door closed behind him my jaw dropped open as the reality of what he said hit me like a moving freight train. His name was Matthew King: trailer four, room eleven. Could this really be happening to me?

Matthew 4:11. Could it really be that simple? I couldn't wait to get back to my room to see what Matthew 4, verse 11 said in my Bible. The anticipation of what just happened made me quicken my pace all the way to my trailer.

Locking the door behind me, I quickly hung up my jacket, grabbed my bible and planted myself on my bed. The unplugged alarm clock was still lying on the table exactly where I had left it that morning. I quickly opened my bible found Matthew 4:11 and read it. I don't know what I was expecting but all this did for me was to make things even more confusing.

The scripture reference was a verse about the temptation of Jesus by the devil and about angels coming and ministering to him. My mind moved from hope and expectation, to writing this whole day off as one big unfortunate coincidence.

As I lay my head on my pillow to go to sleep that night, I pushed aside all of the thoughts and events of the day. I smiled to myself as I remembered that tomorrow was "fly day" and I would be on my way home to see my family.

CHAPTER TWO
THE ENCOUNTER

My two week stay at home streaked by like a sprinter doing the 50 metre dash. During my time at home I did a fair bit of introspection on the way my life was going and my journey up to this point. I had an awesome wife, wonderful family and in general everything was going great. I thought about my parents who had both passed away in 2005, my twenty year career in health care and our hopes and dreams for the future. But the one thing that I didn't want to think about seemed to follow me around and vie for my time and thoughts.

I simply could not deny that the number 11 seemed to play an unusual role in the day-to-day activities of my life. Once I realized what was happening, I seemed to notice it more and more on a daily basis. Along with this strange occurrence, other large events in my life seemed to follow the same pattern. One example of this was that, on November 11, 2004 at 11 am my father called me into his study and said he wanted to have a chat because today was his birthday.

He benevolently gave me his blessing on that day because his own days on this earth were coming to an end. He was slowly dying of bone cancer and he was uncertain how much time he had left in this world. His health seemed to steadily deteriorate over the next few months.

On April 1st, 2005 right around Easter time my mother, who was now living in a nursing home, had a stroke and was not able to eat or swallow any more. We watched our mother's life and vitality slowly drain away and 11 days later she passed away.

The funeral was held four days after her death and all of this proved to be a very difficult time for the entire family. Another four days after the funeral my father took a turn for the worse and three days later he was gone also. My father passed away exactly 11 days after his wife of 55 years slipped into heaven.

The year of 2005 was the hardest time that our family had ever experienced to that point. I went to 7 funerals and a total of 11 people that I knew died that year. The number 11 kept on rolling on relentlessly and there was nothing I could do to stop it.

In 2010, just a few months before I moved up north, we got our final pay increase from $19.35 per hour to $20.11 per hour. Did the year 2011 have some significance for me and my family or was this just another chance occurrence in a long string of unexplainable "number" events. These were the haunting thoughts that I was trying to keep out of my head. It was like a bad dream that had been going on for years now. And for what? I was just as clueless now as the day this all started.

My last Sunday night at home had finally arrived and I was packed for my flight back to Alberta the following morning. My plane left from the Kelowna Airport at 7:50 am, so that meant that I had to be on the road from home by 4:45 am in order to catch my flight. My backpack was ready to go so I set my alarm for 4:15 and drifted slowly off into a sound sleep.

In what seemed like only a few moments, my eyes popped open and I sat bolt upright in bed. I looked at our digital alarm clock and it was flashing the numbers that I had viewed repetitively hundreds of times over the past years. The clock read 4:11. I somehow had an interior alarm clock in my body that was wired to the number 11.

"Oh well" I said to myself, "what else is new?" as I slipped out of bed to begin my journey back to the frozen North.

The first three days back in camp went by quickly as all of the tram crew got back into the swing of things. Construction was just booming and we were moving up to 2000 men every day on their commute to work. Traffic was heavy on the road pretty much all day long and very heavy during the peak hours in the mornings and evenings. During these busy times I noticed some odd behavior from people who were driving past my tram.

From time to time instead of waving to me, they would point to my tractor and swerve to the other side of the road a little bit.

I kept thinking to myself, "Is something wrong with my tractor? Is a tire loose or something?"

I asked Rob and Mike to drive by and check things out on my tram, but neither of them could see a problem anywhere on my tractor.

The following day one of the construction workers walked up to me while I was sitting in my tractor and said, "Hey buddy, what's that strange light reflecting off the box on the front of your tractor?"

I looked at the tractor and then at him and said, "What are you talking about, I don't see anything."

The man then shook his head and walked away mumbling something that I couldn't understand.

The following day after our morning tram run, Raymond came up to me and said, "Hey Walter, there's something strange going on with the generator on your tractor."

"So what do you see?"

"Well, it kind of looks like a reflecting light but when I get closer it looks like it has some kind of a shape to it."

"Are you serious? I've had a couple of other people tell me that they saw some kind of a light or something on top of my genset. This is really weird. Do you still see it?"

"No, not right now" came the response, "but I will tell you if I see it again."

That evening as I lay on my bed I reflected on the events of the day. I thought about Matthew 4:11 which had happened about 3 weeks ago and wondered if these two things could be connected somehow or was I just slowly losing my mind.

Half a world away in the tiny village of Abad in the province of Khuzestan, Iran, located on the northern tip of the Persian Gulf, thirteen men sat nervously awaiting the arrival of their Supreme Commander and Chief.

The conference room in which they were sitting was located in a massive bomb shelter that could house at least 75 people for up to two years. The bunker lay fifteen meters directly under the village centre and could be accessed from two different locations.

The entire village only existed because the Supreme Commander wanted it to exist. He had a plan for its future and vowed nothing would get in the way or stop his will from coming to pass.

The group of thirteen met in this conference room regularly at six month intervals to plan the strategies for the following six months.

This, however, was an unscheduled meeting and that could mean only one thing. Something significant had gone wrong and someone was more than likely in big trouble.

Beads of sweat formed on the foreheads of many of the thirteen sitting around the table. Nervousness may have been the cause or perhaps the fact that the bunker always seemed to be 4 or 5 degrees above the normal temperature.

The group of thirteen came from a variety of backgrounds and geographical locations, but the common trait that seemed to link them all was a blind allegiance to their supreme leader. All the men were extremely wealthy and all of that wealth had come directly via the hand of the one they almost worshipped. Money had no influence among the men in this room. The only thing that carried any weight was summed up in one word and that word was loyalty. Loyalty was the only thing that kept all of these thirteen men alive.

My alarm clock went off at its usual time of 4 am. After turning it off I sat on the edge of my bed and with one hand I turned on the light that hung on the wall and with my other hand I turned off my alarm clock. After waiting a minute or so for my mind to clear and my eyes to adjust to the light, I reached out and put my reading glasses on.

Then I picked up my Bible which was sitting on my dresser and set it on my lap, opening it randomly. Its pages fell open to the book of Judges in the Old Testament. The story I read was about Gideon who was portrayed as one of the heroes of the faith and was a ruler of Israel for forty years.

I started to read in chapter 6 and when I got to verse 11 my mind ground to a complete halt. As I stared at the page in front of me it turned a dazzling white so all of the words on the page disappeared except for the first few words in verse 11.

These were the only words that I could read on the entire page, "And the angel of the Lord came and sat..."

It was as if I were in a trance. My eyes could not move off the words on the page and my body would not respond to what my mind was telling it to do. After a minute or so everything came back into focus and the clock turned to 4:03 am.

What was happening to me? Was I really going off the deep end? After our 4:30 am tool box meeting, we all went out to our tractors to do our morning runs. Cory went first, followed by Rob, Edmond and Mike, with Kevin following behind in his pick-up truck.

All of a sudden I heard a tapping on my glass door. I looked down and saw Raymond stepping up onto the stairs. He said, "Hey Walter, can you see what's happening on top of your generator?"

I looked but could see nothing out of the ordinary.

"Don't tell me you can't see it" Ray said.

"I don't see a thing anywhere."

Ray climbed down the ladder and I followed him out and walked to the front of my tractor. I climbed up onto the heavy, dusty steel bumper. Although I could see nothing, I began to feel the strange sensation that I experienced in my room just before the blinding light hit me.

Without warning, a blazing white light struck me in the chest and I was thrown backwards off the tractor and landed in the dirt on the seat of my pants. Looking to my right I saw Raymond right beside me face down lying in the dirt motionless. As I looked upwards to the front of my tractor all I could see was a brilliant light radiating from a man sitting on my number 3 gen-set box.

As my eyes began to adjust to the light, its brilliance seemed to decrease slightly and what I saw sent ripples of fear right to the soles of my feet. I saw a giant man sitting with his legs crossed and holding what looked like a scroll or something in his right hand.

"Don't be afraid," the man said. "I have appeared to you for a reason which will be revealed shortly to you and your friends. Be at peace. Remember, I am always here for you."

With my eyes wide open I saw this man, who I would guess to be at least ten feet tall, slowly disappear into the dark cool of the morning.

CHAPTER THREE

EVIL LIVES

The side door of the conference room opened, and a sixty-something man walked in and headed towards his place at the head of the table. All thirteen men rose and gave a slight bow as he approached this seat of honor.

Although he was in his sixties, Donald King hardly looked a day over fifty. He was in excellent health and physical condition from years of regular exercise and nutritious eating habits. His natural hair was still jet-black with just a touch of grey and the clothes he wore complemented the way he carried himself. As he took his seat at the far end of the oval-shaped conference table, all the other thirteen waited until he was completely seated before they sat down.

Nobody was quite sure exactly where or when Donald King was born. Although he grew up in the very town that lay fifteen meters above them, no records were kept in the village files, so the exact details of his life were only known in generalities. His father, it was rumoured, was a high-ranking German officer who had been a personal adviser to Adolf Hitler in the last years of World War II. After Hitler's death and the fall of Germany, Donald's father, whose full name was Heinz Donald King, fled to Iran before the roundup of Nazi officers began. He soon met and fell in love with Miriam Pejman, a beautiful raven-haired dark-eyed woman who worked for meager wages in a small corner store run by her uncle.

After the war, times were hard everywhere, including Iran. Although Heinz King was willing to work hard, he still couldn't find any meaningful employment to support himself or his new-found love. After one month of being together with Miriam he decided to move several hours east, where new interest in the emerging oil industry held some hope for jobs that would actually pay decent wages.

The day he left was the last day that Miriam ever saw him. With no news from or of Heinz in the past two months and rumours of Nazi hunters roaming all over Iran looking for foreigners from Germany, things appeared bleak. The reality that Heinz may never come back grew stronger with each passing day, but in the fourth month of Heinz's absence two things were becoming very clear to Miriam. The first was that Heinz was probably never coming back to the village of Abad and the second was that she was now going to have to raise the baby she was carrying all alone. Nothing could be worse in the culture that she lived in than to be a single Muslim woman raising a mixed-race child. Her future did not look bright and Miriam knew it.

Five months later she gave birth to a beautiful, dark-haired, fair-skinned baby boy in the tiny bedroom where she lived behind her uncle's store. The only redeeming thing for Miriam in her situation was that her uncle was a good-hearted person and was willing to bear some of the shame and scorn that would be surely coming their way from the people of the village. To make matters even worse, Miriam chose to honor the memory of her lover and name her newborn son with the middle and the last name of his father. His full name would be Donald King.

Donald King's childhood years proved to be painfully difficult at the best of times. Going to school was a nightmare for Donald. The other children of the village would taunt him relentlessly over the color of his skin, the absence of a father, and worst of all, about his name. He grew to hate the name Donald and would only respond to people if they referred to him as Don.

Throughout his childhood years, his mother Miriam loved him desperately, but she noticed that there was a very dark side to Don. When he became angry or frustrated, his countenance would change and a dark presence that was almost palpable seemed to surround him. This darkness of the soul became so evident that even Miriam was convinced that her child was being controlled, to some degree, by another power.

When Don was 12 years old, one of the school children was making fun of him about his pale skin. Donald turned, pointed, and looked directly into the other boy's face and said "Cursed be the skin on your bones." Within a week the boy's skin began breaking out in pus-filled boils and within two weeks the boy was on his deathbed.

Having witnessed this, Miriam pleaded with Donald to take off the curse. It was only as a result of her persistence that Donald relented and did what she asked. The other boy began to recover that very same day. With each year that passed, the evil within him intensified. He was shunned by the whole village because the people feared the evil that seemed to reside in him.

By the time Don was in his twenties, his whole life revolved around the power that he had over people. He quickly realized that people of influence wanted him and his power on their side and were willing to pay him handsomely for his services. He possessed the ability to bring about whatever was requested or demanded of him by the people around him. If you had a problem Donald and his team would correct it, whatever it involved.

Accordingly, this brutal arm of the Iranian Mafia was born and Don was the number one feared man in his web of terror. His network of "customers" continued to grow but that was not enough for Don. He visualized himself one day being the richest man in the entire world with everyone on the planet bowing to him. During his early thirties he had more money stashed away than some of the oil companies of O.P.E.C. made in a year. Money just seemed to multiply in his multifaceted accounts with all of the oil companies being major contributors. By the time the mid 1980's rolled around Donald was by far one of richest people on the face of the earth. The majority of his wealth stayed in liquid assets.

He never invested his money in anyone else's company but in the scheme of things, if push came to shove, he had great influence in all of them. That, however, was still not enough for Don; he wanted more power and more control so he branched out into the food, water, and beverage industries and became the recipient of billions of dollars annually.

Now in his late 30's Don had become bored with the wealth he had amassed. Somehow he became intrigued with the idea of having a child and living a normal life. He thought that perhaps a family would free him from some of the darkness that seemed to control his life. Over the years he had been only marginally interested in women. The only woman he had any real relationship with was his mother who was now in her mid-fifties and living in an apartment that he supplied. Over the years Don had been physically abusive to his mother and she lived in constant fear of what Don might do to her someday. Don viewed women as very strange creatures and he could not even understand how they survived in this world.

Knowing beforehand that it was a bad idea, he still decided to step over his own self-imposed counsel and pursue his desire to procreate and have a child. Unfortunately this decision created a very large obstacle… he would first have to fall in love with or at least find a woman that he could tolerate.

During the next year he realized the falling in love part could not possibly happen. He had no moral conscience of any kind and killing or maiming was just a part of his job. He would have to resort to "Plan B" and find someone he could tolerate enough to have a child with. And indeed he did. A beautiful dark-skinned Iranian woman named Sonja who surprisingly looked much like his mother did when she was in her mid-thirties. His masterful plan fulfilled, Donald King was to become a father.

Raymond and I peeled ourselves off the ground. We looked at each other in total disbelief.

"What just happened?" Ray said. "How did I get onto the ground?"

"What are you talking about? You're the one who said you saw it first."

"I didn't see a thing" said Ray, "other than a white light and an explosion. I thought your tractor had blown up. What's going on here anyways?"

26

"I'm not sure, Ray, but right now we need to do our morning runs so let's talk later."

I could hardly concentrate on my driving knowing there was an invisible man sitting on the top of my gen-set! I knew right away that this was not a human being but he was an angel from the heavenly realm. I had read about them many times in the Bible and even believed that they existed, but this had been my first physical contact with a spirit being. I remembered his words as clear as a bell "Don't be afraid, I have appeared to you for a reason which will shortly be revealed to you and your friends. Be at peace and remember I am always here for you."

After breakfast Ray and I had a chance to chat in the truck for a few minutes before the guys returned.

"Well," Ray said, "what happened out there this morning?"

Shrugging my shoulders, "I'm not one hundred percent sure but I think I just met a real live angel this morning!"

"What! Are you serious? What did he look like?"

Again I paused for a moment, collecting my thoughts, and then slowly began to speak. "Well, let me see. I'd say he was at least ten feet tall, real big, and I would guess at least 400 pounds. He was wearing pants that were rolled up to his ankles and a kind of t-shirt with long sleeves. He also had a wide belt around his waist and sandals on his feet. I couldn't really tell what color his skin was because there was a brilliant glow around him like an energy field or something. His hair seemed to be very long and it was glowing too. I also noticed that he had something that looked like a scroll that was rolled up in his hand."

Raymond laughed out loud and the only word he could choke out was "unbelievable." Just then the rest of the guys arrived and piled into the truck with their bagged lunches in tow.

As we left the parking lot and headed towards the laydown, Cory gave us a real serious look and said, "So what's up with you two? Let's hear it."

"Well," I said as I looked towards Ray and smiled, "We'll let you know once we figure it out."

CHAPTER FOUR

OFF TO KUWAIT

It did not take long for Sonja to become pregnant. She loved the idea of having and raising a child, but raising it with Don King was a different matter. He was absent most of the time and when he was around, he had no intention of sharing his life with another person. Even though Sonja lived in a beautiful apartment where she was supplied with everything she could ever dream of, Don had already physically abused her and threatened her regularly. She could have anything she wanted except a loving relationship with the father of their unborn child.

As the time came closer for Sonja to give birth she seemed to become more irritable and demanding of Don. The one thing Sonja wanted most of all was to meet Don's mother, and up to this point Don was unwilling to permit it. Don knew that it would eventually happen anyway, so he relented and personally took Sonja to meet his mother.

The two women immediately took a liking to each other, and it didn't take very long for a bond to form. Three weeks later in Sonja's own private hospital room a beautiful healthy baby boy was born. Sonja thought that maybe with the birth of their son, Don's cold heart would open up a little bit and he would let her into his life, but that was not to be.

Don was a man who was driven to succeed and would stop at nothing until he arrived at his goal of becoming the most powerful man in the entire world. He was already well on his way to achieving some aspects of his goal, but other elements of his plan remained elusive. The birth of his son Matthew, or Matt for short, put a smile on Don's face for only a short period of time. It seemed like he was wrestling with constant inner turmoil and the dark side of Don always seemed to gain the upper hand.

Trying to please Don was very difficult for Sonja, so instead of putting her energy into her relationship with him, she was happy to take young Matt to his grandmother's house where there was always lots of love to go around. Sonja totally enjoyed their visits with Miriam and the bond between the two women resulted in a close friendship and the sharing of hearts.

The years crept slowly by and during one of Sonja's visits, when Matt had just turned five years old, Miriam appeared especially distraught. After several minutes of small talk between them, Sonja just came out and said, "Talk to me please Miriam, what's wrong?"

Miriam burst into tears as she told of her recent visit to the doctor and his diagnosis of aggressive liver cancer. According to the doctor she only had a few short months to live, and she had not yet celebrated her sixty-fifth birthday. So far Sonja was the only other person that she had told about her condition, and telling Don was totally out of the question, for the time being at least. Miriam's desire for the last weeks of her life was to go on a short trip with Sonja and Matt, before the cancer began to slow her down. Purposefully, she arranged to take a short three-day trip with her daughter-in-law and grandson to a coastal resort in the country of Kuwait, which was just across the Northern tip of the Persian Gulf.

Although Don was not in favour of the three of them making this trip he finally relented and gave them permission to go. Just to make sure the two women would comply and stay compliant with the conditions he set out, he ordered one of his operatives to follow them wherever they went and report back to him daily. Before the week was out, Miriam, Sonja and Matt boarded a jumbo jet for the tiny country of Kuwait.

The first day in Kuwait was lovely for the threesome. They enjoyed time at the beach where Matt played in the sand and the water for a good part of the afternoon. During this time the ladies had a chance to enjoy one another's company and relish the time they could still have together.

In the evening the three of them had a wonderful meal together and tried several new dishes that were totally new to them. They talked leisurely, enjoying the evening, until they noticed Matt's eyes beginning to get heavy with sleep. Returning to their hotel room, Matt was happy to crawl into the king-sized bed and get lost under the covers.

As the women talked late into the evening, Sonja sensed that Miriam was carrying a very heavy emotional load just under the surface of her calm composure. Of course she realized it was probably the cancer beginning to take its toll but somehow it seemed like it was more than that. It looked like Miriam had a burden to unload that she had been carrying for a long time.

Early in the morning on the next day before the sun had even begun to rise, Miriam stood at the side of Sonja's bed and gently shook her awake. Sonja's eyes slowly opened and as she looked up she saw the streams of tears that were flowing down Miriam's cheeks.

"Please get up and follow me," Miriam whispered as she led her to the balcony that overlooked the gently rolling ocean waves. "I need to talk to you" said Miriam as she poured them a cup of tea and they both sat down on the balcony. "I need to tell you things that I should have told you over five years ago" said Miriam, and for the next two-and-a-half hours she poured out her heart and soul to Sonja about what her life had been like after she had become pregnant with Heinz King's child.

She went into great detail about the formative years of her young son Don and about the darkness that seemed to grow in his heart each and every day. She told stories that were not only hard to believe but unimaginable to the average person. Sonja did not say a word as she listened carefully to story after story about this boy growing into a man. In reality, however, she knew she was hearing the story of a young boy evolving into a monster without a conscience. There was something truly evil that resided inside Donald - something that seemed to consume all of the good and nourish only the evil.

As these stories and descriptions came to an end, Sonja sat speechless with tears running unchecked down her cheeks. For the next few minutes both Miriam and Sonja were lost in their own thoughts, unaware of the presence of a five-year-old who

31

had silently entered the room to announce to the world, "I'm hungry."

Smiles replaced looks of concern and with a quick swoop Sonja lifted her son, squeezed him in a big bear hug and between giggles replied, "So let's go fill that empty tummy right now."

Downstairs in the hotel's lobby, Donald's operative was bored and tired. Why was he sent to follow two women and a little boy around? It felt like a demotion to him, but he knew that loyalty to Donald paid his bills and set him up nicely.

Just as he was walking into the hotel restaurant for some coffee and a quick breakfast, Miriam emerged from the open elevator door. She had come down from their room to make a phone call using the pay phone when she noticed the same man entering the restaurant that she had seen loitering around the lobby the evening before when they had returned to their rooms. Maybe she was correct in thinking that Donald had sent one of his men to follow them! As she proceeded to make her call on the pay phone she also kept her eye on the man seated in the restaurant across from her. Perhaps she had also been right not to trust the security of the phone in their hotel room. She had known that Donald had been monitoring her calls in her apartment for the past several years and she would not be surprised if the same was happening to Sonja in her home. Today was the day that Miriam would have to share her plan of escape with Sonja. Would Sonja be willing to risk the life of her and her son for a life of freedom from Donald? Today the decision needed to be made.

32

CHAPTER FIVE

STRANGE OCCURENCES

As the day wore on I wondered to myself why only a few people saw something on my gen-set but most people didn't. Were some people more in tune with the spirit world than others or was it just a gift some people had to see into the next world?

From some of the stories that Raymond had told me I just assumed that he was one of those people. First of all he totally believed in the spirit world and he said that many of his dreams and visions had spiritual significance. I knew that Raymond believed me when I told him about what I had seen, but what about the other guys on our tram crew? I had no idea about what they believed or even if they believed in a spirit world. I decided that I would keep my mouth shut for the time being, at least until I had more proof. Ray agreed with me, so for the next little while this would have to be our secret.

The first Sunday of our two week shift rolled around as I finished preparing my notes for the upcoming church service that evening. I wondered who would show up and was even more curious to see if Matt was still around and if he would come to church that evening. Well, my curiosity came to an end when only five of the regular attendees showed up. That was OK though, because we had a good evening together and enjoyed one another's company.

I was the last person to leave that evening after straightening out the room and getting all of my stuff into my backpack. Just as I was walking towards the exit door, it opened from the outside and Matthew stepped into the room.

"Hey Matthew! How's it going?"

"OK I guess" he responded.

"I was wondering if you were still around here?"

"Yes I'm still here but I'm not exactly sure how long I will be around."

"Oh, what's up, is your company almost finished its work around here?"

"No, it's a little more complicated than that and that's why I came tonight. Could we talk somewhere privately?"

"Absolutely." I said. So we went back into the church room, closed the door, and Matthew started to share what had been weighing on his mind.

For the rest of the morning and even during lunch both women remained fairly quiet, trying to sort through the conversation that had taken place earlier. Sonja was attempting to digest all the things that Miriam had told her.

Miriam, on the other hand, was wondering how she could pull off her plan with one of Don's men watching their every move. Early in the afternoon Miriam approached Sonja with a warm smile and said to her softly, "could we please talk again as soon as Matt goes down for his afternoon nap?"

"Yes of course" Sonja said, "we do need to talk don't we?" After Matt had used the king-sized bed as a trampoline for the last 15 minutes, Sonja joined him there and made a few bounces with him herself. She loved her son desperately and was a great mother to him. She had decided years ago that she would do anything she could to protect Matt and keep her son safe. After tucking him in under the covers for his afternoon nap, the ladies went out onto the balcony again to talk.

Miriam started the conversation by saying that she loved Sonja like she would have loved her own daughter. Over the past five years the two women had forged a mother-daughter relationship that ran deep within both of them. It was because of that relationship that Miriam knew she must be honest with Sonja and reveal her true motives for the three of them being on this trip together.

Day after day over the past five years Don had steadily walked down his own path of destruction. The darkness inside him seemed to increase as the years went by and only a shell of a human being remained. Words like love, sympathy, and compassion meant absolutely nothing to him any more. Don was at the point where even his handsome five-year-old son could not bring a smile onto his ever-darkening face. Don had become a walking dead man on the inside and each day that passed seemed to push him deeper into the abyss.

Both Miriam and Sonja had seen his progression into the darkness and both had begun to fear even for their own lives. When Miriam had finally revealed to Sonja the reason they had come to Kuwait and that her plan included escaping from Donald, Sonja was more than willing to listen.

Miriam's original plan was very simple. She had been thinking about it over the past three years and was now ready to carry it out. She had saved and exchanged her Iranian currency for ten thousand US dollars. That was the legal amount you could carry on a plane without declaring it. She had also bought some diamonds that she had sewn into the seams of some of her clothing. At least with these it would be enough to get a new start somewhere else in world.

The plan was good except that two things had changed in the past few days. First of all she now had cancer which would most certainly kill her within a few short months, and the second problem was they now had one of Don's operatives watching every move they made both day and night. They would have to come up with a new, modified plan within the next 24 hours before their plane was scheduled to leave for Iran.

Matthew started off the conversation by saying that he was a Muslim and was brought up in the Muslim faith. He told me that he wasn't sure why he had come to church three weeks ago but was glad that he had. He said that he had a story to tell me about what happened to him three Sundays ago.

He began his story by telling me he had just walked out of the dining room when his attention was drawn to a poster on the bulletin board inviting people to come out to a church service that very evening. He said he looked at his watch which read 7:15 pm and then looked at the poster again which said that the service started at 7:30 pm. As he started to walk away something occured that had never happened to him before. Whether it was in his head or whether he heard it with his physical ears he wasn't sure, but a voice clearly and loudly said "Go! Go to that service tonight."

He was in total shock as he turned and looked around to see who had spoken to him. After making a complete circle he realized that nobody was around him and that no person had spoken to him. The event so shocked him that he decided to follow the command of the voice just to see how things would play out.

"And that's the reason I came here three weeks ago" said Matt. "I still don't know what the voice was all about so I thought I might talk to you about it."

Well, Matthew really got my attention with his story. The only thing I could think of to respond with was to tell him a story of my own. I recounted to him what had happened to me over the past few weeks and especially about the part of him telling me that his full name was Matthew King and then saying he was living in trailer 4 room 11. After I had finished telling my story we both just sat there for a minute or two thinking our own thoughts. Things beyond our control were happening to both of us and neither of us had any answers.

As Matthew got up to leave, he said to me, "Could I come to the church service next week even if I'm a Muslim?" I laughed and said "Of course you can come and I promise you that none of us will try to change what you believe, but we will be studying some scriptures out of the Bible." So with that we both went our separate ways leaving with more questions than we had answers for.

I know now that this encounter with Matthew was more than just a coincidence. There was something going on around us that was bigger than anything that we could see. There were forces at work that were shaping the world we lived in and leading us down a path into the unknown.

Both ladies slept very restlessly that night. It was almost impossible to turn their minds off since they only had one more day to come up with a plan that would work.

As the sun rose over the Persian Gulf, its streams of light shone through the bedroom window and onto Matt's face. Sonja was awake already and noticed the light beams dancing on the face of her son. As she looked at the light she thought to herself, "He has the face of an angel." and she offered up a quick prayer to Allah that he would be gracious to them and give them a way of escape.

Just then Matt let out a big yawn, stretched his arms over his head and sat up next to his mother. "Good morning my precious son," Sonja said, "how are you doing this beautiful morning?"

Without any response to her question, Matt simply said four words that ended up changing the course of their lives.

He said, "Mama, where is Canada?"

After a brief explanation of where Canada was, Matt happily skipped out of the bedroom and began his day.

"Yes," Sonja thought to herself, "yes, why not Canada?"

She knew almost nothing about Canada other than its geographical location. But why not? Maybe this was an answer to the prayer she had uttered only moments ago.

Maybe Allah was showing them their way of escape. The thought excited Sonja as she slipped through the bedroom door in search of Miriam. As Sonja entered Miriam's room she realized that Miriam was nowhere to be found and her bed did not even look slept in. "Where could she be?" Sonja wondered.

Having made breakfast for Matt and herself, she walked out onto the balcony to enjoy the sights and smells of a resort town that was just waking up. For the first time in a long while she actually felt excited about what the future might look like for herself and her son. On the other hand, she realized that breaking away from Donald may bring her world crashing down around her. Just thinking about the wrath of Donald caused her mind to freeze up and she immediately broke into a sweat. Sonja pulled her thoughts back to the present tense and then looked down at the face of innocence in the smile of her son. At that moment in her mind there was only one direction to follow and there would be no turning back for them or for Miriam.

CHAPTER SIX

THE SCROLL

Monday morning arrived with my mind spinning in several directions. First of all, I wondered if the angel that I saw on my gen-set was always sitting there. Then I wondered if I could summon him or communicate with him whenever I wanted. Did he have a name? Many thoughts and questions came to my mind for which I had no answers. When I had finished my morning runs, the sun was already above the horizon and its brilliant hues on the clouds proudly boasted nature's creativity. With my stomach growling an early morning wake-up call, I was already contemplating what I was going to have for breakfast as I climbed down from my tractor and headed towards our laydown trailer.

For some reason I turned around and looked at all the trams parked next to each other. My tractor, #3, was located right in the centre of the group of seven. As I looked back, a movement on the top of my gen-set caught my eye. Since I was twenty or thirty metres away from my tractor already, I couldn't quite make out exactly what it was!. Whatever it was started rolling across the top of my gen-set box towards the edge but stopped short of falling off! Pondering what it could be, I turned and started walking back towards my tractor to investigate the strange sight. When I was within a couple of meters of my tractor, suddenly the object started rolling again, but this time it went right off the edge.

Lunging forward, I stretched my arm out and caught it in mid-air before it hit the ground. "What is this?" I thought to myself.

As I opened up my hand, a flash of recognition descended. This looked like the exact same tube or scroll that the angel was holding when I saw him the last time. It was about 30 cm long and seemed to be made out of a heavy, coarse paper. As I stared at it in wonder, the reality hit me that I was standing here holding something that had come from the hand of a real live angel.

At that moment I felt like a little boy who had just found something of great value and wasn't quite sure what to do with it. I wanted to open it immediately, but I resisted the temptation until I had more time to examine it. Carefully I put the scroll behind my tractor seat, then headed for the trailer to go for breakfast with the guys.

The morning crept by slowly with no sign of Miriam. Sonja began to worry, letting her mind wander to places where it should not go. Just before 12 noon the doorknob to their hotel room turned and in walked Miriam. Sonja ran to her with arms outstretched falling into her embrace. Sonja had been worried and was crying, thinking that Miriam was in some kind of trouble since she had been out all morning.

Miriam gently led Sonja over to the couch and the two of them sat down together. Miriam was smiling and in hushed tones began to tell Sonja what she had been doing over the past several hours. The previous night had brought Miriam very little sleep. She felt responsible for the lives of all three of them and she knew she must come up with a plan today. First of all she had to know for sure if the man she had noticed twice downstairs was one of Don's "spies".

At 6 am she had slipped downstairs to see if the familiar face was anywhere to be found. After having no success in locating the man, she thought that maybe the two sightings were just coincidence and that perhaps he was just a guest with the hotel. If that were the case, she thought they could continue with their original plan and never return to Iran again. But just before going back upstairs to crawl into bed again, Miriam decided to go back outside for a breath of fresh air.

She walked out of the hotel lobby's main doors, and as she turned the corner to the right she almost collided with a man that was walking and talking on his cell phone. The man did not notice Miriam walk by him, but she certainly did notice him. It was the same man she had seen twice before and now she had just seen him again. Her heart started to race as she quickly turned into the next available doorway entrance and tried to follow the man with her eyes.

As she watched him walk down the sidewalk, his pace gradually slowed until he was standing in front of a car parked in front of the hotel. With his right hand still holding the device to his ear, his left hand reached down and slowly opened the car door. He sat down behind the steering wheel and continued talking to someone.

Miriam was not sure what to do, but decided that she needed to get closer to see if she could hear what the man was saying. After putting her headscarf and sunglasses on she approached the car, relieved to see that the window was partially open and she could hear the man still speaking. She slowed her pace and listened intently as she passed the open window.

All of a sudden the phone crackled and a voice echoed through its speaker sending a chill of fear straight through Miriam's body. It was the voice of her son Donald.

She didn't have to question herself any longer... this was definitely one of Donald's operatives and he was here to make sure the three of them made it back to Iran safely.

Miriam's thoughts began to run wild. What would they do now? How could they escape with this man following them? She knew their plan had to change but she wasn't sure how to make that happen. Miriam continued to walk down the street until she found a small bakery that was open. As she stepped inside, the enticing smells of fresh coffee and freshly-baked bread filled her senses and a smile found its way onto her face.

She sat down and ordered. She was determined not to go back to the hotel room until she had come up with a plan of action. Her mind raced through many different scenarios and she even considered killing the operative herself, but of course that would never happen. She knew that she could never kill anyone, but on the other hand she also knew that this man would kill her without giving it a second thought if Donald told him to. Donald's men were all loyal and would have no issues at all with killing all three of them if Donald commanded it.

The hours slipped by and yet Miriam had no concrete plan. Her body felt weak and tired from a lack of sleep, and this morning she also began to feel a relentless pain from the cancer that was beginning to wrack her body.

She was still without a plan but decided to return to the hotel room because she knew that Sonja would be worried about her. Just as she was about to get up and leave, the door chimes sounded as the front door opened and three people walked into the bakery and stood together looking for a place to sit. As Miriam got up to offer them her table an idea hit her and the idea personified was right in front of her! The two women and the little girl were covered from head to foot in beautiful outfits worn by the traditional Kuwaiti women. Miriam commented to them on the lovely clothes and asked if clothes like the ones they were wearing were handmade or if they could be purchased at a clothing store. After a short conversation, Miriam had the address of a shop not two blocks away from the hotel that they were staying in.

Finally a plan began to formulate in her mind. When Miriam finished telling Sonja her story and mentioning the general details of the plan, Sonja's eyes lit up and she said with a smile "We are willing to try. We are willing to die trying because we will not go back and be with Donald any longer."

I could hardly keep my mind on my work. We all work a split shift every day so three guys are off after breakfast and three of us are off from 12 noon until 3 pm.

As lunchtime rolled around I carefully took the scroll out from behind my tractor seat and gently wrapped it up in a plastic bag and the three of us headed off for lunch. By the time I got to my room I could hardly contain the excitement welling up inside of me.

I was actually in possession of an object that had been in the hands of a bona fide angel only a few hours ago. I carefully removed the scroll from the bag and laid it gently on the bed. I wasn't exactly sure what the correct procedure was for opening a scroll, but I had a feeling I was about to find out.

Miriam and Sonja continued to make their plans of escape. While Matt had his afternoon nap Sonja told Miriam about the answer to her prayer that morning. Sonja told her of Matt's question about Canada and her intention of making Canada their home.

Miriam was thrilled with the idea, but wondered if she would live to see the reality of life in Canada with her cancer worsening daily. Half an hour later, Matt woke up from his nap and began begging his mom to take him to the beach again since it was their last day in Kuwait. Before long all three of them were on their way to the beach. Suddenly, Miriam became aware that the man consistently tailing them was not far behind. About fifteen minutes after arriving at the beach, Miriam decided it was time to put her plan into action.

She left Sonja and Matt sitting on the sand and headed for the clothing store that the two ladies in the bakery had told her about. As the operative watched Miriam leave the beach area, he seemed unsure of on which of the two ladies he should keep his eyes. He made his decision to stay at the beach simply because he was enjoying a cool drink and sitting in the shade. Miriam was pleased with his decision because now she had the freedom to execute her plan without being watched. She headed directly to shop and quickly started searching for the clothes that might suit their needs. After picking out two beautiful full-length dresses and matching head scarves, she realized that the next item she needed would be a little trickier.

They would have to transform Matt into a five-year-old girl in a full length traditional Kuwaiti dress. Buying the clothes would be the easy part, but getting Matt to put them on and wear them in public would be the real challenge.

Once the garments were purchased, Miriam slipped back into their hotel room to drop them off before returning to the beach. There were still many details to work out if they were going to be successful and escape with their lives. Before Miriam had a chance to return to the beach, Sonja and Matt decided they had had enough of the sun and returned to the hotel. As they entered their hotel room and closed the door behind them, they were startled as a colorfully dressed woman exited from one of the bedrooms with her arms outstretched.

"Well," Miriam gestured, "What do you think?"

Poor Matt didn't know what to think as he hung onto his mother's leg casting her a frightened look. Miriam then removed her head scarf so that Matt could see her face and see that she wasn't a stranger. It still took a few seconds for a smile of recognition to light his face in acknowledgement that this was truly his grandmother.

CHAPTER SEVEN

OPENING MYSTERIES

I sat on my bed looking at the scroll from every conceivable angle, my mind racing ahead trying to guess the contents of the object that I held in my hand. My curiosity finally got the best of me, and I unwound the three thin, paper-like ties that encircled the scroll keeping the two rolls together. I slowly pulled the two rolls apart to their full extension and found myself staring at the scroll that was laid open in front of my eyes. But I still had no idea as to what I was looking at.

I saw words I could not read, pictures that made no sense to me, and symbols that seemed to come from another world. As I studied the almost cryptic writing, I did notice some words and numbers that seemed to be written in English. When I looked at the scroll as a whole I noticed that all the different faces in the corners seemed to be looking directly at the image that consumed the majority of space on the paper.

I was looking directly at it when a strange sensation overtook me and I began to get a little light-headed to the point of nearly losing my balance. Either my eyes were playing tricks on me or it seemed like the picture in front of me was actually moving. I'm glad I was sitting down on my bed because as I looked down at the picture, it appeared to be gaining momentum like two wheels going in opposite directions. As my head and body began to swim in dizziness, I forced myself to turn my eyes away from the scroll. The light-headedness I was feeling soon began to dissipate and I regained my balance.

After taking a couple of deep breaths and being silent for a moment, I thought to myself, "What in the world is going on here? And what have I gotten myself into? Things like this don't happen to ordinary people, do they?" As I thought upon the strangeness of what had just happened to me, I took the scroll, rolled it up and placed it gently inside the drawer that was next to my bed. The scroll and the mysteries it contained would have to wait because I had to go for lunch and then get back to work to finish off my shift.

One of the nice things about driving a tram is that once you know your routes, times, and schedules, there are some quiet moments available to you. When we are waiting for our next pick-up we have some time to think or relax or fill those moments with whatever we want to, and of course I filled those moments with thoughts of what my day had brought to me so far. Of course many thoughts filled my mind about the object that was laying in my drawer next to my bed.

Never in my wildest dreams had I ever imagined to be a participant in things that seemed to be literally "out of this world" and totally out of my control. My nature and personality tend to be very fact-oriented and I need information, routine, and control in order for me to function normally in this life.

These last few weeks had been the total opposite of what my normal routine used to look like and it was beginning to wear on me. It seemed like I had no control over my life any more. The things that were happening to me were not based on facts and information but seemed to come from a different world and frankly it was beginning to scare me. For twenty years I had worked with people with mental illnesses and saw the effects of what a mental imbalance can do in a person's life. Was I now on the verge of experiencing a mental breakdown similar to what the people I worked with for twenty years were experiencing?

Was I beginning to hear voices and see and talk to people or angels that were from another world or really did not exist? Was I in the process of losing my mind? Were all the number 11's I had experienced over the past eight or nine years just signs along the way that I was getting sick and needed professional help? These were the thoughts and the questions that were tugging at my mind and demanding clear answers.

As I broke away from these troubling thoughts, I glanced down at my watch randomly and read the numbers 6:11. I guess it was time to head back to the laydown and put the trams down to sleep for the night. For some reason I wasn't that excited that the day was over and that I had to return to my room.

Rob and I walked down the hallway towards our rooms in trailer #7. He turned and said to me, "Is everything OK with you? You seem a little preoccupied today."

"Well," I said, "I do have a lot on my mind lately, and it has been weighing pretty heavily upon me."

"Is there anything that I can do to help?" he asked.

Even though I was desperate to share with someone what was going on in my life, for some reason I held back and simply responded by saying, "Thanks Rob for your concern, and I will let you know what's going on but just not right now." "Anyways," I said, "you have a poker game to go to tonight and you can't be late for that."

"No problem," said Rob as he opened the door to room #42. As I walked past him I opened the next door which was my room #44. All of a sudden Rob called out to me, "Now don't forget where I live." We both laughed as the doors banged shut behind us.

"You look absolutely amazing!" said Sonja as she walked around Miriam, looking intently and touching the garment that she had purchased. "Do you have another one that I can try on?" Sonja asked excitedly.

"Of course" said Miriam, "and I have one for Matt as well."

As the ladies chatted and laughed together with wide eyes and bright smiles, Matt was lost as to what all the excitement was about. All he seemed to be interested in were the cars he was playing with on the floor. After several minutes of fun with his toys, he noticed the two ladies standing in front of him holding up a dress about his size and asking him what he thought about it.

"Why would I think anything about it?" he thought to himself, until his mother asked him to try it on. The reality of what she was saying suddenly hit him hard and he was not impressed. With one swoop he picked up all of his cars and ran towards the bedroom shouting "NO! NO! NO! NO!" and as he entered the room he locked the door behind himself.

The realization hit both of the ladies at the same time that maybe they should have changed the way they brought up the subject of Matt having to wear a dress. How do you explain to a five-year-old boy that you want him not only to wear a dress in your hotel room but you want him to go out in public with it on and walk through an airport dressed as a girl.

For two hours the women tried to coax him out of the bedroom but he refused to unlock the door and all he would say was, "I will not wear a dress, I will not wear a dress!"

The women realized that forcing him to wear it against his will might draw more attention to them and make them vulnerable. They finally decided to relent from making Matt wear a dress and promised him that if he came out he would not have to wear it at all.

Slowly, they heard the door unlock and Matt emerged with a big grin on his face that seemed to say, "I won! I won!"

As the day wore on the weight of what they were attempting to do began to settle in upon them. Instead of laughter and excitement, forced smiles and tension could be seen on the faces of the ladies. The plain truth of the situation was that their plan was weak at best and only luck or an act of Allah would make their plans of escape a success.

Their flight back to Iran was scheduled to leave at 9 am, but they also had tickets to leave on the 8:30 flight out of Kuwait into Turkey. From there they were hoping to disappear into the population of any country where Donald had less influence and then slowly make their way into Canada.

To make their present situation even worse and even more stressful, the questions of a five-year-old boy kept coming. "Mommy, why are you dressing like that? Are we not going home tomorrow? Will we see daddy soon? Will he meet us at the airport? I want to see him, don't you?"

All of Matthew's questions were ripping Sonja's heart and mind into shreds. Was she sure she was making the right decision? Was this their last day in this world together? Uncertainty assailed her with deadly accuracy and a huge sob that she could no longer hold in escaped her lips. There was still time to change their minds. They could still just go back to Iran and pretend everything was OK and normal. After all they were just returning from a few days of holidays.

Sonja's mind was being bent like never before. She had never had to make such a difficult decision and be responsible to bear the consequences of it by herself. What should she do? Her mind felt like a mass of fragmented and disconnected thoughts randomly floating around in her head.

That all changed suddenly when before her stood her son looking straight into her eyes and saying with the clarity of a church bell, "Mom can you please tell me once more where Canada is?"

Without hesitation Sonja swooped Matt into her arms and looked him in the eyes and said, "I promise you not only to tell you where Canada is, but I will take you there someday myself."

CHAPTER EIGHT

TRAM ANGEL

I stood in the tiny cubicle that was my bedroom, and part of me wanted to go directly to my dresser drawer, pull it open, and further investigate the scroll. The other part wanted to turn around, leave my room and never lay eyes on the scroll again. The encounter with the angel on my tram and now having the scroll in my possession had begun to turn my life and thoughts upside-down.

I liked being in control of my life and I didn't like what these encounters were doing to me. Of course my curiosity got the better of me as I walked over to my desk, pulled the drawer open and reached for the scroll that I had placed there just a few hours earlier. I looked down into the contents of my drawer and a wave of anxiety hit me square in the chest as I pulled the drawer to its full extension.

The scroll was not there or perhaps I just could not see it? I frantically examined every square inch of my dresser drawer and to my utter amazement I realized that the scroll truly was not there. Instantly negative questions started to assault my mind.

Had someone come into my room and stolen it? Maybe the housekeeper had cleaned my room and thrown it out? The questions continued assailing me like the rapid-fire of a machine gun. Maybe this whole thing about the angel and the scroll was just a figment of an overactive imagination. Maybe I was having a massive hallucination. Maybe my whole life really was spinning out of control. Maybe I was on the verge of having a mental breakdown myself. Maybe I was truly going insane.

Sitting on the edge of my bed I could feel my heart beating wildly and my thoughts racing randomly in every direction. Not knowing what was happening to me, one clear thought came to mind; "You are in the process of having a panic attack."

Although I had worked in the mental health field and had observed panic attacks and knew what the definition of one was, I had never experienced one myself. So, here I was almost 2000 km away from home, right in the middle of my two-week shift, sitting in my room losing my mind.

Over the years I had helped others get through some of their panic attacks by sitting them down, telling them to breathe in deeply and slowly and I would speak to them calmly with words of reassurance and hope. So that's what I commanded myself to do right there in my room.

I closed my eyes and began to take long, deep breaths and collect my wild and random thoughts, replacing them with short phrases of positive affirmation. I spoke things like, "Life is good, I am truly blessed, I have a wonderful family, I have a great job. Everything is going to work out fine."

As I began to relax and enjoy the words and phrases that I was speaking to myself, my heartbeat and pulse began to return to normal. I started to smile, as I realized that everything was going to be OK. I'm sure I must have sat there for at least five minutes or more as if enjoying the calm after the storm.

When I finally did open my eyes, it seemed like I was in a new dimension of some kind. The room seemed exceptionally bright and even the atmosphere seemed somehow changed. "Wow," I thought to myself, "maybe I should have these panic attacks more often because it sure does feel nice once they're over."

Just as I was about to stand up from my bed a very loud and clear thought overwhelmed me, or was it an actual voice I was hearing?

A calm and other-worldly voice said "Hi there Walter, how are you feeling?" As I turned and looked towards the door, my jaw dropped open and my eyes bugged out of my head. There in front of me standing by my door was the figure of a huge but headless man. I could only see up to the man's chest and the rest of his shoulders and head extended through the ceiling of my room.

As I sat frozen in fear, not being able to move or speak, the headless man spoke again. "Oh sorry about that Walter," and with that he crouched down and knelt on one knee and continued talking.

"Hey, don't be afraid" he said, "we already met a few days ago, don't you remember?" And of course my thoughts went instantly back to the encounter I had with him as he sat on my gen-set. Yes of course this was the same angel I had seen, but now he was crouching on the floor of my room in front of my door, and I had no place to run.

"Why do you want to run?" the angel asked. "I'm only here to talk. You did say that you wanted to talk to me, didn't you? You had some questions that you wanted to ask me."

My sluggish mind went blank and I felt frozen in time. Here I was sitting in front of an angel and had nothing to say.

"Well," the angel said, "how about I answer the questions you asked me just this morning?"

"Wait a minute. I didn't ask you any questions this morning."

"Sure you did, Walter, you asked me four specific questions and I am allowed to answer all four of them for you. Since you don't seem to remember them do you want me to repeat them to you?"

"Please do."

"Well your first question was 'Am I always sitting on your gen-set?'"

"Wait a minute, that was just a thought in my head and not really a verbalized question to you."

"Well I certainly heard it loud and clear and I'm here to answer it for you if you want me to."

At this point I was too stunned to put up an argument. "Please go ahead, I'm ready to listen."

"Well," replied the angel, "to be honest with you I do spend a lot of time sitting on your gen-set because you spend a lot of time driving your tractor. I figured if I sat there at least I wouldn't have to follow you around everywhere, and then actually, you could follow me. Anyways, Walter, if you haven't figured it out yet, I am your angel and I kind of hang out wherever you spend your time."

I was stunned and amazed at his words. I had always believed that I had a guardian angel just like the Bible said, but now the reality of it was hitting me like a 10 ton truck. All of this was real; I actually had an angel assigned to me to follow me through my life.

"Question #2 was 'Can you summon me when you choose to?' Well, I'm never very far away from you and I always know what's happening in your life, so you would never really have a reason to summon me. But, if you're asking, can you summon me and make me appear before you at your will, then the answer is NO. I have only appeared to you today because I have been given permission and was instructed to reveal myself to you. Listen, you are not God and you can't make me do anything. Only God can release me to do His will."

"Wait a minute, I have more questions about question #2."

"Sorry, you should have thought of them this morning if you wanted more detail.

Question #3 was, 'Can you communicate with me whenever you want to?' The short answer is absolutely yes. You can ask me questions or even give me instructions, but I am not obligated or even allowed to respond to your requests or questions unless I have a clear directive from God to do so."

"Please wait a minute, I'm not sure I really understand what you're saying."

"Well, you're right about that. Rarely do any of you humans fully understand what you have been told, it's not uncommon. Do I have a name was your fourth question? Of course I have a name. All angels have names. Some have secret names but every one of us does have a name. Some of our names have been given to us by God and some of our names have been given to us by humans. I have a name but you already know it. You gave it to me several years ago."

"What? What do you mean I gave you a name already?" Before the last word of my sentence had even come out of my mouth I realized I knew his name and I had always known it. "Your name is Sam and you're 'my angel,' and more than that, you're my Tram Angel."

"Good call," said Sam, "I kind of like the sound of that title 'Tram Angel'. There may be some hope for you yet."

The light-hearted look on Sam's face changed as he looked me directly in the eyes and spoke with a kind of solemnity.

"There is one last thing I need to tell you before the fog of your world settles in on you and begins to cloud your eyes and mind. Whatever happens in your life from here on in is supposed to happen. Everyone has a destiny to fulfil and this is yours unfolding before you. Also, what has happened to you already and will happen to you in the near future is very real and has many far-reaching consequences that you may never know about.

By the way, you do not have a mental illness but some people might think that you do because they cannot understand the things that you will be talking about.

This scroll that was in your drawer I now personally put into your hands because it will be your only earthly link to my world and the reality of my world.

Remember the scroll when times of doubt come and remember I'm only a thought and a question away. Remember II Peter 2:11 when you think about me."

With that, Sam stood to his feet and slowly disappeared into the ceiling above my door. His head and shoulders went in first and then finally all I saw were the soles of his sandals disappearing into the ceiling above my head.

I stood dumbfounded, holding the scroll in one hand and steadying myself with the other hand. "I have a real-live angel," I thought to myself, "and I even named him." As I thought back over the years I could even remember the place and the thoughts I was thinking when I gave him his name. What a day this had been! What a roller coaster ride of emotions I had just gone through. With the presence of Sam still lingering in my room, I laid down on my bed, closed my eyes, and just enjoyed reliving this incredible and surreal experience.

CHAPTER NINE

ESCAPE DAY ARRIVES

The first glimmer of dawn stretched itself over the darkness that had ruled the night. Sleep had been hard to come by for both Miriam and Sonja. Both women stood unwavering in their decisions to escape, but along with that came the worry and the stress of actually carrying out their plans.

The plans were simple: leave for the airport early in a cab, go through customs and security, and wait for the 8:30 flight to Turkey to start boarding. Then quickly go to the restroom, put their full-length dresses and headscarves on, and enter the line-up of people heading for Turkey.

The real challenge would come when they would have to slip by Don's operative without his knowledge as they made their way into the line-up that went to Turkey. As the two women and Matt stood anxiously in the descending elevator with their luggage, they turned to each other and smiled weakly.

"Are you ready Sonja?" Miriam asked as she reached over and gently squeezed Sonja's hand. Sonja gave an almost indiscernible nod just as the elevator came to a full stop and the doors in front of them slowly yawned open. As all three of them stepped out into the hotel's lobby, Miriam instantly recognized Don's operative sitting in the restaurant drinking a cup of coffee.

Putting a smile on her face and drawing in all the courage she could muster, she led both Sonja and Matt right past his table and headed for a booth that looked out over the entrance to the hotel's lobby. As the three of them were having their breakfast, Miriam's attention wandered outside to the activities of the resort town that was now waking up. A small line-up of cabs were forming as guests from the hotel would soon begin their pilgrimages to wherever they were going for the day.

The new day shift doorman arrived and relieved his co-worker who had just finished his night shift. Two men were standing by a white van, smoking, talking, and making hand gestures to one another as another man slowly passed by their window sweeping the sidewalk. Yes, the sleepy little resort town was now waking up to another normal day. But for Miriam, Sonja, and Matt, this day was destined to be anything but normal.

Breakfast over, they exited the restaurant and headed for the main lobby doors that lead to the outside. Miriam noticed that Don's operative was carrying a small overnight bag and was ready to go also.

As the three of them neared the first cab that was standing in the line-up, a white van with no windows pulled up right beside them and screeched to a halt. The sliding side door flew open and before anyone knew what was going on, a man grabbed Sonja and Matt and threw them into the back of the van.

Within two seconds he had his hands on Miriam and was dragging her towards the van. Miriam desperately resisted the attack and in the process lost her balance, falling forward and landing face down on the sidewalk. She began screaming for help as the people around her began to realize that something was not right.

As she lifted her head from the sidewalk she noticed Don's operative running towards her with what looked like a gun in his hand. She then saw the white van speeding down the road with Sonja and Matt inside. The next thing she remembered was a hand grabbing her by the clothes and pulling her upwards and a voice screaming "Get up! Get up!"

To Miriam everything seemed like it was happening in slow motion. Once she was upright on her feet again she realized that it was Don's operative who had pulled her up. He was now running flat out down the sidewalk towards his rental car that was parked behind the line-up of cabs. Within seconds the car he had entered was speeding off in the same direction where the van had disappeared only moments earlier.

Everything that was happening seemed surreal. She was standing by herself on a sidewalk in a foreign country with no idea as to what had just happened. All she knew was that Sonja and Matt were gone and she did not know who had taken them.

Visibly shaken, Miriam was led into the hotel lobby by some staff where she sat down on one of the chairs. The distant wail of sirens grew louder until the whole entryway into the hotel was a mass of flashing lights from the police cars and ambulances that had now arrived.

Miriam was quickly put on a gurney and shuttled off into an ambulance that was headed to the local hospital. En route to the hospital, shock began to settle in, draining the color from her face. All that Miriam could remember from that point on was the prick of a needle going into her arm and within seconds her whole world descended into mind-numbing, inescapable darkness.

Tuesday morning went off without a hitch as we finished up our pre-breakfast tram runs. I had time to think about what the angel had said to me and was thrilled with all of this new information. I found it all very exciting, except the part where Sam had told me that people would probably think that I was crazy when I told them about my experience. It was really something to consider.

How do you tell people about an experience that you can't prove and that does sound like it came directly out of some science fiction movie? To be honest, even my own family might find it a stretch to believe. I had just come in from my last run before breakfast when Raymond climbed the ladder and opened the door to my Tractor.

"Hey, how's it going Walter?"

"No problem. I had a great morning run."

59

"Well, guess what? When I drove by you down by the fuelling station, I saw that light on top of your gen-set again."

"Oh really? Is that all you saw? Nothing else?"

I was secretly hoping he would say that he saw an angel sitting there, because at least then I could back up my story with an eyewitness. But that was not to be. All Ray saw was the light and only for a couple of seconds. As we left for breakfast I wasn't sure that I wanted to tell anyone about what I had experienced. Maybe I would just keep this whole thing to myself.

As I was sitting down having breakfast with Rob that morning, he casually said, "So what's up with the light, the man or angel or whatever it is that's on your gen-set?"

I looked at Rob with a kind of stunned look on my face, as I realized that Raymond had probably not kept our little secret of what I had seen on my gen-set. I guess the word would be out now and I would have to figure out what I was going to say.

"Well that's a good question, but to be honest I'm not exactly sure how to answer you." I didn't want to be dishonest with the guys but I also wasn't ready to spill my guts on what I had just experienced yesterday.

"Well, several people have been seeing a light on top of my gen-set, there's no doubt about that. Ray has seen it a couple of times and five days ago both Ray and I got hit by that light and we ended up on the ground on our butts."

"Well what about the man or angel?" Rob asked.

"That's the part I'm not 100% sure about. Ray said he didn't see a thing but I thought I did see someone or something sitting on the top of my gen-set that looked like a huge man."

I didn't want to lie to Rob but I also didn't want to go into detail about what I saw and heard. I tried to change the subject by asking Rob if he believed in angels or in a spiritual world. To my pleasant surprise, he said that yes, he did, but that he had never experienced an encounter with the other world.

As we finished our breakfast and the conversation started going in different directions we realized we were running late and had to get moving. While walking to the boot room it became clear to me that I was going to have to tell the guys something and that it was going to have to happen fairly soon. The only reason I was so hesitant about telling my story was because I didn't have any proof for it.

The only thing that I did have for evidence was a scroll that I couldn't read and had no idea of what it actually contained. I would have to get it translated somehow and even then, would the guys believe me?

No one else had seen Sam in his true form and I couldn't make him show himself to anyone.

As I was walking back to the crew truck, I heard a voice calling my name from somewhere behind me. Turning, I noticed Matt jogging down the sidewalk towards me.

"Hey Walter, How's it going?"

"Pretty good, and how are things with you?"

"Everything is going OK for me, but I was just wondering if we could get together and talk sometime before the Sunday church service?"

"That sounds great to me. How does Friday at 7 pm in the church room sound?"

"That works great for me" Matt responded.

As we said our goodbyes and Matt turned to leave, I could only wonder what part he played in this series of strange events. He was obviously involved in it somehow, so maybe our meeting on Friday night might be another piece of the puzzle. At any rate that would still give me a couple of days to study the scroll and see if I could figure out its meaning or even possibly understand it. "Well, never a dull moment around here" I thought to myself as the crew truck with all the guys pulled up and I jumped in.

CHAPTER TEN

SCROLL REVELATIONS

Miriam had no idea how long she was unconscious and drifting in the darkness. As she awoke from her slumber, all she could think about was that she needed a drink of water. Her throat was parched and so dry that she did not even know if she could speak. As her thoughts began to return to her in clarity, the scene of the kidnapping replayed itself in her mind's eye. With a gasp her eyes popped open, her consciousness returned, and she found herself staring into the face of her son Donald.

Instantly weeping and wails filled the hospital room as all she could say was, "Sonja and Matt, where are they? Where are they?"

Seeing Donald's face hovering over her only seemed to upset Miriam more. As the wails grew louder and louder, the nurses led Don out of the room and tried to comfort Miriam the best they could. "Where are they? Where are they!" was all that Miriam could choke out in her distress.

"Where were they?" was the same question that Sonja was also asking herself. All she remembered was being thrown into a van and a rag being placed forcibly over her mouth. After that her world went dark and she had no memory of any of the events that followed. Although they were locked in this small room, at least

Matt was here safely with her and there was plenty of food and bottled beverages to drink. She had no idea how long she had been unconscious, but just over five hours had passed since she had regained consciousness.

Sonja could not even begin to guess what was happening to them unless this whole thing had something to do with her husband Donald. Matt was no longer clinging to his mother and had decided to check out the contents of the room. To his surprise, he found some toy cars to play with and even a coloring book with brand new crayons. As he slowly began playing with his new found toys, Sonja concentrated intensely, trying to figure out what was happening to them.

Sonja was also extremely concerned about Miriam. The last image she could conjure up was that of Miriam laying face down on the ground screaming for help. None of this made any sense to Sonja. If Donald was behind this why go to all of the trouble in a foreign country when he had access to them any time he wanted? Or maybe they were being kidnapped and held for ransom since Donald was such a rich man.

"Yes," Sonja thought to herself, "that must be the reason that we were abducted." For a moment she felt sorry for the kidnappers because if Donald ever got his hands on them they would wish that they had never been born. Just as these thoughts were rolling around in Sonja's mind, she was startled by the sound of a faint knocking on the door. Immediately, Matt ran into his mother's arms as the door slowly began to open.

Tuesday evening had finally arrived. It was my favorite day of the week because it was steak night in the dining room. After a great meal and a time of conversation with some of the guys, I hurried back to my room full of anticipation. This would be my first chance to actually study the scroll and see if I could figure any of it out. Back in my room I changed out of my work clothes and got into something a little more comfortable. It was exciting for me to finally lay the scroll open on my desk, and take the time to study it.

As I thought back to the first time I opened the scroll, I remembered having a strange sensation that the image was actually turning. I looked down at the open scroll laying in front of me and I marvelled at the words and symbols, wondering who or what had taken the time to create the scroll.

While scanning the scroll, my eyes finally rested on a certain spot that had a familiar meaning to me. I focused on what seemed to be a scripture reference written in English. The writing was at the one o'clock position on the circle on the scroll. As I looked closer to read the inscription, I just about jumped out of my chair. My eyes were not deceiving me! I was reading the scripture reference to Matthew 4:11. Of course I knew exactly what Matthew 4:11 said. I had read it many times over after meeting Matthew King about a month ago.

Here was the connection to Matt that I was wondering about. Although Matthew 4:11 was written on the scroll right in front of me, I still had no idea where all of this was leading. My attention turned to the 2 o'clock position on the circle as the hair on the back of my neck stood up straight.

I could not believe what I was seeing. It was also a scripture verse and I knew exactly what it said. Only a few days ago I recalled sitting in a trance-like state, staring at the scripture verse of Judges 6:11. The only thing that I could see on the entire page were the words, "And there came an angel of the Lord and sat..." And now, here was the exact same scripture reference written on this scroll. In my mind I finished the incomplete message of Judges 6:11, "And then came an angel of the Lord and sat on the top of my gen-set!"

Maybe these scripture references were here to confirm what was going on in my life? Maybe Matthew 4:11 was the confirmation of the first encounter I had in my room over three weeks ago? And maybe the strange encounter Matthew had coming out of the dining room was actually an angel talking to him? To me at least, it totally made sense that angels still do come and minister and reveal themselves to people from time to time.

My eyes returned to the scroll to investigate the next scripture reference. The last words that Sam spoke instantly came to mind. I remembered his words but had not taken the time to look up the scripture reference. Sam's last words were, "Remember II Peter 2:11 when you think of me" and now right here in front of my eyes was the scripture reference to Sam's words.

I quickly grabbed my Bible and began turning its pages towards II Peter. Of course I could not read the writing of the actual words on the scroll but my guess was that it was probably at least a portion of II Peter 2:11, and I was about to find out. I thumbed through the pages of my Bible, finding the verse and sure enough it was a reference to angels, and more than that, for me it was a reference to Sam. It says, "Whereas angels which are greater in strength and might."

"Yes," I thought to myself, "that's exactly how I'm going to think about Sam, as a strong angel and as a mighty angel." As far as I was concerned all three of these scripture references confirmed all the angelic activity that had seemed to be going on in my life over the past several weeks.

Looking down at the scroll at the remaining scripture references, none of them seemed familiar to me in any way. But what I did notice was that each and every one did contain the number 11 except the one on the very top of the circle which said 12:01. As I continued to study the circle image and all the numbers, of course it became obvious to me.

The image in front of me represented a clock of some kind. It had twelve distinct settings like the hours on any clock, ending at 12:01. Well, I really had no idea whether it ended at 12:01 or began at 12:01. All I knew for sure was that the first three scripture references on the clock seemed to confirm what was going on in my life in regards to angels. At least now I seemed to have some scripture references to the last nine hours on the clock, which might give me some clues to their meaning. What an exciting evening I had just experienced here in my own room. Although there were still many more questions than I had answers to, at least a couple of things had become clearer.

The nurses were able to calm Miriam down after a few moments. The wails subsided but she was still visibly distraught that Sonja and Matt were not there with her. After the next half hour or so, the door to her room opened and a well-dressed gentleman walked in and introduced himself as an investigator from the local police department. He made it clear that it was very important that he be able to talk with her as soon as possible and get as much information as he could if they were to have any chance of finding her daughter-in-law and grandson. Miriam concentrated and calmed herself down as much as she possibly could. After an hour of questions and conversation, Miriam doubted that she had given him any helpful information. She, of course, mentioned nothing of Don's operative who had been following them around for the past 3 days.

After the investigator finished his questioning and walked out of the room, Donald advanced towards Miriam through the open door and sat on the edge of her bed. A wave of nausea hit Miriam as Donald's cold black eyes bored into her in an attempt to expose the very thoughts of her soul.

Was this actually her son sitting on the edge of her bed or was it someone else that was just living in his body? Miriam could not stand to look into the face of her own son, and making eye contact with him was even worse. The presence that Donald exuded was dark and evil and Miriam had spent a lifetime watching this persona destroy her son. In her opinion, the man that sat beside her was not even her son any more. The true soul of her son had disappeared slowly over the years and this evil imposter had completely taken over his life.

After several moments of silence, Donald opened his mouth and spoke his first words to his mother. Instead of words of compassion and endearment, they were words of suspicion and accusation. "Well, mother dear," Donald said, "you have been a busy woman haven't you? And now, here you lie in a hospital bed all by yourself with your daughter-in-law and grandson nowhere to be found. Now why is that? Can you explain that to me please, mother dear?"

Miriam had been in this position many times before in the presence of her son. She knew that the only thing that was stopping

Donald from striking her in the face was that they were in public. She also knew that it was only a matter of time before she was back on a plane to Iran with Donald. Little did Miriam realize how quickly her thoughts of being in a plane back to Iran would materialize. She was yet unaware that Donald's personal doctor from Iran was already in the hospital consulting with the attending physician and plans were being made to catch the 10 pm flight out of Kuwait back to Iran.

Miriam knew that it was pointless to resist Donald's questions because she would just end up making things worse for herself. Somehow the thought of having cancer and only having a short time left on this earth comforted her, because with Sonja and Matt gone she had absolutely nothing left to live for. Her only thoughts and prayers were for the two people in this world that she truly loved. And her only prayer from here on in was that Sonja and Matt would somehow stay alive and their dream of starting a new life in Canada could somehow come to pass.

CHAPTER ELEVEN

BACK TO IRAN

The door to the small room swung completely open. Two men entered the room and stood next to each other in front of Sonja and Matt. Although they were imposing figures, there seemed to be an air of respect and order that followed them.

"Good evening Sonja and Matthew," the older and slightly taller of the two said in almost perfect Farsi. "We trust you have been comfortable enough even though the room is small. This must be very difficult for both you and Matt, but we will explain and answer all of your questions as fully as we are able. First of all let us introduce ourselves. My name is Jacob or Jake for short, and this is my young friend and co-worker David. Please believe me when I say it truly is a pleasure to finally meet the both of you. We also want to say that we are terribly sorry about what happened to your mother-in-law back at the hotel. Our plan was to bring all three of you, but with Miriam's resistance and the Mafia man bearing down on us with a gun, we had no choice but to leave without her or we all would have been dead. We truly are very sorry that we failed to get all three of you out safely."

Fear and confusion caused Sonja to erupt into tears but she managed to choke out the words "Who are you and what do you want with us?"

The two men pulled up chairs, sat down and endeavoured to answer her questions as best as they could. Jacob was the older of the two (at 38 years of age) and the spokesman , and David was very young, having just turned 21 a few days ago.

As Jacob looked into Sonja's eyes with compassion he said,

"Let me start at the beginning of a very long story. As you know already, your husband is not only a very wealthy man, but a very powerful and influential man all around the world. His influence and status seemed to grow daily. Unfortunately, he has created a world around him based on fear, cruelty, and terrorism.

Over the past several years he has caught the attention of many other countries that are committed to fight terrorism and bring him to justice. For the past fourteen years I have been assigned to gain as much information as I can on Donald and his activities back in Iran. This also included watching Miriam's movements and interactions with her son Donald. And for almost six years now I have also been trying to gain information about Donald through you and your son.

For the past two years David has been my co-worker and our assignments have been to gain information and try to keep you safe and alive if we possibly can. When we became aware of your plans to escape and leave Donald, we had to do something. Your plan would not have worked and Donald would have probably killed all three of you.

We decided to kidnap you in order to keep you safe, and you know what happened next, and here we are without Miriam. It was our hope to keep you all safe and out of Donald's hands."

"But what will happen to Miriam?" Sonja blurted out, "I'm sure Donald will come for her soon, we have to help her!" Both men dropped their heads and stared at the ground without responding.

Jacob then lifted his head, looked Sonja in the eyes and said, "Donald has been in the country for over six hours and he's already made plans to return to Iran on the 10 pm flight with Miriam. He is also turning this city upside-down looking for both of you along with the help of the local police. Since you have become kidnapping victims, everyone will be looking for you and we can trust no one. You will be safe here for the time being at least, and within the next few days we will get you out of the country."

"Where will you take us?" Sonja asked weakly.

"We have made arrangements and everything is set to get you into Israel. You will be safe there." said Jacob.

Sonja's hands covered her face as she began to weep. What

was happening to her world and what would their futures look like? Mostly, she was thinking of Miriam and the dark future that awaited her.

Miriam sat on the crowded plane on her way back to Iran aware that she was glad for one thing. There were only single seats available on this flight, so she did not have to sit beside Donald or one of his thugs. It gave her time to think about Sonja and Matt and the wonderful five years that she was able to spend with them, but she also thought about just how short life was. Her days on this earth were coming to an end and her hope and desire was that she could live them out in quietness and peace.

As the plane landed on Iranian soil and everyone made their way through customs, Donald did not speak a word to Miriam and once outside, he disappeared into a waiting car that sped away. Miriam was left standing on the sidewalk as another car pulled up to the curb and two men got out to help her into the car.

Miriam watched the road signs go by from the back seat and she realized she was not heading in the direction of her apartment. Where Donald was taking her, she could only guess. With no idea of where she was going, or how long it would take to get there, Miriam closed her eyes, made herself comfortable, and tried to get a little sleep. It had been a very, very long day.

Wednesday and Thursday rolled by fairly uneventfully, and I was beginning to get excited about meeting Matthew later on in the evening. I wondered what was on his mind and also how he fit into all the strange events that were happening around me. I had managed to deflect most of the angel questions from the tram crew, but at some point soon I was going to have to give them the whole truth. Maybe my meeting with Matt tonight might shed some light on what had been going on. I guess I would soon find out.

I arrived at 7 pm in the lounge room that we use for our church service on Sunday nights. Matt was not there yet, but there were a couple of guys chatting and one other fellow reading a book in the corner chair. As I was waiting for Matt, I started flipping through some of the books that were in the tiny library that was in the room. Soon the two fellows talking left the room.

Suddenly the room seemed uncomfortably quiet. It was now 7:15 pm and Matt had still not arrived. Maybe he had forgotten, I thought to myself, or maybe he just got held up somewhere? Just as I was putting a book back onto the shelf, the person that was sitting in the corner chair started to speak to me. I turned to look at him, he stood up and extended his hand towards me.

"Hi, you must be Walter."

We shook hands and I said to him, "Well hi there. Yes, my name is Walter, but I don't think we have ever met before. You don't look familiar to me."

"No, we haven't officially met" he said, "but I have heard a lot about you."

"What do you mean by that?" I asked.

"Sorry about all this," he said. "My name is Dave and I'm a good friend of Matt's. He asked me to come here at 7 pm and meet you and tell you that he was running late, but would be here as soon as he could."

"Oh," I said, "nice to meet you Dave. Do you work with the same company as Matt does?"

"Yes, we do work together, and we've known each other for a long time."

"That's great" I said. "I've only known Matt for a month or so, but he seems like a really nice guy. We were just going to meet here tonight and talk. I'm not sure what was on his mind."

"I'm sure he'll be along shortly."

With that we both sat down and continued to chat. Actually it was Dave who took control of the conversation and steered it wherever he wanted it to go. He would ask the questions and I would answer them as best as I could. After over an hour of talking with Dave, I was getting a little frustrated and tired of where this conversation was going. I almost felt like I was being interrogated so I started looking for an excuse to leave. For someone who I had never met before, I felt he was being too pushy and too direct with the questions he was asking me.

Finally I said, "Excuse me please, but I have to go now, and I guess I'll have to catch up with Matt some other time." As I started gathering up my jacket and backpack, David's phone rang.

"Just wait a minute" Dave said as he held his phone to his ear. While I waited I could hear the person on the other end of the phone speaking in a foreign language and Dave would also answer in that language. After a minute or so Dave clicked off his phone, saying Matt had just called and that he would not be able to make it this evening. He said that Matt also asked if it were possible for the three of us to meet tomorrow at the same time.

I felt like saying to Dave, "I'd love to meet with Matt but I would rather not meet with you," but as I pondered the question for a moment I reluctantly said,

"Sure, OK. I'll be here at 7 pm tomorrow."

As we shook hands and exited the room I thought to myself, "Who is this guy anyways." It felt to me like I was a pawn in someone else's chess match. I did not like that feeling, and I certainly did not like the first impression that Dave had given to me. "Oh well," I thought to myself as I walked down the sidewalk to my room, "maybe tomorrow would bring some answers to the many questions I still had in my mind." I had only two and a half days left in my two week rotation and I sure was looking forward to going home.

CHAPTER TWELVE

THE DREAM

After another hour of answering Sonja's questions, Jacob and David finally left with the promise to return in the morning with any updates on Miriam if they heard anything. The men had told Sonja that she may have to stay in this room with Matt for up to five days and also be ready to go at any time within a few minute's notice.

Matt had fallen soundly asleep during the conversation with Jacob and David. Sonja was thankful and beginning to believe that these men actually seemed to care about their wellbeing. She knew that they worked for the Israeli government in one way or another and it looked like Israel was going to be their new home, for the time being at least. Even though Israel was the sworn enemy of Iran, she had a sense that everything was going to be OK. She also seemed to feel that somehow this must be the will of Allah for their lives.

As she thought of the conversations she had just had with Jacob and David, she was amazed at their apparent honesty. Other than withholding the exact details of who they worked for in the government, they seemed to be holding nothing else back in regards to what they wanted from Sonja and Matt and how they were willing to help them find a new life. She was also amazed at the length of time that she and Miriam had been under surveillance without either of them knowing what was going on. As she sifted through these things in her mind, the thought hit her that these two men who were complete strangers to her had more information and probably knew her better than her own husband Donald did.

As exhaustion hit her, she yawned and settled down in her

bed. Trying to quiet her mind, it felt like her thoughts had been on a race track all day long. Sonja closed her eyes and a picture of Miriam's smiling face filled her mind. She offered up a prayer that Miriam would find strength and hope in the days that lay before her.

Sleep came only sporadically for Miriam as the thud and jerk of the car tire hitting another pothole would jar her awake. As far as she could tell they had been driving for well over an hour, possibly two. She was still unsure of where they were until she caught the image of a small sign in the headlights of their car.

As she read the sign she was taken aback, because the sign read 'Abad 64 km.' Was she actually on the way back to the place where she had grown up and raised her son Donald? If this was their destination, it would be the first time in over twenty years that she would be returning to the place of her youth. It held some good, but mostly difficult and painful memories for her.

When Donald was in his late teens and started making lots of money, he moved his mother Miriam to the apartment she currently lived in, over a two hour drive away from Abad. She remembered that day like it was yesterday and she had never been able to shake the memory of that moment.

After moving her things into the apartment, Donald looked straight into her eyes, shook his finger in her face, and said, "You will never go back to Abad or even have contact with any of the people there again, because if you do, I will kill you myself." It was a memory that haunted her and she could not shake it or forget his words. For twenty years she had never returned or even contacted any of her friends or relatives that still lived in Abad.

Was she now on the way back to the village of her childhood? Why would Donald be taking here there now? Too many questions and not enough sleep fogged Miriam's sluggish brain and not only that, the pain inside her body had grown in intensity as this extremely long day never seemed to end. As the car began slowing down, she glanzed out the window and noticed that they were entering a town or a village of some kind. They turned a corner and continued down the street when a flash of recognition hit her. She was on the same street where she had grown up living with her uncle and working in his store. At this point Miriam was not even sure if her uncle was still alive or if his store and small house were still standing. Memories flooded her as they drove by place after place that she recognized even in the dark. It was hard for Miriam to imagine, but here she was! She was actually in the place of her childhood! She was home in Abad.

Saturday's work day came and went quickly. I was only a day and a half from heading home and my thoughts drifted in that direction. I had not gained any new information from the scroll over the past few days, as far as I could tell. I had looked up all of the English Scripture references, but came to the conclusion that I had no idea what they were trying to say to me.

From the number of words on each scripture reference, you could tell that some were only parts of verses and some were the verse in its entirety. I guess my next step was to at least try and find out what language these were written in.

Since I was totally computer illiterate and did not even own one, I would have to rely on others to help me figure it out. As I was pulling on my jacket, the thought came to me that maybe I should at least take the scroll to my meeting with Matt and Dave. I was secretly hoping that Dave would not show up with Matt that evening because I did not have the greatest first impression with him.

I carefully put the scroll in my backpack, did up the zippers, and headed out my door to my 7 pm meeting. When I arrived and walked towards the lounge door, I noticed that both Matt and Dave were already there and sitting down.

As I walked through the door, both guys stood up, we shook

hands and greeted each other. Before our conversation even got started, Matt leaned forward and whispered in my ear, "Can you please follow us outside for a moment?"

I was a little bit confused about the strange request, but said, "Sure I can," and followed the two of them outside into the parking lot. Once outside Matt turned and said to me, "Sorry about all of this, but I will explain why, if you trust me for just a few minutes."

"Sure, no problem," I said and with that Matt lead me to a 1-ton crew cab truck. He opened the front door on the passenger's side and then motioned for me to get in. Matt then went around to the driver's side and Dave got into the back seat. After the doors closed behind us, Matt turned to me and said, "It's now safe to talk in here." I was not sure what he meant by that, but I had a feeling I was about to find out.

"First of all," Matt said, "I know you already met Dave yesterday and probably didn't get the greatest first impression of him, but we have been friends for over 20 years and he's closer to me than any brother could be. He's really not in agreement with me talking to you here tonight, but I insisted because I don't know who else I can talk to about what I have to say.

Strange things have been happening to me lately and I remember you mentioning that you have had similar experiences over the past month. I don't know where else to turn because I think fate has brought us together for some reason.

To make a long story short, I have been having a recurring dream, or maybe call it a nightmare, over the past week. It is so real and vivid that it wakes me up and I can't get back to sleep. Needless to say I've had a rough work week through lack of sleep and it has really left me physically and emotionally drained. I thought that if I could maybe share the dream with you, that you might have some insight into its meaning."

"Well, I'm certainly willing to listen, but I don't know if I will be able to help you figure it out or not" I replied.

"I get some pretty strange dreams myself sometimes and I don't know what they mean or even if they have a meaning. But go ahead, Matt, I'm all ears."

Matt started to speak, but I noticed Dave was holding a mini electronic device in his hand that had a small red light flashing on it. I didn't know what it was and I didn't want to interrupt

80

Matt to find out. After a little background information on his dream, he began to recount in as much detail as he could, the main content of the dreams.

"The dream always starts out like this. I am jogging down a dirt road with trees and swamps on both sides. I'm having a great run and enjoying myself in the beauty and solitude of nature. While I continue running, I notice a sign on the side of the road and it is written in the Hebrew language, which I do read and write fluently.

But it's a very strange sign because it doesn't make any sense to me. I stop and look at it closely and the words on it seem to change order and sequence, but the meaning remains the same. The sign reads:

The Beast's Pit #13 – 11 km ahead

Pit #13 – The Beast – 11 km ahead

#13 the Pit and the Beast – 11 km ahead

None of this makes any sense at all to me, so I keep on running and try to forget about the strange sign.

As I turn the next corner on the gravel road, I see someone standing in the middle of the road holding something in his hand above his head. As I get closer I notice that the person standing on the road is a giant man, at least 10 feet tall, and he is holding a sword above his head that has the words 'DRAGON SLAYER' engraved onto it. I also notice his belt and what it says on it. It has three words written on it and this is what they are: 'Strength And Might.'

For some reason I also notice that the first letter of each word is capitalized and bolder than the rest."

As Matt finished his last sentence, the revelation of what he had just said hit me right between the eyes. He had just quoted part of II Peter 2:11 which were Sam's last words to me. Not only that, the bold letters that Matt had just described in his dream spelled out the word SAM. My tram angel actually seemed to be the angel in Matt's dream. I could hardly believe what Matt was telling me.

As he continued recounting his dream to me he said, "As I stop and look at him, I ask him a question and say, 'What is your name and who are you?' In response to my question, he points to his belt with his left hand and says, 'This is my name.' Then he brings his right hand down from above his head and points the sword directly at me and says, 'The question is not who I am but the question is who are you, Dragon Slayer?'

With that, the big man takes the sword with one hand on the blade and one hand on the handle and drops to one knee, bows his head and holds the sword towards me and says, 'Take the sword Dragon Slayer for it belongs to you.'

By this time I am starting to lose control of my thoughts and feel paralysed with fear. I don't know what to do, so instead of taking the sword that the big man offers me, I get up and run down the road without looking back. But as I run I feel like a coward and shame hits me like a tidal wave.

Before I turn the corner on the road I look back with regret, but the road is empty and the big man is no longer there. I keep running and thinking to myself, I don't understand anything that is going on around me.

When I turn the next corner and head down the long straight stretch, I notice an animal standing in the middle of the road. When I finally get close enough, I notice that it seems to be a little lamb standing there all by itself. It looks lost and lonely, so I stop my run and reach down my hand to touch it. While I am in the process of doing that, the lamb looks up and turns its face towards me. I am shocked as I see the lamb has the face of a man.

All of a sudden the lamb moves towards me and attacks my legs and tries to bite me. Then many lambs with the faces of men start coming out of the bush and surround me and try to bite me. I start to kick and hit them with my fists, but I am secretly wishing I had taken the sword and had it to fight with. There were far too many of them to fight. So I choose to run again thinking that maybe I can outrun them, but they all follow me and are not too far behind.

As I turn the next corner I see a barricade across the road and a sign in front of it. It seems like I can not get around the barricade so I stop in front of it and read the sign.

The words on the sign say, 'The end of the road has come. This is Pit #13. You have run 11 km.' I turn to look behind me and see that the lambs are still running towards me and will reach me in a matter of seconds. I turn once again to see if I can get around the barricade, but my feet are stuck in sinking sand and I cannot move in any direction.

All of a sudden the earth starts to move like we are having a massive earthquake. Right before my eyes the earth in front of me erupts into a massive fireball just like a nuclear explosion has taken place. I feel the blast of heat and power that should have disintegrated my body, but I am totally intact standing there with my eyes wide open, watching the scene unfold before me.

Out of the fireball and pit which the nuclear explosion created, I see what looks like a creature or beast emerge from the embers. It has great wings with great power that lifts it out of the pit and into the earth's atmosphere. It had seven heads and a long tail which moved back and forth like a snake.

I had no human category to put this beast into but the best I could do to describe it was that it was half snake and half dragon. As the beast turned its flight direction towards me, I also noticed it had a human rider on its back with the reigns in his hand.

I looked at the surreal sight and I noticed the man had a king's crown on his head and two small horns protruding through the crown. As the beast flew directly towards me, the man's face suddenly came into focus. I stood there still stuck in the sinking sand, paralysed with fear as the eyes of the rider met with mine.

I am now looking directly into the face of my father, Donald King! And that's the point where I wake up every time, totally wet with sweat and shaking like a leaf. The dream feels so real to me, I would swear that I am conscious and that it is really happening to me."

With that Matt lifted his head and his eyes met with mine as he said, "So what do you think Walter, do you think I'm totally losing it or do you think that the dream has some kind of significance?"

"Wow! What an incredible dream. I've never heard anything like that before in my entire life. But before I answer your question, I have a few things to show you and to tell you about. I also have a feeling we might understand things a little bit better after I tell you what's been happening in my life lately."

CHAPTER THIRTEEN

UNCERTAIN FUTURES

As the car slowly rolled to a stop, the back door opened and a man gestured for Miriam to exit the car. She stepped out and the man put a blanket over her head and led her down a small alley and through an open door. They then stood in silence for a moment until she heard what she thought to be elevator doors opening. After three steps forward, she heard the sound of the doors again and all of a sudden her dark world turned to light.

The blanket was removed from over her head and yes, she seemed to be in an elevator going down. When the doors opened once again, she exited the elevator and was lead down a long hallway with only an occasional door on either side.

"Where could I possibly be?" she thought to herself. As her guide stopped in front of a door, he inserted a key into the lock and then swung the door wide open. Without saying a word he motioned for Miriam to enter the room and then gave her a slight bow as he reached for the door handle.

The door closed behind her, the click of the deadbolt found its resting place, and she was now alone. As she looked around, she noticed that the room was small but comfortable, and best of all it contained a single bed where she could rest her exhausted body and mind. From all she could tell it must have been at least 2 or 3 o'clock in the morning and she was now yearning for sleep.

She laid her head gently on the pillow, her evening prayers going out silently for Matt and Sonja. She missed them desperately, but somehow knew inside that she would probably never see them again in this life.

Sonja thought she was still dreaming when she heard the sound of knocking on a door. When the sound grew a little louder she realized it was not a dream, but that someone was actually at her apartment door.

She quickly slipped out from under the covers, and went to the door saying in hushed tones that she would be ready in a moment. Sonja wanted to let Matt sleep for as long as he could because it had been a very long and traumatic day for him also. As she returned to the door she spoke to whoever it was on the other side and said, "Please come in quietly because Matt is still sleeping."

With that the key turned from the outside and the lock opened to Jacob standing on the threshold. "May I come in please?" he asked in not much more than a whisper.

As Sonja motioned for him to come in, he closed and locked the door behind him, and then headed for one of the chairs that encircled the small kitchen table. Both of them sat down and he began to explain that they had a little more information on the approximate location where Miriam was being held.

Jacob explained that Miriam had been taken to the town of Abad after leaving the airport in Iran, and as far as they knew she was still there somewhere, but her exact location was still unknown. Jacob then asked Sonja if she knew anything about why she would be taken to Abad.

Sonja paused for a moment and tried to recall what Miriam had told her about Donald and her early years in their small town. Jacob seemed to be fascinated with the story as Sonja recounted the things that Miriam had told her just a few days ago. After a few more questions which she answered as best she could, Jacob thanked her for her cooperation. He then excused himself saying that he would return later on in the day or in the evening.

As the door closed behind him, Matt let out a big yawn and said, "I'm hungry mommy, what can I have for breakfast?"

Smiling, Sonja responded to her son's request with a "Well, today young man, you can have whatever you want of anything that is in our fridge, and you can also have as much of it as you want."

Miriam's eyes slowly opened and consciousness began to emerge. She had to think for a moment to orient herself as to where she was. As the events of yesterday began to replay in her mind, they soon led her to the reason as to why she was lying in a small room in a strange bed. She was somewhere in her hometown of Abad, but her exact location was still a mystery.

As Miriam turned on the light and walked throughout the small room, she noticed a few things that seemed very odd. On the wall above the small table hung two large paintings, and on closer investigation, the images on the canvases appeared to come alive in Miriam's mind.

On the first painting were images of strange looking creatures out of mythology somewhere, mixing with the human race and tormenting and torturing the people depicted in the scene. The second painting was of a man wearing a long black hooded robe with his arms outstretched towards a multitude of people who were bowing in his presence. Other than his eyes, his face was obscured in the shadow of the hood covering his head. But his eyes seemed to command the full attention of the entire painting. They were eyes that depicted evil, and that evil seemed to control the destiny of the people that were bowing before him. If paintings could speak, these two certainly had some kind of magical power to draw the observer directly into the scenes.

Miriam broke her gaze away from the paintings and forced herself to turn her back to them. She stepped away and walked towards a clothes rack that contained at least a half-dozen beautifully-made robes, each out of a different type of material. The robes were all snow white, but had different colored threads embroidered around the necks and also around the bottom hem down by the feet. Each robe was beautiful and hand-crafted to perfection. Where did these robes and the two pictures come from, Miriam wondered. She was positive they had not been in the room when she had arrived during the night, but here they were right in front of her this morning.

As Miriam was thinking of the strangeness of the robes and paintings being in the room, a knock on the door shifted her attention towards the door as it swung open from the outside. The same man who had brought her here was now standing in the doorway, holding a tray of food in one hand and Miriam's suitcase in the other. As he handed her the tray, Miriam asked him if he knew what time it was.

Without responding verbally, he held out his arm so she could read the numbers on his wristwatch which read 10:45 am. Miriam put the tray on the table, thanked the man for the food and asked him if he could please bring the suitcase in and lay it on the bed. The man became more agitated as she talked with him and asked him for help with her suitcase. Without any warning the man took the suitcase and slid it across the floor until it came to a stop against the bed.

With a shocked look Miriam glanced up at the man whose mouth was now wide open, his finger pointing directly into it. The man had no tongue and was in no mood for conversation nor able to answer Miriam's questions. The whole room shook as the door slammed shut, and the man stomped angrily away down the hallway.

What kind of a place was this, Miriam thought to herself and why had her son Donald brought her here? Perhaps it was better for the time being at least that she didn't have the answers to her own questions.

As the day wore on, Sonja could see that Matt was getting restless from being cooped up in the small apartment. He was bored playing with the few toys that he had, and he wanted to go outside into the sunshine and explore something new.

Sonja had also tried to answer the many questions of a five-year-old. She tried to answer questions like, "Why are we here, mommy? Where are we? Where is grandma? How long do we have to stay here? Is Daddy coming to pick us up soon?"

All of Matt's questions were difficult to answer and Sonja could see that he was beginning to get frustrated. Late in the afternoon Jacob returned with a bag of fresh food and also some new things for Matt to entertain himself with. Sonja was thankful for his thoughtfulness, but had a question for him that was playing on her mind. She wanted to know if they had any more information on Miriam and on how she was doing.

As Sonja and Jacob sat on the couch to chat, Matt seemed to be enjoying the new toys that he was the grateful recipient of. Jacob began the conversation by saying that David had been following Miriam since they had left Kuwait. They also knew for sure that she had been taken to Abad and that she was probably still there somewhere. Jacob also said that he suspected that Abad was a meeting point or safe location of some kind for Donald and his men. They had no specifics of its exact location but at least they were making progress in tracking Donald and his activities. Jacob also told Sonja that there seemed to be an unusual amount of activity in the town and the faces of several of Don's operatives had been spotted throughout the day.

Jacob's guess was that there may a gathering or meeting that evening or possibly the next day, and they were still trying to find out the exact location of that meeting. Jacob also said that they had no new information on Miriam's whereabouts but they were fairly sure that she had not been taken out of Abad. He also told her that because of the new information that she had given them about Abad, new resources from the Israeli government were going to be focused on Donald and his web of terror.

Jacob also mentioned that their time of departure for Israel was imminent, and it would probably happen within the next 24 hours. Sonja was thankful for all the kindness and updated information that Jacob had given her. The only thing that was still weighing on Sonja's mind was Miriam's welfare and thoughts of her future. Sonja, regrettably, realized that once they left this apartment for Israel, she was sure there would be absolutely no hope of ever seeing Miriam again.

CHAPTER FOURTEEN

A JOURNEY INTO THE PAST

The day quickly passed as Miriam rested and relaxed through the afternoon hours. She thought it must be at least 4 or 5 pm by now because she was actually starting to get hungry after her late breakfast. She was enjoying her afternoon of solitude when it was suddenly disturbed by a firm rapping on the door.

The door opened slowly and the figure of the man who had brought her the breakfast and her suitcase filled the doorway. He was holding an envelope in his hand and motioned for Miriam to come towards him and take it from him. As she reached out to take it from his hand, she noticed that his face was bruised with small bandages in three places.

It looked to Miriam like he had been in a fist fight with someone or that he had been severely beaten. As she took the envelope into her hands, he again bowed slightly, backed out of the doorway and then closed it gently.

Miriam looked down at the envelope wondering if she had been the cause of the man's beating. He had become frustrated with her questions and had reacted with anger at their last meeting. Her heart went out to him and she hoped that she was not the cause of his misfortune.

As she opened the envelope and began to read its contents, she was surprised to see that it was handwritten by her son. It was a short letter giving her instructions about the upcoming evening.

The letter was direct and to the point and this is what is said, "Dear Mother. I'm so glad you could come and visit me here in Abad.

We have a wonderful evening planned for you and you will be one of the guests of honor along with a couple of other people. I hope you liked the pictures I put in your room last night. I painted them myself. As for the robes, pick one out and bring it with you when you come for the last supper. Also, please wear the beautiful Kuwaiti gown that you bought while on vacation. I want to see how it looks on you.

Please start getting dressed right away because someone will be there soon to bring you to the celebration.

See you soon, from your loving son, Don."

Miriam finished reading the letter and a cold chill went down her spine. What did Donald have planned for her this evening and what was he talking about when he mentioned the "last supper?" Miriam's peaceful and enjoyable afternoon had just come to an abrupt end as she thought about the meaning of the letter.

The more Sonja thought about Miriam, the more concerned she became about her welfare. She did not even want to think about the fact that Miriam was with Donald and that he probably knew about all their plans of escape. If only Miriam had not struggled to get away from Jacob and David, they would all be here together and soon be on their way to freedom and a new life. But it was not to be. She was not here with them and she missed her so. Sonja wept softly as her heart went out to Miriam, wishing for things that might have been.

It did not take long for the knock on the door to come. Miriam was ready to go, as she had already picked out one of the white silk robes and was wearing the Kuwaiti gown that she had purchased only a couple of days ago.

As she looked toward the open door, there stood her escort to supper, bandages and all. With a slight bow and an outstretched arm he pointed in the direction that they should go. Both of them walked down the long hallway and then stopped at two large, beautifully carved wooden doors. Miriam entered into a world that she never knew even existed when those doors swung open.

It seemed like she was stepping into a historical museum with the decor representing the middle ages. As her eyes travelled around the room, there was too much information to take in all at once. The room was filled with paintings, artifacts, sculptures, and statues of great men throughout earth's centuries. Their many names and faces covered the walls with their stories and exploits of conquest. Miriam recognized many of the names like those of some of the Pharaohs, the Caesars, and men like Alexander the Great and Napoleon Bonaparte. She also came across a section of Middle Eastern kings and military leaders from her own region's past. Names like Nimrod, Sargon, Hammurabi, Sennacherib, Antiochus IV and then of course Nebuchadnezzar which was probably one of the Middle East's most famous kings and world powers.

Her eyes continued to drink in the centuries of earth's political and military leaders, until she came to a section that portrayed some of the world leaders and powers of the 20th century.

The names and pictures of men like Jozef Stalin, Pol Pot, and of course Mao Zedong who had killed an estimated minimum of fifty million people, hung on the walls boasting their accomplishments and contributions to the world's history. Unfortunately Miriam noticed that the leaders portrayed in this section of history seemed to have a very negative impact from the things they accomplished. The leaders portrayed here were the ones that seemed to bring devastation to their own countries and the people that they were trying to rule.

These leaders, in Miriam's mind, were evil and wanted to rule by fear, terror, and intimidation. They sought total control and power over the minds and wills of their own people. As Miriam came to the end of the section of the political powers of our century, there was one person who had a section to himself. Her eyes fell on the different artifacts and symbols which represented this leader's era, and she noticed that the swastika was the main symbol that center-pieced this section of the room.

Flags and pictures which looked like originals covered every square inch that was available, and a large portrait of Hitler himself was the centerpiece of the exhibit. Just looking at the pictures and the artifacts of the World War II era brought tears to Miriam's eyes. "It must have been a horrible period of time for those living in Europe" she thought to herself, and was very thankful that she had been hidden away in the tiny village of Abad as the war years were going on.

She walked into what seemed to be the last section of exhibits, gasping in horror as the first picture she saw hanging on the wall was a picture of herself holding a tiny baby in her arms. Memories flooded Miriam's mind as that moment in time replayed itself in her mind.

She remembered the moment just like it was yesterday, when her uncle was showing off the first black-and-white camera that had come into their tiny village and this was the very first picture that was ever taken by that camera. She stood in stunned silence looking at parts of her own life replaying themselves on the walls in front of her, and she soon realized of course that this was not her history being immortalized but it was the history of her son. It was his life's story being recorded in the annuls of this museum.

As she came to the end of the chronological history of her son, a life-sized framed portrait of Donald stood on a table. As she stared into the eyes in the portrait in front of her, she was amazed at how lifelike the picture was, until one of the eyes winked at her and the mouth started to speak.

"Hello Mother dear," said Don as he stepped out from behind the empty picture frame. Miriam was in total shock and speechless as Donald walked around the table and stood in front of her.

"Welcome to my world Mother. I hope you enjoyed your self-guided tour of my museum. Have you enjoyed your tour?" Words were slow in coming for Miriam, but finally she managed to respond by saying,

"Well, yes I did find it interesting, but also very disturbing."

Donald laughed at his mother's response, and said to her, "Well, I do hope you find the rest of the evening 'interesting and disturbing' as well." With that, Donald clapped his hands twice and said with a loud voice, "Let us begin the festivities!"

Instantly brighter lights came on and people were scurrying around everywhere, setting up tables and chairs, moving things around, and preparing for something that appeared to be well planned out.

"Come Mother and sit down with me. We haven't talked for such a long time. Please come and tell me all about your trip to Kuwait, I'd love to hear about it. Tell me about all the fun and exciting things you and my family did together."

Miriam knew that lying to Don would be useless. He probably already knew everything about their plans and intentions, and he only just wanted to hear it from her own lips.

"Well, I'm not sure where to start to tell you about our trip."

"Why don't you start here," Don said as he reached into his pocket and pulled out ten thousand dollars in US currency, and then opened a small bag and poured out several diamonds onto the table. "This would be a good place to start," Donald said. "Yes, why don't you just start here?"

Miriam took a deep breath, whispered a quick prayer and started telling Donald the truth of what the intent of their holiday had been. As she continued telling him the story of her plans, she made it sound like she had talked Sonja into leaving with her. She was trying to take all the responsibility of the escape plan just in case Donald ever caught up with Sonja and Matt. When she came to the end of her story, she noticed that Donald's demeanour had changed drastically and there was no longer a smile on his face.

"Well mother dear, that was a very interesting story. Do you have anything else that you would like to confess to me while you are being so honest?"

Miriam thought for a moment as she was not quite sure as to what information Don was actually fishing for.

"Do I have to start every conversation around here?" Don said. "Please tell me about your doctor's visits." Miriam was surprised by Don's statement. How could this man know everything about her personal life and even about a private conversation with her doctor?

Miriam told the truth and ended the story by saying that she had only another month or two at the most to live.

With that confession, Donald burst into deep laughter and responded to her by saying, "Oh mother dear, I'm sure you do wish you had another month or two to live, but I'm not sure that even I can arrange that." With that statement Donald just walked away laughing and Miriam sat there trying to figure out and understand what his comment meant.

Miriam looked around the room and she noticed that tables and chairs had been added and it had been transformed into a dining hall complete with linen table cloths, candles, and music. She stood up just as the chimes of a clock began to sound. She counted the chimes and when they came to six, they stopped, and only the echo of them remained.

Donald stood up on the portable platform where the head table rested, and raised his hands calling everyone to attention.

"Welcome all my friends, come and dine, for tonight we have a very special evening planned."

Miriam watched as people came from all different directions and found their places at the two tables that were set up below the head table. Everyone stood behind their chairs and waited as Donald shook hands and greeted some of the guests.

When he was finished welcoming people he called out to Miriam and said, "Please come Mother, you have a special seat with me up at the head table." Miriam followed the lead of the others till she stood behind the chair that was at Donald's right side.

Donald then called out a man's name and said, "Please come and sit at the head table with me." As the man approached the head table, Miriam's eyes opened wide and her mouth fell slightly open. She knew this man from somewhere, she thought to herself. Yes, this was the same man that had been watching them while they were in Kuwait.

Ascending the platform he was directed to the first chair to the left of where Donald was sitting. "Everyone please take your seats," Donald said, "so we can begin tonight's festivities."

As Miriam sat down next to her son she noticed that there was still a chair and place setting prepared for one other person.

Donald continued his speech by saying to everyone, "As you can see we have two very special guests with us here tonight. But in fact we have a third guest which will be a great surprise to all of you, I'm sure. Please," Donald said, "come in and take your place up at the head table." All the heads in the room turned as a fairly frail older gentleman started walking up the aisle between the two guest tables and then on towards the empty chair which was beside Miriam.

Miriam's eyes followed the man that was walking towards her and she noticed that her heart rate was increasing as there seemed to be a familiarity about him. All of a sudden the man stopped in his tracks, looked up towards Miriam and said, "Is that really you, Miriam?"

With that statement a flood of recognition hit Miriam with full force. Leaping to her feet, she looked directly into the eyes of the man, instantly realizing she was gazing into the face of her former lover. There standing right in front of her was Heinz King, Donald's father, whom she had not seen in forty years.

CHAPTER FIFTEEN

TOGETHER AT LAST

Miriam stood speechless while Donald continued speaking to this audience, "I would now like to introduce someone very special to all of you. In the last three weeks I have been reunited with this man, and without any hesitation I would like to introduce my father, Heinz King."

With that statement a collective gasp went through the small crowd and people started whispering and pointing in amazement at the frail man walking toward the table.

As far as anyone knew, and even as far as Miriam herself was concerned, it was believed and confirmed that Heinz King was killed in Iran shortly after the end of World War II. Apparently that was not the case, because here stood the living proof that Heinz King, high-ranking Nazi officer and personal adviser to Adolf Hitler, was still alive and well. As Heinz slowly made his way to take his seat beside Miriam, he could feel the eyes of every person in the room staring at him.

Miriam was not sure what she should do. Should she throw her arms around her former lover in joy or should she slap his face in public for abandoning her all these years. Her thoughts and emotions were scrambling in all directions and she had no idea how to react. He sat down on the chair next to her, so she also sat down and both looked straight ahead not knowing what to do or say.

Donald continued giving his speech to those in the room, but Miriam did not hear a word that he was saying. All she could think about was the man who was sitting beside her and all the questions she had for him.

As Donald continued speaking, Heinz turned towards Miriam and in not more than a whisper said, "I'm so very sorry Miriam for abandoning you. I never knew we had a son."

Tears filled Miriam's eyes at his words, but she could not bring herself to turn her head and look at him.

Donald finished his speech, then called for the meal to be brought out and the head table was to be served first. Even though Miriam was hungry, there was nothing on the plate in front of her that appealed to her. Too many things had happened to her in the last hour and right now food was the last thing on her mind. As she turned her head slightly to look at Heinz's plate, she noticed that his food was also untouched and he was just sitting quietly looking down into his lap. Miriam pondered the situation they were in, realizing that this might be her only opportunity to actually speak to Heinz.

Gathering her courage, she turned her face completely towards Heinz and began to speak quietly to him.

"I had no idea you were still alive," she said to Heinz, "where have you been for all of these years?"

Heinz slowly lifted his head, turned his face towards Miriam. "I have been a fugitive, running and hiding in every country in South America over the past 40 years. It is much too long of a story to tell in a few minutes, but there are some things that I think you should know. I have been chased like an animal all these years by those Nazi hunters because there are a few people that are still living that know the truth of who I really am."

"When I met you," Heinz continued, "I thought that finally I might have the chance of a new life without all the baggage of my past haunting me wherever I went. You have to believe me when I tell you that you were the best thing that ever happened to me in my entire life. I should never have gone out to look for that job, I should never have stepped foot out of Abad. I'm sure we would have survived somehow. But I did go and that's when the Nazi hunters caught up with me and everything changed. I was a wanted man and was being chased by people who would never give up their search for me as long as I was still alive. They were relentless over the years, but somehow I managed to stay one step ahead of them until three weeks ago when I found myself on a plane bound for Iran.

How Donald found me and how he even knew I existed, I have no idea even to this day. He told me nothing about you, so I didn't even know if you were alive or not. For the past three weeks he has been questioning me about my past with you and also about my growing up years with my mother and father.

He has had doctors examining me, doing blood tests, and giving me all kinds of psychological examinations. The tests and examinations never seem to end. But I think he has now come to the conclusion that I have been telling the truth.

Although I am not proud of my history and never carried out any of the actual deeds or the plans of my father, I am still the son of my father. This is hard for me to say, but it is the truth and I think that you should hear it from me instead of Donald."

Heinz looked directly into Miriam's eyes and with a steady and calm voice said to her, "I am the illegitimate son, and in the direct bloodline of the one and only Adolf Hitler." With those words finally registering in Miriam's brain, a wave of nausea and light-headedness hit her body hard, and all she remembered was her world going dark as she slid off her chair and onto the floor.

The day dragged along slowly for Sonja and Matt. Although they had been treated well and had plenty to eat and drink, it was still hard to be cooped up in a small place for an indefinite period of time. Both Sonja and Matt picked away at some of the food that Sonja had prepared for supper, but for some reason neither of them had much of an appetite.

As Sonja cleaned up the dishes that they had used for supper, she heard a small knock at the door and then saw it open quickly as Jacob slipped into the room and locked the door behind him.

"Sorry I don't have any news from Iran," he said to Sonja, "but I do have information on the time of our departure to Israel. We have the confirmation to leave in about four hours, right around midnight. I just wanted to give you some forewarning so you would be ready to go when the time comes. I can't stay and talk right now but I will return in about four hours and then we'll be able to talk.

Jacob locked the door behind himself as he left, and Sonja thought to herself, "Only four more hours to wait and then our world will change forever, and only four more hours to wait and any chance of seeing Miriam alive will also be gone forever.

Several people rushed to the platform to help Miriam off the floor. The doctor was called and arrived in only minutes. By the time he got to see Miriam she was already sitting in a chair and regaining some of her strength.

The combination of stress, lack of sleep, not enough food, and the introduction of Heinz King back into her life proved to be too much for her already-weakened condition. Over the past couple of days she could feel the cancer beginning to take its toll on her body, but she was determined to put on a brave face. She secretly wished she could have more time to actually get to talk to Heinz in private, but she was not sure if that was going to happen. Donald seemed to have his own plans for everyone's lives and she was not sure where she fit in.

"Well," Donald said as he rose to address the crowd, "now that all the drama has died down, let's move along to the program that has been prepared for this evening."

As Miriam looked down the table past Donald, she noticed the man that had been following them in Kuwait was visibly agitated and was sweating profusely.

Donald finished speaking to the people in the room and he turned his attention to the man on his left asking him to stand. The man stood but his eyes remained glued to the floor in front of him.

"As you all know," Donald continued, "Loyalty and excellence in our job performances are a top priority in our line of work. There is no room for error and you all know that I demand and expect my instructions to be carried out perfectly. Well, sadly, this evening we have to deal with some issues that have led to unfortunate events that have included the kidnapping of my entire family. These are the kind of things that will happen when we are not focused on the job. Today I have chosen to be gracious to this man who has failed me, even to the loss of my family. I have decided to give you a choice," he said to the man, "as to what your punishment will be. Your first choice will be to lose your tongue and your right hand, since it was your eating and drinking that distracted you from your job. And if you choose this option both you and your family will live. Your second option is a bullet to the head, which is quick and easy, but it also means a bullet to the head to all of those in your immediate family.

Miriam felt another wave of nausea coming on as Donald finished his judgement upon the poor man. She held the table in front of her to steady herself.

Heinz immediately saw what was happening to her, so he put his arm around her to help steady her in case she fainted again. Miriam had always known that her son was a cruel and evil man, but now she was actually experiencing the full force of what that meant.

To Donald this was just business as usual, another day, another dollar, Miriam could not even begin to conceive that this was the son that she had raised, and that he had turned into the evil monster that now stood before her.

"Well," Donald said out loud to the man, "what is your decision, will you take option number one or will you take option number two?"

A groan escaped from deep within, but the man stood up straight and looked into the faces of his peers and said, "I will take option number one."

"Wonderful!" Donald intoned with a smile on his face, I was hoping you would choose that one. Doctor, can you please join us on the platform, I think we will need your assistance soon. But before we begin that, I would ask my mother and father to please leave the room for a while, because we do need you conscious for the rest of this evening's festivities."

As Miriam and Heinz were led into a side room, Miriam burst into tears, thinking to herself, "How could this actually be happening right before my eyes? Could the son I brought into this world really be the grandson of Adolf Hitler himself?" From what she had just seen and heard there certainly was the possibility of that being the case.

CHAPTER SIXTEEN

STOLEN MOMENTS

Several moments passed by in relative quiet. Donald had quit speaking and an odd silence had descended on the dining room that they had just left.

Miriam decided to take this opportunity to speak to Heinz and try to catch up on the past forty years that they had been separated. Neither of them had ever married and for the majority of their lives they had lived a very lonely existence.

As Miriam spoke of her past and briefly told Heinz about Donald's growing-up years, tears appeared and flowed freely down his cheeks and onto the floor. He could only guess how their lives together might have been if he had never left Abad to go and find employment.

When Miriam came to the part of her history where Sonja and Matt came into her life, her whole countenance changed and it was a pleasure for her to tell the story of her last five years. She beamed as she told Heinz how much joy and laughter they had brought into her life. As she finished the very brief telling of her last forty years, she noticed how good and healing it was for her to share her life story with Heinz even though they had not seen each other all these years.

There was still a spark of affection inside her for the man she used to love. When Miriam had finished her story, Heinz began giving a brief history of what his life had been like, and what being a fugitive felt like. He then recounted to Miriam the war years when his father seemed to be in control of the world's destiny.

Of course being the illegitimate son of Adolf Hitler was kept very quiet and only a handful of people knew the truth.

Heinz's father considered him a failure in every way. Heinz had no ambition to follow in his father's footsteps and was repulsed by the things his father was doing to the Jews and other minority groups in Germany. He actually tried to reason with his father to put an end to the brutal regime he had created but it was of no use; his father appeared to be controlled by an evil force that was bent on the destruction of anyone who was not of the Aryan race.

Heinz was then given the role of a personal advisor to the "Fuehrer" but in reality it was a position in name only and over time Hitler himself even refused to acknowledge him, let alone take any advice from him.

When Heinz finished telling his story, Miriam's mind drifted off and she started thinking about Matt and how similar his life might have been if he continued growing up in the shadow of his father, Donald. But Matt was not here and for that she was eternally grateful. Hopefully Matt would have the opportunity to grow up and have a normal childhood like any other five year old boy should have a chance to do.

For both Miriam and Heinz these few moments together brought some healing to their long and lonely lives. Heinz spoke soft and tender words to Miriam and she responded like she would have over forty years ago. Although nothing could change the predicament and situation they were in, at least maybe they could get through it together and enjoy the little time that they did have.

Finally, the side door opened and the man with no tongue and bandages on his face handed Miriam the white robe she had brought from her room. He gestured for her to put it on in the small washroom that adjoined their room.

As Miriam exited the washroom wearing the white robe, Heinz noticed how beautiful she still looked, even at 65 years of age. The man opened the door that led back into the dining room and he pointed towards it, giving Heinz and Miriam a slight bow. The dining room which they had left only forty five minutes ago had been completely transformed. What was a dining room an hour ago and a museum two hours ago now looked like a ghostly courtroom of some kind with dimmed lights and somber music playing in the background.

As the two entered the room, Miriam slipped her hand through the crook of Heinz's arm and hung onto him to steady herself. Heinz looked down into Miriam's eyes. It was like he was looking deep into her soul and he liked what he saw.

For the first time in forty years, Heinz felt like he was at home and did not have to run any longer. He bent down and tenderly kissed Miriam on the cheek, whispering into her ear "I will never abandon you again Miriam, and whatever happens tonight, we will go through it together."

Heinz and Miriam stood motionless on the perimeter of the room they had just entered, and it began to come to life all around them. Hooded men in long black robes began to enter the room from a variety of locations. Each seemed to know their destination and soon thirteen hooded men sat around the oval-shaped table that was placed in the middle of the room.

Others followed, wearing long grey robes, and sat down behind the table where the thirteen men were seated. The sight of all the hooded men sent a chill of fear down Miriam's spine and she was glad that she was holding on tightly to Heinz's arm. Several minutes ticked by as all the men sat quietly with their faces gazing at the floor. Suddenly, the background music stopped and all the men slipped off their chairs and onto their knees and then into a typical prayer position with their foreheads on the floor.

Heinz and Miriam continued observing what was happening around them, while a hooded man walked out of the darkness and stood behind a podium that was set up in front of the oval table. Miriam directed her gaze towards the man. She realized that the man standing behind the podium looked identical to the man that was portrayed in the picture that had been hung in her room.

She continued to study the figure of the man, but it was his eyes that captured her attention and drew her into another world. As the man behind the podium began to speak, he removed his hood and addressed his followers by saying, "Rise up my brothers and take your places with me as we take another step towards the destiny that is being prepared for us. Take your seats, remove your hoods and we will begin."

Heinz and Miriam watched the man behind the podium take his followers through different recitations and incantations that almost sounded like prayers that were being directed to someone. Miriam could not keep her eyes off the man that was leading this ceremony, because to her it looked like Donald standing there, but yet it seemed like a completely different person that was speaking through him.

All of the men in the room were completely absorbed in the things Donald was saying to them, to the point that Miriam thought they were in a mass trance or hypnosis of some kind. As Donald came to the end of his incantations, the energy in the room built to a crescendo. All of a sudden simultaneously the entire group of robed men stood to their feet. With one motion and one voice their right arms extended upwards and outwards in front of them and in unison they recited the chant, "All Hail Apollyon, Angel of Light."

The men's voices subsided and an eerie silence filled the room. All the robed men slipped onto their knees and then bowed with their foreheads to the floor. A bright light entered the room and hovered over the place where Donald was kneeling.

He stood with the light encircling him and he seemed to glow with the brilliance that the light gave off. The light grew brighter and brighter, so much so that Heinz and Miriam had to shade their eyes from its intensity and turn their faces away from the source.

Whether the voice came from the light or whether Donald was actually speaking, the two of them could not tell. All they knew for certain was that they heard a voice speaking and it was coming from the ball of light.

The voice boomed, "I am Apollyon, Angel of Light. On this day, forty five years have passed since our defeat occurred at the end of WWII. Twenty five more years must pass before our final victory comes and the seventy years of waiting will be accomplished. Today all the centuries of time will converge and the spirits of the great men of the earth will possess and empower this man who is my chosen vessel. At the close of this next twenty five years, Donald will lead us into the last great war and then into the 'Final Solution' for all mankind. Tonight the blood of the innocents and the spirits of the great men will come."

As the bright light that surrounded Donald slowly vanished, a radiant glow on Donald's face remained. It was very apparent that something had transpired while the light had surrounded Donald and that things from beyond this world were taking place right before their eyes

The evening crawled by slowly for Sonja and 11 pm was right around the corner. She was now sure that sleep would not come. On the other hand, Matt had been soundly asleep for the past three and a half hours. There had been no word from Jacob since he had dropped by for a few moments after supper. The anticipation of going was hard for Sonja to accept because she knew that once they left they would never see Miriam again.

Her thoughts constantly returned to Miriam and she wondered what was happening in her life this very moment. She wished she could see her just one more time and tell her that they were OK and how much she had grown to love her. As Sonja closed her eyes she brought back the image from a few days ago of Miriam standing in the long Kuwaiti gown that she had purchased. It brought an instant smile to her face as she recalled the memory and the fun she had while wearing it.

While Sonja was still deep in thought she felt a strange sensation on her hip. As she opened her eyes to investigate, there stood Matt tugging on the belt that was around her waist. "Matt," she said, "why are you not sleeping?" "

Well," Matt said, "I was just talking to grandma and she told me to come over and talk to you."

Sonja was perplexed at the words of her son. What was he talking about? Where did he see his grandma? But instead of taking him back to bed she said, "come and tell me all about what grandma said to you."

"Well, I saw her in a big room and there were a lot of big rocks that were piled nicely in the middle of the room. First she was wearing the gown she bought when we were on holidays with her. Then I saw her wearing a beautiful long white robe with colors around the collar and the hem.

She told me to tell you that everything was OK with her and that you don't need to worry. She said that she loves us very much and that she would always live in our hearts. Then a man who was also dressed in white came and stood by her and held her hand. I didn't know who the man was, but grandma looked very happy. They both waved to me and she said, 'We both love you very much. Now go and tell your mom about our visit.'" Matt concluded.

Sonja was in tears as the simple message from her son found its way into her heart. For some reason her five-year-old son would dream dreams or speak words to her that would help through difficult moments and it was almost like he could see into their futures. From that moment on Sonja knew that everything was going to be OK for both her and Matt. The only question that remained in her mind was, who was the mystery man that was holding Miriam's hand in Matt's dream?

CHAPTER SEVENTEEN

HARD CHOICES

Heinz and Miriam pondered all the different things they had just seen, but they were not quite sure what to make of them. It was totally obvious to them that Donald was being controlled and manipulated by forces that were spiritual and that belonged to a different dimension. Up to this point in Miriam's life she was not even sure if she believed in a spirit world but after the events of this evening her way of thinking was definitely changing.

After a few moments passed, Donald's voice rose above the buzz of conversation that filled the room.

"Order, we will have order in this courtroom," he said. "As you all heard," Donald continued, "today is the 45th anniversary of a failed attempt to bring in a new world order. But today is also the first day of the last twenty five years where our dreams of a new dawning and a new world order will come to pass.

As you also heard Apollyon say, the spirits of the great men of the earth will come tonight as a sacrifice of the innocents is offered. Blood must be spilled this evening to commemorate the next twenty-five years of earth's history.

But first of all, we must establish where my mother and father stand in this court of law. Please step forward, mother and enter the judgement stand, and we will plead your case."

Miriam stepped forward onto a small raised platform which had a wooden railing fastened around it. She was now looking directly into the face of her son Donald.

"Since we have only a limited amount of time to try your case before the midnight hour, you must keep your answers to either a yes or no as you respond to the following questions.

"Are you my biological mother?"

"Yes" said Miriam.

"Did you support the path I chose to follow during my growing up years?"

After a few seconds of thought, Miriam simply said, "No."

"Have you been supportive of me during my adult years?"

"No," Miriam responded.

"Over the past several months have you been planning to abandon me and flee the country?"

"Yes," came the answer.

"Did you willingly try to convince my family to abandon me and try to turn them against me?"

"Yes," Miriam responded. She knew there was no point in trying to explain her actions to Donald, and with her option of only yes or no answers, her guilt had been established before the questions ever began.

"Heinz King, please step forward and stand beside your lover and answer the following questions with only a yes or no answer.

"Are you my biological father?"

"Yes," Heinz responded.

"Are you also the son of the one and only Adolf Hitler?"

"Yes."

"Did you abandon my mother before I was even born?"

"Yes."

"Did you support your father in his quest to make the world a better place to live in?"

"No."

"Did you actually work against your father in his attempts to bring in the 'Final Solution' to the world's problems?"

"Yes" Heinz responded firmly.

"I have one final question for both of you, but I want you to answer it individually. The question is, are you proud of me as a son and do you endorse the work that I am doing to make the world a better place to live?"

As Heinz and Miriam looked at each other, both knew the only answer they could give was to say no.

So both of them in turn gave the simple answer of "No."

With that answer, Donald struck the podium he was standing beside with a gavel and said with a loud voice,

"This court will now rule. From the answers you have given, this court finds you guilty of three major crimes.

First of all, this court finds you guilty of the abandonment of your son.

Secondly this court finds you guilty of conspiracy to break apart my family unit.

And thirdly this court finds you guilty of insurrection and of actively trying to stop the work of making the world a better place to live in."

"Now that this court has found you guilty of these three charges, you still have a chance to speak your mind. To the charges brought against you, you still have the right to say, guilty or innocent.

What do you have to say about your indictment?"

Miriam and Heinz looked into each other's eyes, knowing they had to play Donald's game to the end, so with one voice they turned to Donald and simply said,

"We are innocent of these charges."

"Wonderful," Donald said with a big smile on his face.

"I think we have found our 'innocents' for this evening's festivities. But before we continue on, I am feeling very generous and forgiving this evening.

I am going to give you one more opportunity to put all of your unhappy past and guilt behind you. If you both will yield to only one request that I have for you, I will let both of you walk out of this place together to live out your lives however you choose, without any further interference from me. The choice is simple and the choice is yours. All you have to do is bow down and worship me like all my loyal followers do.

That is not too much to ask for a life of freedom is it? Nothing else will be required of you other than this simple act. It's your decision."

Heinz looked deeply into Miriam's eyes and he desperately wanted to have more time with her, but he also knew he would have to sell his soul to Donald in order to get it. As he continued to look into Miriam's eyes, he knew she would follow him in whatever decision he made.

Was he going to compromise his whole life and Miriam's also for the chance of a few weeks or months together or was he going to be true to his own conscience and soul?

As he turned his face towards Donald and looked him straight in the eyes, he said, "We cannot yield ourselves to your temptation. We will not bow."

With these words spoken, Donald's face lit up and he said with a loud voice, "We have our 'innocents.' Let us prepare quickly, for our time of great power has arrived and the spirits of the great men of the earth await us."

When Donald finished speaking, a flurry of activity took place around them and Heinz was handed a white shirt and a pair of white pants to change into. Heinz took the clothes and headed for the side room to get changed.

Miriam intercepted him, threw her arms around him and said, "I love you and I want to tell you that you made the right decision for both of us." As they held each other close, the forty years of separation and hurt seemed to vanish away and all that remained was this moment in time where everything was perfect and just the way it was supposed to be.

When Heinz returned from changing into his clothes, the room had once again changed and the decor resembled that of a dungeon with an altar made of stone being its centerpiece. All of the men including Donald had once again covered their heads with hoods and were in the process of some kind of prayer and meditation. As Heinz and Miriam stood next to each other holding one another's hands, Miriam's thoughts and prayers went out to Sonja, but more so for Matt.

Poor little Matt knew nothing of the evil that his father was involved in, and for that she was eternally grateful. She also knew that Allah was watching over them and that he had a plan for all of their lives, but especially for Matt's. As she reached out in her thoughts towards Sonja and Matt, her prayer was that they would know that she loved them totally, and that they should not worry about her, and that everything would be OK. She smiled as pictures of Sonja and Matt came alive in her mind. She let her mind wander to the precious moments she had experienced with them over the past five years. As she thought of them, she decided that these would be the pictures she would hold in the front of her mind if these were to be the last few minutes of her life.

Miriam looked up towards Heinz, smiling, and said, "I am so glad we finally found each other and that we get to spend the last few hours of our lives together." As Heinz embraced her and kissed her on the forehead, Donald's voice rose above the prayers of all the hooded men.

"The time has come my brothers. It is the midnight hour and for this purpose we have come into this world. The time has come for Apollyon to rise to power and with him we will rise also as the rulers of the entire world.

Twenty-five years from now every nation will bow to us and Apollyon will rule with a fist of iron over those who oppose him and an open hand of love to those who obey. It all begins tonight.

At the stroke of midnight this world will change forever!"

As Miriam looked at the clock on the adjacent wall and took note of the time, the realization came to her that she only had about eleven minutes left on this earth.

What is a person supposed to do or think when you realize you have just eleven minutes left to live? Her heart had forgiven Heinz once she heard his story and understood what he had gone through.

But her heart was still hard towards the son she bore and raised by herself through all of his growing years. She still had malice towards the son that abused her and turned her into a prisoner in her own home. She detested him for the countless families he had destroyed and people he had killed and maimed over the past twenty-five years.

Was it possible to forgive Donald for what he had done or for what he was about to do to them? Those were the thoughts and questions that were running through her mind with only six minutes left to live.

"These must be the important questions one thinks about when they are about to breathe their last breath" Miriam thought.

What would she do in these next six minutes or did it really even matter? Her son did not deserve her forgiveness but still the question kept running through her thoughts, "Is it possible to forgive?"

She did not have the answer to her own question as Donald led both her and Heinz up the stairs and made them kneel on the altar that stood in the middle of the room. Heinz and Miriam knelt next to each other, as the cold stones of the altar pressed into their kneecaps, and each of them could feel the touch of a steel barrel resting on the back of their heads.

Donald stood behind them holding a Luger pistol from WWII in each hand, while the chimes of the clock began to sound as the last minute of their lives had arrived. A calm peace seemed to flood into the very soul of Miriam and she was not afraid any more. Deep inside Miriam's heart of hearts she had answered the question that had haunted her for the past ten minutes.

As the chimes struck twelve times, she lifted her eyes and spoke two simple words. She said, "I forgive" as her world went dark and time stood still.

CHAPTER EIGHTEEN

SHAKING THE NATIONS

Matt was still awake as his head lay gently on Sonja's lap. The last hour had passed by very slowly and there seemed to be a sadness of heart that had attached itself to both of them. All of a sudden Matt sat up straight beside her and said, "I think that grandma and grandpa are OK now and that they are very happy."

The thought had never occurred to Sonja that the man that Matt had seen in his dream might actually have been Matt's grandfather.

As Matt continued to speak, Sonja was a little taken aback by her son's next question which was, "Is my daddy a bad man?"

Sonja looked into Matt's eyes but she was not exactly sure how to answer that question.

"Well, Matt," Sonja said, "your daddy has done some things to other people that have not been very nice."

"Is that why grandma had to forgive him?" Matt responded.

"Yes, Matt, forgiveness is very important and in our lives there will be many times when we will need to forgive."

"I'm so happy that grandma forgave daddy. Now they're happy."

What was Matt seeing that made him say the things he said? Matt seemed to have some kind of insight into things that most people were blind to, including herself.

As Sonja pondered the things that her son had just brought to light, she looked at the clock that was beside her bed which now read 12:01; a new day had just begun.

June 21, 1990 was now one minute old as the blood of the 'innocents' had been shed and was now slowly making its way down the altar and onto the floor.

Donald waited in expectancy as the two limp bodies of his mother and father lay on the cold stone slab. With his hands raised in worship, he waited for Apollyon to appear and fulfil his promise of the spirits of the great men coming to indwell him. The moments ticked by and Donald realized that somehow a blockage had occurred in the other dimension and that something was delaying Apollyon from appearing.

He lifted up his voice for wisdom from the other world, and the answer to the problem came quickly. He was shocked as the impression came into his mind.

The words of the impression said, "Your mother forgave you before she died, and it's her forgiveness that will not let us come to you."

Donald was stunned as the implications of the impression gripped him. To this point he had assumed that Apollyon was all-powerful and that he made the rules that everyone played by. Apparently that was not the case, Donald thought to himself.

"What shall I do?" he said out loud, "to bring your presence and to fulfil your will?"

Again an impression came and the words clearly said, "Renounce your mother's forgiveness in your life and we will come."

The moment Donald renounced his mother's forgiveness, the atmosphere in the room changed and Apollyon entered in a dazzling white light.

"A new day has dawned," he said, "and together with the spirits of the great men of the earth, we will rule the world. Prepare yourself, Donald, for they are about to come and when they do arrive the earth will shake and many will die because of this day."

On June 21, 1990 at thirty minutes past midnight, a massive earthquake rocked the northern part of Iran that could be felt throughout the whole country. Some estimates placed it as a 7.7 magnitude earthquake that killed at least fifty thousand people and injured at least one hundred and thirty five thousand.

It was the largest earthquake to ever hit Iran since the early

1700's and it wreaked havoc over the whole northern regions of the country.

As the earth shook, Donald stood upon the altar with his legs spread over the still warm bodies of his mother and father. As the earth continued to rumble, Donald could physically feel the spirits entering his body one by one.

Instead of it being the euphoric feeling he thought it would be, the entering of the spirits brought darkness and confusion and an actual pain and discomfort started to grip his entire body. As the torment in his body increased, he felt like he was ready to explode.

He raised his hands and in a loud voice he spoke to the spirits that were still coming and said, "Enough! Stop! I can't take any more."

Having spoken these words, the earthquake subsided and Donald staggered down the altar stairs. As his consciousness began to leave him, he collapsed at the bottom of the stairs and fell to the ground with a loud thud. The hooded men quickly rushed to assist him and they carried him away to his private quarters.

Sonja and Matt were now fully awake as they experienced the earthquake that had just hit northern Iran. Although the epicentre of the quake was several hundred kilometres from Kuwait, it still had the intensity to cause minor damage in the countries that surrounded Iran.

Within a minute after the earthquake subsided, a knock on the door came and Jacob entered the room and locked the door behind himself.

"Are you both OK?" Jacob asked Sonja and Matt.

"Yes," Sonja responded, "we are both fine, but I feel for the people who live close to the epicentre of this quake. I have never felt one this big before and it really scared me."

"Yes," Jacob said, "I totally hear what you are saying. This has been one of the biggest ones I have ever experienced."

Jacob sat down at the table and motioned for Sonja to join him. As the two sat together, Jacob began to explain the plan they had for getting her and Matt out of the country and into Israel.

"As you already know," Jacob said, "there is still a nationwide search going on for you and Matt. And not only that, Donald is using his own power and influence to locate both of you even as we speak. This earthquake will play into our favour because as the morning light comes and we find out more details, the attention of the border officials will shift away from you and onto the natural disaster.

It will be impossible for us to get both of you out of the country by air for the two hour flight that would get you close to Israel. The airports are still on high alert and Donald's eyes and men are everywhere and on every border crossing. In one hour from now we will leave and head southwest through Kuwait City.

We have arranged to have you both smuggled out of Kuwait and into Saudi Arabia. We cannot travel through Iraq right now because tensions are building between Iraq and Kuwait and border crossings are becoming more difficult. We can still get you out through Saudi Arabia.

Unfortunately, to get to Israel by road is a very long process. It is over twelve hundred kilometres and can take up to twenty four hours, depending on road conditions and border crossing waits. Our plan is to get you through Saudi Arabia and into the city of Amman in Jordan. There you will have to stay in a safe house for a couple of days until safe passage can be arranged into Israel. The truck that will take you out of Kuwait and into Saudi Arabia has been designed with a smuggling compartment. It is quite small and it might be difficult for Matt to stay quiet and motionless, especially during the two border crossings." Jacob then handed Sonja a brown bag that contained two small bottles of fruit juice.

As Jacob leaned in closer towards Sonja, he spoke in hushed tones so Matt could not hear what was being said. "You are to give Matt one bottle of juice to drink one hour before each border crossing. Each bottle contains a mild sedative and it will put Matt to sleep for about two or three hours. The driver of the truck will be able to communicate with you, and he will let you know when you should give it to Matt. After I drop you both off and you're safe in the truck, we will not see each other for a while. But the next time we do meet, it will be in Israel, your new home."

Sonja was glad to be leaving the small apartment, but was not looking forward to being stuck in a tight compartment for the next twenty four hours. Matt was happy to leave also and was wide awake as they drove through Kuwait City with all of its lights and tall buildings. As the lights of the city slowly faded behind them and the darkness lay before them, both Jacob and Sonja sat quietly thinking their own thoughts.

For Sonja there was no turning back to the life she once knew and for Jacob this also meant a new beginning. For the past fourteen years of his life, his job had been to gather information on Donald and Miriam and over the past five years, Sonja and Matt had also been put on his job description. Now with Miriam's location unknown and Sonja and Matt soon to be in Israel, he was sure his life was about to change also.

Nearing the transfer point, Jacob slowed the car down and pulled off the highway into an exit that led into a truck stop and rest area. A few words were exchanged between Jacob and the driver as Jacob placed an envelope into the driver's hands.

Within two minutes Sonja and Jacob had said their goodbyes and Sonja and Matt were hidden in the one meter wide by three meters long smuggling space that had once contained the now nonexistent refrigeration unit. Inside the compartment was a small pot with a lid on it which was presumably used as a toilet. A bag of food also sat on the narrow bed that was just wide enough for one small person to lie on.

The tiny room also contained one twelve volt light that kept the room from being pitch black. It also seemed to have some source of fresh air as Sonja felt a slight air movement against her face.

"Like it or not," Sonja thought to herself, "this is going to have to be home for at least the next twenty-four hours."

As the truck slowly pulled out onto the highway and picked up speed, a man's voice came through an intercom system. "We are one and a half hours away from the Saudi Arabian border crossing, so keep your son awake for the next half hour and then give him the juice."

As the truck bounced down the road in the early hours of the morning, Matt was actually excited to be on a adventure in the middle of the night.

CHAPTER NINETEEN

A FIGHT FOR CONTROL

For the next twenty-four hours Donald lay tossing and turning on his bed. Since the moment the spirits had entered into him, he seemed to have very little control over his bodily functions and the thoughts of his mind. It was like the spirits were fighting amongst themselves for dominion over who would control and be able to manipulate Donald to do their own bidding.

Eventually Donald, through the strength of his own will, was able to rise above all the other voices and spirits and make them subservient to him and him alone. As he rose up off his bed he knew that something was very different inside him. In some respects, he did not even feel human any more. His body seemed to pulsate with a new energy and vitality that he had never known before. As he walked towards his dresser and looked into the mirror above it, even his appearance seemed to have changed.

The euphoric feelings that did not come when the spirits entered him were now there in full force and he felt like he was now invincible and that nothing could stand in his way. As Donald walked out of his room he was determined that he would put his new powers to the test. Without saying a word, and by only projecting his thoughts, he said inside of himself, "The first 5 people that see me will rush towards me and fall on their faces before me in worship."

Before he had even finished the thought in his head, someone was already running up the hallway and falling before him, face to the ground.

Within the next thirty seconds there were five people laying in front of him prostrate on the ground. As he smiled to himself and was enjoying the moment, he also noticed that he was reading bits and pieces of the thoughts of the people that were laying in front of him. He could almost feel their fears and the emotions as they lay before him.

Donald entered the room where the sacrifice of his mother and father had just taken place twenty-four hours ago, and he sensed a new and powerful presence that was lingering in the room. Without any incantations, recitations or worship, Donald simply projected his thoughts once again and said inside of himself, "Come Apollyon, Angel of Light."

In seconds Apollyon entered the room, surrounded in light.

"I have responded to the request of your thoughts" Apollyon said. "I can see that your power has grown since you have been indwelt by the spirits and that you are now learning to use it properly. You must always remember that you are powerful, but you are not all-powerful and never will be. We will work together over the next twenty-five years to bring in the 'Final Solution' for all of mankind, but you will always remain my servant and you will serve me, obeying whatever I say."

And with that, Donald knelt before Apollyon in reverence not because he wanted to, but because the will of Apollyon compelled him.

Crossing the border into Saudi Arabia was uneventful. Within twenty mutes of drinking the fruit juice, Matt was sound asleep. As far as Sonja could tell, the actual border crossing was a mere formality and there were no line-ups at four o'clock in the morning. Once the truck was in motion again and heading north toward Jordan, Sonja decided that she would try and get some sleep herself. The only problem for her right now was that she had to figure out how to fall asleep while standing or sitting on the hard, cold floor. Since Matt was sleeping on the only thing that looked like a bed, she thought she would try sitting and sleeping first.

The hours crept by slowly as Sonja slipped in and out of consciousness trying to get some sleep.

All of a sudden, Sonja was jarred awake out of her semiconscious state as she heard Matt's voice calling out in his sleep,

"Daddy, daddy, daddy!" Matt tossed and turned on the bed.

Sonja gently shook him to wake him up out of his dream.

"Hey Matt, everything is alright, mommy is here and everything is going to be just fine."

Sonja took Matt into her arms, and he began to settle down as she rocked him back and forth and whispered reassurances in his ear. "You must have been having a bad dream," Sonja said to Matt, "but everything is OK now. Do you want to tell me about the dream you had, son?"

Matt finally relaxed and was happy to be in the comfort of his mother's arms, so he slowly began to recount the dream that had been very frightening to him.

"I was in the same room that I saw grandma and grandpa in last time. I knew it was the same place because I could see Daddy standing on the pile of rocks that was in the middle of the room. All of a sudden many bad men came flying through the air and started to fight with Daddy.

They were poking and hitting him and I think they were trying to push him off the pile of rocks. Some of the bad men seemed to even go right inside of Daddy and disappear into his body. When the bad men were fighting with him, the ground was moving and it seemed like Daddy was going to fall down.

All of a sudden Daddy shouted 'Stop!' to the men and the ground stopped moving and the bad men flew away. I heard Daddy calling for me to come and help him.

I want to go but I don't know how. We have to go and help! He is in trouble and he needs our help!"

As Sonja pulled Matt close to her once again, she could only guess the significance or the meaning of the dream. Matt was so innocent in all of this but he was too young for her to tell him the truth about what his father was really like. For the next half hour, Matt was content to stay in the arms of his mother as she hummed and sang some of his favourite childhood songs.

An hour had already gone by since Matthew, Dave, and I had gotten into the crew truck. The story of Matthew's dream was fascinating and I could see that at least bits and pieces of it obviously fit into the information which I had gotten from the scroll.

As I looked back at Dave, I noticed that he was still holding the mini electronic device in his hand.

"Before I speak, I want to know what that device is that you are holding in your hand."

"Well, it's a voice recorder. This is also the first time that I have heard Matthew's dream in its entirety and he asked me to record it for him."

My next question for both Dave and Matt was, "Why are we sitting in this truck instead of being inside the room?"

Both Dave and Matt looked at each other and started to speak to each other in what I presumed was the Hebrew language. It almost sounded like they were having an argument of some kind, which actually went on for two or three minutes.

When their conversation ended, Matt turned toward me and started to speak. "Our story is far too long to tell tonight and it goes back to when I was a child over twenty-four years ago. As for your question of why we are sitting in a truck instead of inside, well I'm sure you are aware that we live in a very high-tech world.

Someone's eyes and ears have the potential of literally being anywhere without our knowledge. Because we didn't want to take the chance of our conversation being heard by anyone else, we decided to talk in the truck where we are one hundred percent sure only the three of us are hearing this conversation."

To me this seemed like the guys were going a little bit overboard with their secrecy, but I guess it did make sense to talk in a quiet and private place.

"I kind of feel uncomfortable with you recording me, at this point at least."

"No problem," said Dave as he tossed the device up to Matthew who put it away in his coat pocket.

I could tell that Dave was still not in favour of the three of us having this conversation, but Matthew was desperate for answers to his dream.

I started off the conversation by asking Matthew if he had shared the details of our last conversation with Dave. When he responded that he had, at least I now had a starting point to begin the story of my last week here at work.

I started retelling my story with the exact quote that the angel had spoken to me when I encountered him sitting on my gen-set.

His words were, "Don't be afraid, I have appeared to you for a reason which will be shortly revealed to you and your friends. Be at peace and remember, I am always here for you." I looked at Dave's facial expressions and I could tell that he was not very impressed.

His cynicism was written all over his face and I could only imagine what he was thinking. I could not blame him because if someone were to tell me a story like the one I was telling, I would probably be thinking the same thing as well.

"Well," I said to Matthew, "after we talked last Sunday night, I sure had a lot of questions and a lot of things rolling around in my mind. I didn't have many answers, but I knew for sure that you had a significant part to play in whatever was happening around both of us.

The next morning I went to work as usual and completed my morning tram runs. As I was walking back to the laydown trailer to head for breakfast with the guys, I looked back towards the parked trams and I noticed something was sitting on the gen-set of my tram.

I looked back to see what it was and it started rolling towards the edge and I caught it in mid-air before it hit the ground.

I could not believe what I was holding. To me it looked like the exact same thing that the angel was holding in his hand when he gave me the message I just told you about."

"So do you have the scroll in your possession?" Matt asked excitedly.

"Let me finish my story first, before I answer any of your questions. Anyways, later on in the day I opened it up and tried to figure out what it all meant.

Of course I could not understand what the scroll said, because it was written in a different language, other than what seemed to be a few scripture references that were written in English."

As I continued my story of what happened to me that evening and how Sam had entered my room and answered the four questions I had asked him, Matthew and Dave stared at me in total disbelief like I was a crazy person. Although I knew that it all did sound crazy, at least this time I had some proof to verify what I was actually talking about.

When I had finished my story, over an hour had gone by and I had not lost their attention.

"Anyway, to answer the question you asked me earlier, yes, I do have the scroll and it's right here in my backpack."

CHAPTER TWENTY

HOT HANDS

Two and a half hours had gone by since Matthew had shared his dream with me and I had told them of the things that had happened to me in the last week. It was now dark outside and it was getting late. My days started at four in the morning so I was already going to be down to six hours or less of sleep tonight. Matthew and Dave were very excited and really wanted to see the scroll, but I knew that if I took it out we would be here for the next few hours.

"Listen," I said to them, "we don't have time tonight to sit down and study the scroll because I have to work in the morning and so do you."

"Please, can we just see it and look at it for a couple of minutes?"

I reached for my backpack, noticing that the cynicism had left Dave's face and he was genuinely interested in seeing the scroll. I placed it on the seat in between Matthew and myself, unzipped the zipper and pulled it open. As the backpack opened, a burst of bright light radiated out of the opening and filled the front part of the truck. The intensity of the light startled us and we all leaned away from it.

"What's happening to my backpack?" I asked.

"What have you got in there?" Matt quickly responded.

"All that's in there right now is my Bible, a notebook, and the scroll." As I reached my hand towards the top of the backpack and into the light, I could feel a fairly intense heat coming from the inside of the pack. Matthew and Dave felt the same thing. It reminded me of people sitting around a campfire warming their hands in the heat of the fire.

I looked up into Matthew and Dave's faces, and I could tell by their expressions that they were stunned with what was going on right before their eyes.

"Well," I said to both of them, "I'm not sticking my hand in there to get the scroll out, but feel free to give it a try yourselves!"

Matthew and Dave looked at each other wondering which one would be brave enough. It was Dave's hand that moved closer to the top of the backpack and disappeared inside.

As soon as it had completely disappeared inside, he pulled his hand out shaking it violently.

"Ahh!" he shouted, "it burned me! Give me some water!" With that, he flung the back door open, jumped outside and began pouring water from a water bottle over his hand.

Dave shuffled around outside doing a little dance as he continued pouring water over his hand. Matthew and I looked at each other in quiet amazement and just shrugged.

"I guess the scroll did not want to be seen this evening," I thought to myself. So I zipped up the zipper and both the light and the heat disappeared instantly.

Matthew grabbed a flashlight and we both got out of the truck and went to see how Dave was doing with his burnt hand. As we shone the light on Dave's hand, there were definitely three burn marks on his fingertips where he had touched the scroll and had tried to lift it out.

A flash of anger came across Dave's face and it was directed towards me.

"What did you burn me with?" Dave demanded.

I was a little taken back at his reaction.

"What did I burn you with? I had nothing to do with this"

Dave stepped forwards towards me but Matthew moved in between us and started speaking to Dave in Hebrew.

"I guess it's time to go back to my room" I thought to myself, so I grabbed my backpack, said, "See you later," and headed down through the parking lot.

As I pondered the things that had just transpired, the thought hit me that some people like Dave still will not believe even though he saw the light, felt the heat, and burned his hand in the process.

"People can be funny" I thought to myself, "they will believe only what they want to believe even if the evidence is contrary.

Oh well, only one more day to go and I'll be on a plane heading home."

As Donald thought of the struggle that he had just gone through for the past twenty-four hours, all he could remember were bits and pieces of memories as the spirits were in the process of indwelling him. Unbidden, the image of his son came to mind and a broken memory of Matt calling out his name saying, "Daddy, daddy, daddy." What a strange memory, he thought to himself. Was it real or was it just a figment of his imagination?

Whatever it was, Donald now wondered if it was actually possible to contact Matt with his newly-endowed powers. It was an idea that he would have to follow up on since there had been no news and no leads to follow since the kidnapping had occurred several days ago. Donald knew that the reality was that Sonja and Matt could be anywhere in the world right now, but he also knew that with his resources, he would eventually find them no matter how long it took. It was not that he wanted to be a husband or a father to his family, but somehow deep inside he knew that his son Matt had some role to play in his upcoming leadership of the world. Yes, he would find them, even if it took the next twenty-five years to do it.

To Sonja it seemed like an eternity since they had climbed inside the stifling hidden compartment. She had got almost no sleep during the night and now it was mid-afternoon. It had already been three days since they had seen the sunlight and both Sonja and Matt were desperate to take a walk in the sunshine and breathe fresh air. The driver had been friendly enough and kept them informed as they were going through different towns on the long road north.

They had already passed through the towns of Hofar al Batin, Ash Shuba, and had just driven through Rafha. As the intercom crackled, the driver's voice came on and said that he needed to sleep for a couple of hours before they continued on the trip.

He then said that he would be pulling over at the next rest area that was just a few miles ahead. Sonja responded that she had understood him, but she also pleaded with him for them to please come out and be in the sunshine while he slept. As he did not respond to her question, she assumed that he had been given instructions by Jacob that they were to stay hidden. The truck slowed down and finally stopped. Sonja heard the driver's door open and then close behind him. Within a minute the panel to the hidden compartment was removed and Sonja and Matt stepped out into the covered box of the cargo truck.

"Don't talk to anyone," the driver said, "and if someone asks, just tell them you are waiting for your husband to wake up from his nap."

Matt and Sonja stepped into the warm sunshine, smiles breaking out on their faces as they looked around and began to investigate their strange new surroundings. Before the driver got back into his truck to go to sleep, he gave Sonja some Arabian money to buy some food and snacks from the local vendors. He also told her to wake him up before it got dark if he happened to oversleep.

The two hours of sunlight and being in the outdoors did wonders for both Sonja and Matt. They sampled some of the local food, bought a few little souvenirs, and just enjoyed the break from being cooped up in a confined space.

As the sun was about to set, Sonja knew that she should go and wake their sleeping driver so they could continue their journey. She was feeling a little bit uncomfortable because over the past half hour or so she had noticed the same man walking by them at least three times. She recognized him as being one of the local street vendors, but now it seemed like he had a special interest in them. As he turned the corner and disappeared out of sight, they quickly made their way back to their truck and woke up the driver. Sonja conveyed her suspicions and he quickly got them back to their hiding spots.

Instead of leaving right away, the driver wanted to see if someone would begin to look for Matt and Sonja. Sure enough, within a couple of minutes he noticed a man walking along the lineup of trucks looking for something or someone. The driver continued to wait until the man walked away and was out of sight. A couple of other trucks pulled out to leave the rest area, so the driver also pulled out and followed close behind them. The two trucks ahead of him turned south and so he turned south also. If the man was keeping track of which way the trucks were going at least this would hopefully throw them off to some degree. Several miles down the road, the driver turned his truck around and headed north again and drove straight through the rest area.

There would be no stopping now until they were over the Jordanian border which was at least another five or six hours away.

Within half an hour, a car came to a screeching halt as it entered the rest area and truck stop. The man inside exited his car. He began to walk up the row of street vendors calling someone's name.

For the past three days one of Donald's operatives had been cruising the highway and showing pictures of Sonja and Matt to anyone he could. This had been his first response to any of his inquiries and the adrenaline was pumping through his body. The two men found one another and they headed back to the car so that they could talk in private.

Donald's operative took the initiative and was rapid-firing questions towards the street vendor. "Were these the two people you saw?" He handed him a picture of Sonja and Matt.

"Yes, I think so" the vendor said.

"You think so?" the operative screamed back at him. "Is it them, yes or no? I want to know for sure!"

The vendor clutched the picture once again, this time coming back with a clear, "Yes, it is them." He then told the operative that he had seen them three times and as far as he knew they had disappeared into one of the three trucks that had headed south down the highway. Two of the trucks were transport trucks with trailers and the third one of the trucks had only one large white box on the back.

Don's operative quickly told the man to get out once he had given him all the information that he had. As the vendor left the car, he turned around and held out his hand in hopes of receiving a tip of some kind. He stooped down and looked into the car but he realized he was looking into the barrel of a gun pointed at his head.

"Here is your tip, I am giving you your life back, now get away from my car."

With that the car sped away and turned south to follow the three transport trucks.

Don's operative was a greedy and selfish man with only thoughts of self-promotion. This was his chance to prove himself and move up in the organization if he were to bring Sonja and Matt in by himself. As he sped down the road going south, he figured it would take him at least an hour to catch up with the trucks. The vendor had given him the truck descriptions and the plate numbers of the first two trucks, but he just got a partial plate number on the box truck as the licence plate had been covered in mud. It took just over an hour to catch up with the two transport trucks that were still travelling together.

After waving the lead truck over and talking to both of the drivers, he discovered that the box truck had turned around and gone north shortly after leaving the rest area. Don's operative was enraged and was screaming out loud as he ran back to his car. Once inside, he pointed his car north and put the gas pedal to the floor, not releasing it until he was going almost two hundred kilometres per hour.

For the first ten minutes of the car chase back north, Don's operative was screaming curses and threats that were not only directed to the passengers of the truck, but also to himself for being so stupid and letting the truck get so far ahead of him. He was now not sure if he would be able to catch up to it before it crossed the Jordanian border. This also put him in a difficult situation. Should he phone ahead and have someone stop them before they got to the border, or would he be able to catch them and get the glory for himself? In an instant he had made his decision. He pushed the gas pedal down a little bit further and the speedometer went up past the two hundred kilometers an hour mark.

Sonja also noticed that the truck they were travelling in seemed to be going a little faster. They had no idea if they were being followed, but they were not going to take any chances. They were making a run for the border and they were moving as fast as the speed limit would allow.

CHAPTER TWENTY-ONE

THE MOMENT OF TRUTH

The last Sunday of my two week shift had just ended and most of our tram crew was heading for supper. I had read the menu board earlier on in the day and I was looking forward to the roast turkey dinner that was being served this evening. I only had one hour to eat and get ready to go because the church service started at 7:30 pm and it was now already 6:30 pm.

As the four of us sat around the table and were enjoying the roast turkey, out of the blue, Edmond asked me a direct question that made three pairs of eyes leave the plate of turkey in front of them and look directly at me. "So, when are you going to tell us about the things that have been happening with you and your tram?"

"That's a good question," Cory said, "I think we would all like the answer to that one."

I was glad that I was in the process of chewing a mouthful of turkey because that gave me about fifteen seconds to figure out what I wanted to say. The three guys waited patiently for me to finish chewing so I could answer the question.

"OK," Mike said, "Let's hear it."

"Listen, I do owe you an explanation of some kind. Unfortunately, I can't explain it in the next five minutes and I'd like everyone to be present at the same time so you will all hear the same story. I'm going to talk to Kevin tomorrow and get him to set up a time when we can all get together after we come back in two weeks. Sorry, but that's the best I can do for right now."

As we finished our supper, I excused myself and said,

"I have to get going now or I'll be late for church; see you all in the morning." I hurried down the sidewalk towards my room, wondering if Matthew would show up at the church service this evening. I still had the scroll in my backpack since our hand burning experience yesterday and I wondered how Dave's hand was doing today.

I arrived in the church room a little early and was pleasantly surprised to see that not only was Matthew there, but Dave was there as well.

"Hi guys, so how is everything going? It's nice to see both of you again." With that I extended my hand towards Dave and we shook hands.

He pulled me in closer and said, "I want to say that I'm sorry about what happened yesterday. Will you accept my apology?"

"Of course I will, it wasn't that big of a deal." We stepped back.

Releasing our handshake Dave said, "Look at my fingertips." He extended the palm of his hand towards me. I noticed immediately that everything looked fine and there were no burn marks on his fingertips whatsoever. "Two minutes after you left, all the pain and discomfort left me instantly and all the burned flesh became like new right before my eyes. I can't explain it and can hardly believe it, but all I know is that it did happen."

I knew exactly how Dave was feeling. For the past month, my life had become a series of unexplainable events that I knew were real but for which I had no rational or logical explanation. It is strange to have to accept things you don't even believe in, or experience things that you cannot prove to anyone else. Dave just had one of those things happen in his life and was now trying to figure out where to put that in his belief system. For me it had been a little easier to accept because I did believe in the Bible, but for Dave, he was a 'facts' man only and he did not have any room in his theology for unexplainable events to occur.

As I was shaking hands with Matt, a couple of the regular attendees of the church services walked in, so I made the introductions so at least everyone knew each other's names. Within the next five minutes everyone arrived that was coming, so we started the service and our topic for the evening was, 'Do miracles

136

and unexplainable events still happen in the 21st century?' Needless to say it was a very interesting topic to discuss and people's opinions varied from one extreme to the other.

The truck carrying Sonja and Matt reached the outskirts of the border town of Al Quaryyat. It looked like they would make the border crossing before midnight. As they entered the town, the driver noticed that there seemed to be an unusual amount of activity and a high volume of traffic. There appeared to be a traffic jam in front of them that led to the road where the border crossing was located. The driver communicated their situation with Sonja, and she could sense that he was very nervous about the situation they found themselves in. As the box truck continued idling in one place, the car that had been pursuing them was making excellent time. Don's operative was only fifteen minutes behind them and he was gaining ground fast. He had been driving at an average of two hundred kilometers an hour for the past two and a half hours and was now hopeful that his quarry would be just around the next corner.

The lineup of cars started to form behind the box truck, but the driver knew that their situation did not look good and that he should have never let Sonja and Matt out of the truck to stretch their legs that afternoon. Inside the smuggling compartment, Sonja began to perspire as her mind began to imagine all of the negative scenarios that might occur in the next few minutes.

Her mind wandered to places it should not go, so she did not even hear her son saying, "Mommy, mommy." Matt then reached up to where his mother was standing and started to pat her on the hip in order to get her attention.

"Yes Matt, what is it?" she said as she broke away from her wondering thoughts. "What do you think happened to all the people in the earthquake? Do you think they will be OK?"

She thought about Matt's question for a moment, when an idea flooded through her mind as she quickly turned around and hit the intercom button. She was sure that the reason for the border crossing delay was due to last night's earthquake and all the humanitarian aid that would certainly be flowing into the quake zone. Then Sonja told the driver to find a police officer or someone who was controlling the traffic to let them through so that they could join the earthquake relief effort. Within seconds Sonja heard the driver's door open and then close behind him. It did not take long and soon the truck began to inch forward as it was being led around the lineup of traffic by a policeman.

Don's operative entered the border town and he ran into the same lineup the box truck had just got out of. He got out of his car and looked down the lineup of parked vehicles. He could see the top of the box truck and realized that the truck was moving. Without a second thought, he reached under the seat of his car, pulled out his handgun, tucked it into his belt under his jacket and started running down beside the lineup of parked cars. The man was desperate now to catch his quarry before they slipped out of sight into a different country. He was breathing heavily as he arrived at the place where he had last seen the truck. His eyes desperately searched for the large white box that was on the back of the truck. Being unable to see it he peered beyond some immigration buildings and saw the taillights of the large white box truck disappear around a corner into the country of Jordan.

He swore and cursed and mumbled out threats of retribution as he made his way back to his car. What should he do now? He could not cross the border and continue his pursuit because he had no idea of where the truck was now headed and it was also out of the jurisdiction that Donald had given him. Another question now came to his mind. Should he make contact with Donald and tell him of these events or should he forget this day ever happened? He had made an inexcusable error because of his pride and now it was impossible to correct it. As he thought of the possible ramifications of telling Donald about what had transpired through the day, the decision became quite obvious. He would get back into his car, drive south, and try to erase this day from his memory.

The church service ended just before nine o'clock. Even though the guys were tired everyone hung around and chatted before heading back to their rooms. After everyone had left, it was only Matthew, Dave and I standing in the middle of the room.

I was very surprised that Dave had come with Matt that evening. My guess was that he did not come for the church service, but for the possibility of seeing the scroll. Dave was the first one to speak and as he shook my hand he said, "To be honest, I'm glad I came to the service tonight. Although I do not agree with most of what was said, it was interesting to see how and why people believe the way they do. It also made me look inside myself and question my own motives and the reasons that I believe or don't believe in certain things. Anyways, after last night only a blind man or a fool would not look at the evidence and stick to his own way of thinking".

"Well I'm glad you came," I said to Dave, "and I'm also glad that you got something out of what was said this evening." I turned towards Matthew and I could see on his face that he was excited about something.

"Guess what!" Matthew said with a big grin, "Last night was the first time in over a week that I have had a sound sleep. No dreams or nightmares and I woke up this morning feeling fresh and well-rested. I had almost forgotten what it felt like to sleep through a full night uninterrupted."

"Hey that's awesome," I said to Matthew, "I'm glad you had a good night's sleep."

"So what do you think guys? Should we try and look at the scroll again tonight? I have not touched it or moved it."

"Sounds great," Matthew enthused. "We can go to my room and check it out there if you want to."

"Sure, let's go, We won't have enough time to study it in detail, but at least tonight we should be able to get a good look at it."

As we walked towards Matt's room, my thoughts went back to the first time we met when he had told me his full name was Matthew King and that he lived in trailer #4 and room #11. Amazing things had happened in my life since that evening exactly a month ago.

When we arrived and entered Matthew's small room, he immediately offered me his only chair and he and Dave both sat on the bed. I placed my backpack on the floor in between us and unzipped the top of it.

Tonight there was no light, no heat, but there seemed to be an anxious expectation from both Matthew and Dave. I reached my hand into the backpack and removed the scroll carefully, while Matthew and Dave's expressions registered awe and wonder as I laid the scroll on the small table.

Without saying a word I unrolled it to its full extension and held the ends in place so that we all could see it clearly. After a few moments of total silence, Matthew and Dave's eyes slowly came up off the sheet of paper that had kept them spellbound. With his index finger pressed against his lips, Matt motioned for us to go outside once again.

No words were spoken until we found a private spot where we could all talk freely.

"Listen Walter, you have something in your possession that is truly unbelievable. I'm not sure what it all means, but I know that we need to keep it safe. It is all written in Hebrew and we would be more than happy to translate it for you if you want us to. We also need to make at least one copy of it so that we can translate it and not have to have the original in front of us."

I thought for a moment. I knew that they were right and that we did need to make at least one copy of the scroll. I also knew that from this point on we were going to have to trust each other.

As I responded to Matthew's request of having a copy of the scroll I said, "I will agree to make a copy of it on one condition and that is, only one picture will be taken of it for translation purposes and that at least for the next two weeks you will show it to nobody else." Matthew and Dave had no problem agreeing to the condition that I had set out, so with that in place we returned to his room and he took a close up picture of the scroll with his digital camera. As I said my goodbyes and turned to leave for the evening, I was excited for the fact that soon we would know exactly what was written on the scroll.

CHAPTER TWENTY-TWO

HEADING HOME

The Monday morning tram runs came and went in a flash and I was now finished my two week shift. The one question I still had not answered in my own mind yet was "Am I going to take the scroll home, or leave it here at work?" I tossed that question back and forth and finally decided that I would take the scroll home. I knew my family would love to see it and we also had some friends back home that could speak and write the Hebrew language. I still wasn't sure if I was going to tell anyone other than my family about my experiences over the past couple of weeks, but if I did at least I would have some evidence with me to back it up.

My flight from work into the Edmonton Airport was totally routine. I had just completed the first leg of my eight hour journey and now had a two hour wait between flights. I found a quiet spot to sit and read the newspaper I had just bought.

Many thoughts from the past two weeks crowded my mind. It was still hard for me to imagine that the things I had experienced were actually true and had occurred, not only in my life, but also in the lives of others.

As I thought about Matthew and Dave I could only imagine their curiosity and excitement as they were going to study and translate the scroll over the next couple of weeks. As I sat in a quiet corner of the airport, I thought about Sam, my Tram Angel. I could clearly remember every word that he had spoken to me and I often wished that I could have another face-to-face conversation with him since I still had so many questions, and very few answers. From what he had told me, I knew I could ask him the questions, but I also knew that he needed permission to reveal himself to me and answer them. I sat there thinking about Sam and wondering if he was sitting with me here in the airport.

As that thought passed through my mind, an announcement came over the loudspeaker saying, "Paging passenger Sam Matthews, last call for Sam Matthews flying out of gate #4 flight #11. Your plane is now fully boarded. Last call for Sam Matthews gate 4 flight 11." My ears perked up with that announcement and a big smile came to my face. This must be Sam's answer to my thought "Is Sam here with me right now?" The name Sam, the name Matthew, and the numbers 4 and 11... yes, Sam was here.

The box truck continued to make its way northwest towards the city of Amman, Jordan. Sonja and the driver felt much better now that they had crossed the border. It was only another hour to the drop off spot where the driver would be happy to leave his human cargo behind. Sonja and Matt would be happy also as they would finally get out of the moving tin can that had been their home for the past eighteen hours.

Just over an hour later the truck came to a stop and the engine ground to a halt. Sonja could hear two people talking through the walls of the compartment, but she couldn't understand their language. Within a couple of minutes the wall that had confined them was removed and Sonja and Matt were quickly led into the back seat of a waiting car.

"Where are we going now?" Sonja wondered, as the car headed down the highway into the darkness of the night.

I got settled into my seat for my fifty-five minute flight from Edmonton to Kelowna. I made sure I had my glasses and earphones with me so that I could watch television. As the plane took off and we reached cruising altitude, I turned on the TV set and plugged in my earphones. Flipping through the channels, I stopped at a news station and began to listen to some of the events that were happening in the world around me.

A story came on that sounded interesting to me. I focused my attention on the television and settled in to watch and listen as the newscaster was talking about the biggest company buyout in history. I listened with interest as the newscaster gave a brief history of what had transpired to make this deal happen.

He said, "Late in the 1990's Global Ventures and Abaddon Industries had teamed up to become the world's largest food and beverage distributor and over the last ten years they had also become the largest import/export company of oil and gas in the entire world. Their assets would probably reach the trillion dollar mark by the end of the decade.

For the past six months, starting in the fall of 2012, they had been working on a deal which was now finalized. The two companies could merge into one and its new name would become Apollyon Global."

The newscaster went on to say that the governments of many nations were concerned with the fact that one company was so large and held the distribution power to the most important commodities on the planet. The collective thought of the global community was that with all the power, money and influence of this one company, it would not be very hard to bring the nations of the world to their knees. Yet it was happening, and not only that, it was now a done deal and Apollyon Global had become a reality.

As the newscaster finished his brief history on the biggest deal of the twenty-first century, he said they would air a prepared statement by the sole owner of Apollyon Global, Donald King.

The moment the newscaster spoke the words 'Donald King,' the hair on the back of my neck stood up straight. Could this actually be the same Donald King that was in Matthew's dream? Was this Donald King, the owner of the largest company in the world, the father of the Matthew King that I worked with up north? The implications could be staggering if that were the case, and if so, Matthew had a lot more of his history to tell me when we got back to work.

As the newscaster switched locations, the image of a sixty-something year old man came onto the screen. The satellite video feed was coming from the capital city of Tehran in the country of Iran. Donald King began his short address to the world. I could see the facial similarities and expressions in both Donald and Matthew and I was convinced that these two men were father and son.

"My name is Donald King," he began. "I was born and raised in this beautiful country of Iran. It has been my hope and dream for the last fifty years that we can all live in a world of equality and peace. As my company, Apollyon Global has now become the largest in the world, I believe that my dreams can become a reality.

From this point forward and over the next few years you will see the earth's resources begin to flow in new directions. The poorer nations of the world will begin to experience a slow but steady growth to a new prosperity of goods and services and the richer nations of the world will continue to enjoy their prosperous way of living as well.

I challenge the governments of the world to bring their nations into the twenty-first century and begin to work for the good of their people. We must all work together for the greater good of all humanity and seek the mutual benefit of all the nations of the earth.

I promise that I, Donald King, and Apollyon Global will do our very best to usher in a New World Order that will ultimately bring equality and peace to our planet."

The video feed ended and the newscaster made closing comments as the news station went on to its next story.

I leaned back in my seat and pondered the words of Donald King. To me it sounded like he had just made a political statement and had thrown out a challenge to either follow his dream or face the consequences. Somehow his speech did not sit well with me and there was something about him as a person that seemed to repulse me. I didn't know why I thought that but yet I did. I usually give people the benefit of the doubt, but in this case I had a strange feeling on the inside that this man could not be trusted. There was not only something untrustworthy about this man, but there was something almost evil about Donald King.

My mind continued to think about the ramifications that a company like Apollyon Global could have upon the world. I would have to agree with the global community that a company that size could bring the nations of the world to their knees. Maybe that was Donald's plan from the beginning; to be able to rule the world without a shot being fired. I would definitely have to talk to Matthew about his father when I got back to work but for the time being at least, I was going to enjoy my two weeks off and the rest of my flight home.

Sonja and Matt slept soundly in the back seat of the car, as the hours slipped by. With all the business of the earthquake relief effort happening, it was decided that there would be no waiting in a safe house in Amman, but a direct border crossing would happen within the next hour. The Israeli border guards had been notified and they were waiting for their arrival.

Dawn started to break over the awakening desert. The car pulled up to the Israeli border crossing and was quickly waved through. Sonja and Matt slept soundly as the car continued on its way to its final destination. Jerusalem would be their new home. The car pulled up to the King David Hotel, which was located just outside the walls of the Old City. As the driver roused Sonja and Matt out of their slumber, he opened the back door of the car and helped them onto the sidewalk in front of the hotel.

"Shalom," he said to them. "Welcome to Israel and Jerusalem which will be your new home.'

CHAPTER TWENTY-THREE

HOME AT LAST

The rest of my trip back home was routine and uneventful. I was very much looking forward to my next two weeks off and it would be great to see my family again. As I walked through the door of our home, I was greeted by hugs and smiles from my wife and two youngest sons. Our oldest son and daughter were still away in University, which did not get out for Christmas break for another month. Since it was still fairly early in the evening, the conversation quickly turned to my last two weeks of work. I began to tell the family about my story.

All three of them listened quietly and patiently until I started recounting the part where I had found the scroll on my gen-set. Once I mentioned the word scroll, both boys started firing questions at me, and of course the first one was, "So did you bring the scroll home?"

I responded with a "Yes of course I did and it's in my backpack, but you don't get to see it until I finish telling my story." I began telling them the part about when Sam came into my room and answered the four questions I had asked him. I noticed the faces of both of my boys had skepticism written all over them. I could understand why they were responding to my story in that way because all through their growing up years I had told them wild adventure tales with them being the characters in the stories.

With my sons now fourteen and sixteen years old and it being at least three years since I told them their last adventure tale, I could understand why they were skeptical. I'm sure they were thinking I was just making up another story for them, and a wild one at that.

They graciously let me finish without too many more questions until I got to the part when two nights ago my backpack was glowing like it was on fire and Dave got his hand burned.

"Come on, dad," my sixteen-year-old son Andrew said, "we're not ten years old any more. You're just making all of this stuff up aren't you?"

"Well, I know it's going to be hard for you to believe, but yes, all of this actually happened to me over the past two weeks. Sometimes I lay awake at night and ask myself the same question, 'Is all of this stuff really happening to me?' but yes it is, and I still can't explain why."

I finished my story, then handed my youngest son John the backpack and said, "Open it up and take out the scroll."

He unzipped the top and pulled it open, looking inside before he placed his hand into it to retrieve the scroll. As he pulled it out, he turned it over and over in his hands checking out every square inch of it. Then, with one hand on each side of the paper, he fully extended it and placed it on the table in front of him.

"Well, what's all of this supposed to mean?" John asked. "It's all in a different language and I can't understand a word."

"You're absolutely right John, it's all in Hebrew and so we'll have to get it translated before we can figure out what it actually says."

The scroll conversation wound down and the eighteen hours of being awake began to catch up with me. I yawned and said, "Let's leave all this until tomorrow when we have more time to check things out."

After saying my good-nights to the boys and closing their doors behind me as I left their bedroom, my wife, Lisa, and I would now have a chance to catch up and talk about the things that had happened in her life over the past couple of weeks.

The car pulled away from the King David Hotel and someone familiar walked through the hotel doors towards Sonja and Matt. "Welcome to Jerusalem," Jacob said with a warm and friendly smile on his face. "It's very good to see both of you again." He gave them a hug and welcomed them to their new home.

"Come with me" he said, "and I will help get you settled into a room here in the hotel where you can relax and enjoy yourselves for the next couple of days." Sonja and Matt followed Jacob through the hotel lobby. The thought hit Sonja that they had finally arrived in Israel and were safe from the long arm of Donald King.

As they entered their hotel room, Matt found the remote control for the television set and started to click buttons until he found something that put a smile on his face. Jacob and Sonja then sat down on the couch and Jacob asked Sonja how the trip had gone. Sonja gave a brief review of their last twenty hours ending her story by saying that she was so glad that they had finally arrived and that they did not have to stay in the safe house in Amman.

Jacob then told Sonja he had been following them during the whole trip. It had been his job to make sure that the truck made it safely into Jordan and then to also make sure that they made it into Israel as well. He told Sonja how close they had come to being discovered by one of Don's operatives and how close he was to catching them at the Jordanian border crossing. Jacob continued saying he had been in between the truck and Don's operative and was only ten seconds away from intercepting him in the lineup for the border. As the truck had made its way through the border crossing before Don's operative could reach it, he abandoned his pursuit, went back to his car and headed south, back into Saudi Arabia.

While Jacob and Sonja continued chatting, both of them tried to relax and unwind after the last twenty hours of nonstop stress. They were physically exhausted and it was nice for them to relax a little and talk without any agenda. Although Sonja knew that it was Jacob's job to watch over her, she enjoyed the fact that somebody actually seemed to care about her and the welfare of her son.

For the past five years she had been emotionally starved for the kindness and affection that Donald had never once given to her. She had felt totally alone and unloved other than the times that she and Matt were able to visit with Miriam. A tear came to her eye as she asked Jacob if there had been any news about Miriam and her whereabouts. Jacob sadly responded that there had not been any word, but that David was still watching for her and that they would let her know as soon as they found anything out.

Sonja thanked Jacob for all of his help and told him that she was truly grateful to him and David for their protection. Jacob got up to leave and he told Sonja that he would be the one helping them over the next few weeks as they got settled into their new home and their new country.

"I would like that," Sonja said to Jacob as he left their hotel room and she locked the door behind him.

Over the course of the past four days, David had lived on very little sleep. He napped for short periods of time either in his car or in the small room he had rented in the town's only hotel. The problem with being a stranger in a small town was that everyone knew you were there and were aware of everything you did. Unlike a city where you can blend in, a small town was like a large family where everyone knew your business and kept a watchful eye on you.

Everyone knew about the stranger in town and so David was quite sure that Donald knew also. During the last three days David had been observing people's movements in the community and was almost sure he had located an entrance or a meeting point to Donald's operations. Although he was booked for one more day at his hotel, David was feeling very uneasy about his presence here in this small community.

Over the past several days, David had also investigated the terrain and geological features of the area that surrounded the small town of Abad. About three kilometres northeast of the town stood a small hill with an outcropping of rocks that gave a good vantage point of the small town. The rock bluff stood at the edge of an endless desert that stretched as far as the eye could see. Because of the urgency he felt within himself to leave, he followed his instincts, packed his few belongings and checked out of his room. As he drove through the town just one last time, he wanted the people to notice that he was leaving in order for word to spread that the stranger had finally left town.

David drove about ten kilometres up the main road that went east, then he pulled over to the side of the road and waited to make sure that he had not been followed. As dusk started to descend upon the Iranian landscape, the colours were truly stunning with the sun slowly sinking below the horizon and darkness following in its path. Once the skies were completely dark, David turned his car around and headed back towards Abad.

When he found the small dirt road that led past the rock bluff, he turned off his lights and drove the two kilometres to his final destination. He had already predetermined a hiding spot for his car where he would sit with his high powered night vision binoculars pressed again his eyes. This would be his last night to gather any information on Donald and his activities, and he would have to do it from a distance.

Little did David know that while he watched for any unusual movement in the town that lay below him, two men were in his former hotel room looking for anything that might give them a clue to his identity and his purpose for being in Abad. They searched every square inch of the hotel room and even took fingerprints off some of the items that he had touched. They also had access to the security camera at the hotel that had been installed at Donald's expense. This was Donald's town and nothing happened in it without him knowing.

As the night wore on, David noticed a fair amount of traffic activity going on in the town below. David had already counted six different vehicles stopping and then leaving in front of the location he suspected of being a meeting place. The midnight hour approached and the town seemed to fall asleep, its activity slowly grinding to a halt. Now only a sporadic car or person could be seen on the streets and David himself was ready for some sleep. He told himself that he would stay awake until at least midnight, when he noticed a car beginning to move from the edge of town and begin to make its way down the highway going east. He watched it slow down as it approached the small road that he had turned off onto. Instantly David's weariness disappeared and adrenaline started pumping through his veins. The car he had his eyes on was coming down the small road right towards him!

Many thoughts started running through David's mind. "Is my car hidden well enough? Did someone put a tracking device on my car? Has my position been compromised?" David waited and watched as his heart pounded wildly in his chest. His right hand firmly gripped his semi-automatic pistol with a clip of fifteen rounds of ammunition. He watched the approaching car as it got closer and closer and was now only one hundred meters away. Steadily the car moved closer and was only fifty meters away, then thirty and then the car slowly drove past the rock bluff and continued down the small dirt road. Once it had completely passed his line of sight, David moved his position and continued watching until it came to a complete stop about two hundred meters past the rock bluff.

Both front doors opened and two men exited the car with shovels in their hands and walked about twenty meters into the desert. For the next five minutes all that David could hear was the distant sound of two men talking to each other and two shovels being forced into the desert sand. It was obvious to David what was happening and he did not like the possibility of what he might have to do once the men left.

After the digging stopped, the two men walked back to the car, opened up the trunk and carried what looked like a body to the prepared grave site. With a thud, the body hit the bottom of the hole in the ground. The men then returned to the car and a second body was lifted out of the trunk and was carried and dumped into the same shallow grave. Within two minutes the hole had been filled in and the men returned to their waiting car. As they turned the car around and headed down the same small road past the rock bluff, David was thankful that he did not need to encounter these two men.

The car slowly made its way back to the main highway and headed west towards Abad. David watched carefully to see where it would end its journey. As the car pulled into the same area where it had left from, David had a strong suspicion that he might have possibly found another location that Donald was working out of. David finished writing down the final details of the information that he had gleaned over the past few hours. He knew that his next job would be the most unpleasant of all. He must go down and actually see the corpses and photograph them before his evening work would be finished.

CHAPTER TWENTY-FOUR

SCROLL TRANSLATION

Three days into my time off we had the opportunity to go and visit some friends of ours that could read and write Hebrew to some degree. Kris and Ty invited us over for supper and later in the evening we would relax in the wood-fired sauna that Ty had built. After we had enjoyed the home-cooked Mediterranean style supper, conversation moved from topic to topic effortlessly.

As the evening wore on and the fire in the wood stove had warmed the cedar room to a very hot ninety degrees Celsius we made our way over to the small, rustic cabin that was built to resemble an old prospector's home out of the 1800's. Ty was a retired carpenter/artist and everything he put his hand to build or create turned out exceptionally well. While enjoying our sauna together I asked Ty how his linguistic skills in Hebrew was these days. To my pleasant surprise he responded by saying, "Well, I am a little rusty but I still could hold my own in a conversation and my reading skills are also pretty good."

My next question to Ty was if he would be willing to translate some Hebrew into English for me when we got back into the house. "No problem," he said, "I'll give it my best try anyways."

After returning to the house, I sat down with Ty and handed him the scroll to look at as the ladies made coffee and got some snacks ready in the kitchen. Ty sat staring intently at the scroll that lay before him and I could tell by his facial expression that he was very intrigued by the piece of paper that his attention was fixed upon.

After three or four minutes of silence his eyes left the paper and looked directly at me and asked, "Where did you get this?"

"I'll gladly tell you, but first, what you think of it."

Ty turned his eyes back to the scroll and said, "I'm not sure what to think about it. It's obviously scripture verses from both the Old and New Testaments in the Bible, but it has its own flavor to it. I have never seen any Hebrew written like this in my entire life. I can pretty much read it, but it seems to me that this style of writing was the ancient template of where our modern Hebrew language comes from."

As Ty went into his room to get his Hebrew Bible, the ladies came in with coffee and snacks on a tray and set them down on the coffee table.

"Where was Ty off to in such a hurry?" Kris asked.

"I think he went to his room to get his Hebrew Bible so he can compare it to the words that are written here on this scroll" I responded.

"What's this scroll all about?" Kris asked as Ty came back into the room and sat down.

"Yes, please tell us," Ty said.

As I told my story, I was not sure of what the reaction would be or if we would still have friends at the end of the evening. It took me an hour to recount the details of the past month and a half and when I finally finished, there was a long silence that lingered as Ty and Kris tried to make sense of what I had just told them. The coffees we had started to drink were now stone cold and the warm pastries did not look as appetizing any more.

Finally, Ty looked me in the eye and said, "So let's translate this thing and maybe we can figure it out." With those words the ladies collected the cups full of cold coffee and returned to the kitchen to get some fresh coffee as Ty opened his Bible and began the translation work.

David climbed down from the rock bluff and headed towards the shallow grave. He dreaded the thought of what he might find beneath the few inches of dirt. As he followed the men's footprints that still remained intact pressed into the desert sand, he soon came to the spot where the two bodies had been buried. David slowly knelt down beside the grave and carefully began to remove the sand that covered the final resting place of the two nameless victims.

This was the last thing on earth that he wanted to be doing, but it was a part of his job and he knew he must complete the task. It only took forty-five seconds of digging to find what he was looking for. As David readjusted his flashlight and carefully removed the sand from around the victim's faces, a blast of recognition hit him and he was almost positive he was looking into the face of Miriam. David let out a groan and turned his face away from the bodies as he tried to keep himself in control. After a moment of getting his thoughts together, he turned once again towards the grave and took pictures of the two faces along with hair and blood samples.

He was about to cover the two corpses up again when his eye caught the reflection of an object as he readjusted his flashlight. With his hands he carefully brushed the sand away, finding a heart-shaped pendant that was still around Miriam's neck. Gently he lifted Miriam's head and removed the pendant and chain and held it in his hands. He shone the flashlight on it and inspected it more closely and he noticed a small latch that seemed to hold the heart together. With a gentle push from his thumb, the heart opened up and the smiling faces of Sonja and Matt shone in the flashlight's beam. Now there was no doubt, he had just found Miriam but who was this man was this mystery man?

Sonja yawned and stretched as she threw the covers off herself and sat on the edge of the bed. She had no idea how long she had slept, and even had to think hard to orient herself as to where she was now. The past few days had become a blur to her but she distinctly remembered Jacob saying to her, "Welcome to Jerusalem, your new home." Yes, they really were here, where she and Matt would be safe at last.

She got up to check on Matt, quietly slipping into his room and saw he was still sleeping soundly. She had no idea what time it was, so she went in search of a clock to satisfy her curiosity. Once she realized it was three o'clock in the afternoon, she decided to wake Matt up before they got their sleeping patterns totally out of sorts.

She also wondered if Jacob would stop by today and check up on them and see how they were doing. But as the hours slipped by and another day came to an end, it was just Sonja and Matt in their hotel room. "Tomorrow," Sonja thought to herself, "we will go and explore this strange new country they call Israel."

It was hard for them both to sleep that evening. Matt drifted off to sleep around ten pm and Sonja finally drifted off about midnight. It seemed like minutes had just gone by when Matt came running into her room around four am saying, "Mommy, mommy, I had a really bad dream."

Matt jumped up on her bed and she held him close and said, "Do you want to tell me about it?"

"Well," said Matt, "It was scary. The necklace with the heart on it that we gave to Grandma was floating through the air and many people were trying to grab it. But then Mr. Jacob came and gave it back to you and you started to cry. I don't like dreams like that," Matt said as he snuggled in closer to his mother. "Can I sleep here with you for the rest of the night, mommy?"

"Of course you can son," Sonja said as she held Matt tight and both of them tried to get a little more sleep before a new day started. But it was not to be for Sonja. Matt drifted off to sleep very quickly, but Sonja could not get Matt's dream out of her mind.

By now, Sonja realized that Matt's dreams were significant and somehow he was gifted with seeing things that others could not. Since this dream had scared Matt, Sonja wondered what the dream meant and what it had to do with Jacob. Whatever the dream meant, she could only guess, and the one thing that she knew for sure was that there would be no more sleep for her for the rest of this night.

Matt woke up early, just after eight am. He was filled with excitement as they quickly ate their breakfast and got ready to explore the city of Jerusalem.

As they walked out the main doors of the hotel, they were greeted by a man introducing himself as one of Jacob's co-workers. Since Jacob was not available to be with them today, he had been instructed to be their guide for the day and to take them wherever they wanted to go. Of course Matt started jumping up and down excitedly saying, "I want to go to the big castle!" as he pointed towards the walls of Jerusalem.

"Of course you can," the man laughed as the three of them started walking towards one of the gates that entered the old city. Both Sonja and Matt were awestruck as the three of them wandered through the old city streets drinking in the sight, smells, and sounds of this ancient city. There was something new to see around every corner and Matt tirelessly led the way until he realized he was very hungry and wanted to stop for lunch somewhere. They settled in to enjoy their first authentic Israeli meal and Sonja was pleased that her son was having a wonderful day.

Ty finished translating the scroll into English and his conclusions were the same as mine. All of the scripture verses on the time wheel were either parts or whole scripture verse references. The verses were easy enough to translate by just reading them out of an English Bible, and now I knew exactly what they meant. Ty wrote down each reference so I now had a direct and literal translation of what the scroll said. I figured that this must be the easy part, because now we had to figure out how these references tied into a much larger mystery. Anyway, it was time for Lisa and I to go home after a very full evening of good food, storytelling, and getting one step closer to figuring out what the scroll had to say.

Three thousand kilometers away, in the province of Ontario, Matthew and David had made the same discoveries from the picture they had taken of the scroll. Since they were both fluent in reading and writing Hebrew, it did not take them very long to translate it.

They had spent the first couple of days of their time off reading and studying all the chapters surrounding the scripture references on the scroll, but could make no sense of any of it. Only the first four references that had already come to pass made any sense. They were already looking forward to going back to work so we could compare notes and maybe figure this out. But for now the only thing to do was to keep thinking about the references but try to enjoy the rest of their time off.

CHAPTER TWENTY-FIVE

9:11

Two weeks slipped by very quickly and before I knew it I was thirty-four thousand feet in the air flying back to Northern Alberta. I was not exactly excited about having to tell the guys at work about the things that had been happening to me over the past couple of months. What I was excited about was that I would be able to talk to Matthew again and find out more about his father and family history.

I kept thinking about Donald King, who was the sole owner of the now largest company in the world, Apollyon Global. As the words Apollyon Global swished around in my brain, a paralyzing thought flooded through my mind. The word Apollyon was also in the scripture reference at the six o'clock position on the scroll. With that word connection formed in my mind I almost came out of my seat on the plane.

"Why didn't I see that earlier?" I thought to myself. But the thoughts kept coming. As I quoted the scripture reference to myself in my mind, another word stuck out as if it were calling to me. The word was Abaddon, and instantly I realized that this was the name of Donald King's former company that had just merged to create Apollyon Global.

My mind was now racing, causing me to squirm in my seat at the possibilities of the meaning of these two words.. Then, to make matters even worse, another word association possibility came into my head. It was the word "king". Could the word "king" in this scripture verse actually be referring to Donald King, the world's most powerful man? Without thinking I put the table tray down in front of me, grabbed a pen and paper and started to write. I had already memorized all of the different scripture references and time allocations, so I started to write out the six o'clock position.

"And they had a king over them, the angel of the bottomless pit, whose name in the Hebrew is Abaddon and in the Greek, Apollyon. Revelation 9:11." My mind was swarming with different thoughts. Could all of this actually be true? Was this a 9:11 warning coming to the world? Was Donald King the angel of the bottomless pit? Was this warning connected to Matthew's dream of his father bursting out of Pit 13 riding a dragon in a kind of nuclear explosion? Could Pit 13, 11 kilometers to go, in Matthew's dream be a clue to something?"

I had to slow my mind down, because I was starting to hyperventilate right there in the 737. I closed my eyes and let my thoughts go to different places and times. I would have a lot of time to think about what the scroll was trying to say to me, but for right now I had to stay focused and try to enjoy my flight back to work.

Sonja and Matt had totally enjoyed their day exploring the old city and getting a taste of what Israeli life might be like. Sonja was excited to be in this strange new land with her son. Here they might be able to blend in with the general population and have a fresh start at life. She wondered when Jacob would return and help them make the transition she was so excited about. She realized it would not be today since Matt had already gone to bed for the night and she was sitting on the couch wondering what her and Matt's future would be like.

As she let her mind wander, her thoughts were interrupted by a very quiet knock on the door. She quickly moved towards the door, pressed her ear against it, and quietly said, "Yes? Who is it?" At first there was no immediate response, but then she heard a voice saying in low tones, "It's Jacob, but I can come back in the morning if you'd like."

With that, she unlocked the door, swung it open and said, "No, please come in, I could use some company and Matt has gone to sleep already."

Jacob entered the hotel room and they both sat down on the couch. Sonja began telling him about the lovely day that they had and thanked Jacob warmly for sending someone over to show them around. Sonja's eyes finally met with Jacob's as they sat in the living room, and she realized that Jacob's eyes were not following her story of the day's excitement, but had a look of sadness and empathy in them.

"What's wrong, Jacob?" Sonja said as she searched his eyes for any clues as to the reason for the sadness he expressed.

Before Jacob could even say a word, Sonja broke into a quiet sob and she covered her face with her hands. "You've brought me Miriam's heart-shaped necklace, haven't you?"

Jacob sat stunned with his mouth wide open as he pulled the golden necklace out of his sport jacket's front pocket. "How, how did you know?" he managed to stutter.

Sonja did not hear him as she was already so lost in her grief. Miriam was gone forever and now she would have to face life without her best friend by her side. All of the not knowing and the built-up emotions burst like a dam, and the tears flowed down from her eyes like a raging river.

Sonja threw her arms around Jacob's neck and wept freely. How long they remained embraced she had no idea, but when Jacob finally left for the evening, she noticed his sports jacket was saturated from the flow of her tears.

Once Jacob had left, and the door to the hotel room was locked, Sonja just stood there looking at the heart-shaped pendant that lay in the palm of her hand. She remembered the day that she and Matt had given the pendant to Miriam with the pictures of them on the inside. It was on Matt's fourth birthday and since that day, Sonja had never seen Miriam without it. She had worn it everywhere, even if it didn't match with the clothes she was wearing. It was actually Matt's idea to give it to his grandma after he had seen it in the jewellery store window.

When he had given it to his grandma, he said to her, "Now you can take us anywhere and we will always be in your heart."

As the words of her son replayed themselves in her mind, a fresh batch of tears found their way down her cheeks, but this time they fell onto the uncaring floor.

I got off the plane in Edmonton and headed to the ground transportation that would take me to another private airport hangar. I was surprised when I ran into Edmond and Mike who were already waiting for the shuttle. I quickly got my ticket and headed over to the revolving exit doors to join them so we could leave on the same shuttle. As we headed out and got on board for our 5 minute ride, Edmond said to me,

"So, have you been listening to the news for the past couple of days?"

"Actually, I haven't, what's up?"

"Things are really heating up in the Middle East. Not only is Israel threatening Iran with an all-out air strike, but seems it is imminent and will happen before the end of 2015. The situation is so tense that the United Nations has asked Donald King, the president of Apollyon Global, to talk to both sides and see if a peace deal can be brokered. It sounds like a great idea to me," Edmond said, "and if anyone can do it, he probably can make it happen."

I could not believe what Edmond was telling me. I had not heard anything about that over the past couple of days, but obviously it was happening and Donald King seemed to be right in the middle of it. We all stepped out of the shuttle and into the waiting room where we would catch our next plane. I could not get my mind off the things I had just heard, especially about Donald King. I desperately needed to talk to Matthew King and see where he fit into this whole puzzle. The more I thought about it, the more I believed that Matthew was a major player in this scroll mystery, and now it would be his turn to let me in on the things that were going on in his life.

Sleep did not come easily for Sonja that night. Thoughts of Miriam crowded the corners of her mind and a myriad of questions that needed answers floated aimlessly around in her head.

How did Jacob get the pendant? Was Donald now coming after her? She knew that Jacob could have some of the answers to her questions, but she also knew that she may never have the answers to all of them. Deep inside of her Sonja knew that she was being torn apart by all the things that had happened to her since she had married Donald. But she also knew that she had to be strong for her son Matt and that he was more important than falling apart herself.

So with a deep breath and a clear focus in her mind, she said to herself, "Sonja, you will be strong for your son from this day forward. You will live with purpose and not live in the heartaches of the past. You will remember the good times and learn from the mistakes of the past, and you will be the mother that Matt needs from this moment on. I make this promise to Matt and also to myself."

With new resolve and a fresh outlook on life, Sonja rolled over in bed, closed her eyes, and was soon sleeping soundly. A new day would come and she would be ready to meet it, whatever it brought.

CHAPTER TWENTY-SIX

BLACKMAIL

My first evening tram run went smoothly and I was soon making my way back to the dining room for supper. My mind was crowded with all the thoughts and information that had come my way in just the past few hours. I needed to find Matthew and Dave and see if we could get some perspective on exactly what was happening.

While having supper with Mike and Edmond, they asked me how my two weeks off had gone and then asked if I had seen anything unusual on my gen-set that evening. I knew that they were just having fun with me, but I also knew they wanted to hear my story. I responded to their ribbing by saying,

"You'll have to wait until tomorrow when all the rest of the crew gets in."

As we finished our supper and were just about to leave, I turned around and saw Dave come through the dining room doors and make a beeline straight for me. When he arrived, we shook hands and he said,

"We need to talk right away."

After putting my tray of dirty dishes away, we found a table off to the side where we could sit and talk privately. David looked distressed and anxious as we sat down.

David started the conversation. "I'm not sure what's going on, but ever since we started translating the scroll, our lives have been turned upside-down."

I could tell that Dave was in real turmoil and his body language was expressing it very well.

"I don't even know where to start telling you about it. For starters, ever since we found out what the scroll said, I've had a migraine headache. My doctor has no idea what is causing it and I'm swallowing pain relievers like they're candies.

I've been in an accident back home and totalled my car, my basement suite sprung a leak and I was ankle deep in water. Then to top it all off I got food poisoning in a restaurant and was sitting on a toilet or laying in bed for two days. And that is only a few of the worst things that have happened to me over the past two weeks.

It hasn't gone any better for Matthew either. He is laying down in his bed right now because he has been running a fever of one hundred degrees for the past week, and can't seem to shake it. This morning we met in the airport in Toronto for our flight out to Edmonton, but for some reason he can't talk. He must have laryngitis. I told him to stay home and come when he is better, but he wouldn't hear of it. He wanted to get back to work so that he could talk to you and see if we could get this scroll figured out. I don't like this scroll any more. We've had nothing but trouble since we've translated it."

"I have a ton of questions for both of you," I said to Dave, "but especially for Matthew. When do you think we could get together?"

"He wants to see you now! That's why I'm here, to bring you to his room. I'm not sure how much talking he will be able to do, but we can go and see him in his room anyways."

We were walking down the sidewalk towards trailer number four when a strange wave of heaviness seemed to swirl around my feet. All of a sudden, I felt like I had two twenty pound weights strapped onto my legs and it was starting to slow me down.

"What's wrong with you?" Dave asked.

"I'm not sure. I was fine just a minute ago, but now I feel like my legs have lead weights tied to them."

"So it's happening to you too," Dave said with the beginnings of a smile on his face. "Welcome to the sick club."

As we walked down the trailer hallway and came to room eleven, I could feel a dark presence by the door and my legs were feeling heavier by the moment. Dave pushed the door open and stepped into the room. I felt a gust of wind rush past me, disappearing into the hallway. Entering the room, we could not believe what we were seeing! Matthew was laying on the top of his bed, holding a Bible in his hand and looking like a corpse that was ready to be buried.

Dave quickly moved beside him and started to shake his shoulders shouting, "Matthew, Matthew, wake up!" He continued to shake him and call his name, and Matthew's eyes finally began to focus and a gurgling sound came out of his throat.

"Help me up," Matthew said in a raspy voice.

We got Matthew into a sitting position and handed him a bottle of water. I asked Dave if I should go and get the paramedics.

Before Dave could respond, Matthew grabbed Dave's arm, shook his head and croaked out a "NO!" Dave and I looked at each other and we decided to wait a few minutes and see if Matthew got any better. If he didn't, we would get the paramedics whether he wanted us to or not. Within a few minutes, Matthew had gotten significantly better and was even beginning to say words we could actually hear and understand. Within ten minutes of entering the room, Matthew was speaking in full sentences at normal volume and was looking much better.

At this point I asked Dave, "So, how is your headache?"

Dave thought for a moment, then answered my question by responding "I can't believe it, it's totally gone."

"My legs are fine too," I said as I moved them around just to make sure. "So, what do you think just happened to us?"

Both of them just shrugged.

"We have no idea, but we haven't felt this well in days."

I looked at Matthew and Dave, and I said, "We desperately need to talk and catch up on what's been happening to us over the past couple of weeks. I have so many questions to ask you both that I don't even know where to begin.

The morning started out bright and cheerful for Sonja. Even though she'd only slept a few hours, her resolve and the promise that she had made to Allah and herself seemed to completely transform her disposition. She smiled and hummed her favorite song as she scurried around the hotel room tidying things up and getting breakfast ready for her son. Matt emerged from the washroom, walked straight up to his mother and gave her a hug around her waist. This was a little out of character for Matt so early in the morning, but she gladly drank in the affection that her son was giving her. Still with his arms around her waist, Matt looked up into his mother's eyes and said,

"Has Jacob brought you grandma's heart yet?"

Sonja was stunned as the words came out of his mouth, but without missing a beat and without having an emotional breakdown, Sonja simply said,

"Yes he did, Matt, he brought it last night and now we know that grandma is in paradise and that everything is OK."

With that news, Matt let go of his mother's waist and said, "Let's eat so we can have another fun day."

Sonja smiled and laughed as she tickled her son and said, "I'll race you to the breakfast table."

Far away from the eyes and the ears of the world and the news media, three individuals sat around a table talking about things that could change the course of the world as we know it.

The Prime Minister of Israel was the first to speak as he introduced his Defence Minister to the newly-appointed representative of the United Nations, Donald King. Since face-to-face negotiations were impossible between Israel and Iran, it had been decided that Donald King would be the sole mediator between the two nations. Every communication from either side would go through Donald and he would become the peace broker for the entire world. As the introductions and pleasantries ran their course, the Israeli delegation laid out their proposal for lasting peace in the Middle East.

Of course it came with an ultimatum that Iran immediately abandon its nuclear ambitions and then Israel would not order the air strikes against Iran's nuclear facilities. Donald graciously listened to the well thought-out Israeli proposals for peace and then thanked them for putting so much time and effort into the proposal.

"Unfortunately," Donald responded, "it's not quite that simple. The Iranian government has already given me an answer of 'no' to any of your demands in regards to abandoning their nuclear programs. But since we are all here together, I'm sure the three of us can come up with a plan that will satisfy everyone.

I also have a plan and vested interest in the outcome of these negotiations. I did not become the most powerful man in the world to be thwarted by two tiny nations that cannot get along. Now, here is a peace proposal that I'm sure you will find you can live with, in time anyways.

You'll have to think back with me a few years in order to understand what I'm saying to you. The year was 1996 and your own nation was at the height of the strategic relocation of your own nuclear arsenal. Everything went according to plan until the final nation-wide tally was taken and one nuclear missile was unaccounted for.

At first it was thought that a clerical error was made, but upon closer inspection, #11 missile was nowhere to be found. This created such a panic in your military and government that your nation's largest cover-up took place and remains to this day.

Unfortunately for you, #11 remains a real bomb and has been in my possession since 1996. Do either of you even know about the reality of #11? But there are others in your government who do know and I think it would be in your best interest to have a long conversation with them.

And just in case you think I'm bluffing, ask those who put the bomb together why they put a plaque on the inside that reads, 'Revelation 16:16' and named the bomb 'Armageddon.' I'm sure you will begin to see things my way. Actually, today we will be making peace between Israel and Iran because that's the way I want it. Number 11 is securely hidden somewhere in Iran, and let me tell you this in no uncertain terms; the first Israeli plane to cross Iranian air space to target its nuclear facilities will be a signal to me to detonate #11 and the whole world will think you dropped it on poor Iran.

You do realize that each bomb leaves its own footprint as to where it was built, and you will bear the responsibility of it. Of course a deal must work both ways, and I propose that I will stall the completion of the Iranian nuclear facilities for the next few years.

As you well know, I already control and own most of the food, oil, and beverage industries in the entire world, and I also have the ability to make things happen, when and where I want.

I will give you two months to evaluate the lack of progress that will be happening in Iran's nuclear facilities and then we will go public with our peace plan.

You have two months to accept my peace offer or you can expose your government's seventeen year cover-up. The choice is yours. I will get what I want in the end anyway."

"This is blackmail," the Israeli Prime Minister shouted as he slammed his fist on the table. "We will not bow to your demands."

The meeting was now over.

CHAPTER TWENTY-SEVEN

PICK UP THE SWORD

"I want to talk about what just happened to me over the past hour." Matthew said firmly. "I've been sick for a week and have been running a steady fever. So, when I get here to work, things just go from bad to worse. I can hardly walk or stand up and the only thing that I have the strength to do is to lay on my bed. I told Dave to go and find you and as soon as he left the room, I must have passed out.

The next thing I remember is the lambs with the faces of men that I saw in my previous dreams surrounding me on my bed and biting me. There are so many of them that I can feel my life slipping away, and I am slowly coming to the point of death. I can feel my heart stopping and my breathing is getting very shallow. At this point the only thing that I can think of to do is call out for help.

As I say, 'Someone please help me!' all of a sudden the lambs stop biting me and a bright light appears in my room. From the light I hear a voice saying, 'Pick up the sword, dragon slayer, and you will live.' But I don't see a sword anywhere and all I see is a bible on the table next to me.

So with all the strength I can muster, I reach over and pick it up and move it onto the bed with me. That's exactly the moment when the bright light disappears, the lambs disappear, and you guys come walking through the door. Now, fifteen minutes later, no more fever, I can speak normally, and I'm feeling fine.

Would someone please explain all of this to me?"

Dave and I looked at each other, shrugged and I said, "Sorry, but we have no idea about what is going on either." As I was thinking about what Matthew had just experienced, it dawned on me that he did actually pick up a sword. I remember reading in the book of Ephesians where the word of God, or the Bible, is described as a sword.

As I mentioned this to the guys, Matthew said, "Are you serious? Please show me where it says that in the Bible."

I took his Bible and found the book of Ephesians. I was quite surprised to see that two verses in the Bible had been underlined.

The first one was Ephesians 6:11 which said, 'Put on the full armor of God so that you can stand against the devil's schemes' and the next verse that was underlined was Ephesians 6:17 which says, 'Take up the sword of the spirit, which is the word of God.'

I asked Matthew why he had underlined these two verses in Ephesians. With a puzzled look on his face, he looked at me, "I just bought that Bible at the airport yesterday and I've never even opened it."

It had been a long day for all of us, so we decided to meet tomorrow after supper and hopefully then we would get some of our questions answered.

Just as Sonja and Matt were making plans to head out of the hotel and explore the city for another day, they heard a knock and both raced to the door and flung it open. There stood a stunned Jacob looking at two faces were full of excitement and ready for adventure. Jacob was pleasantly surprised to see the change of demeanor in Sonja since she had just received the news of Miriam's death the evening before.

"Have you had breakfast yet, Jacob?" Sonja asked.

"Well no I haven't," Jacob replied. "I was thinking I would get some a little later on in the morning."

"Well sit down," Sonja said, "I will quickly make you some."

Jacob sat down at the table and Sonja busied herself in the kitchen. Matt made his way to the table, sat down, and started asking Jacob some questions.

"So what is your last name, Mr. Jacob?" Matt asked.

"Well, my full name is Jacob Cornelius Rosenberg."

"Do you have a wife and children?"

"As a matter of fact, I was married for six years, but sadly, my wife and unborn child were killed in a bus explosion almost three years ago."

"Do you still miss them?"

"Yes Matt, I think about them every day."

Matt continued asking questions until Sonja came out with Jacob's breakfast. It had been good for Jacob to talk about his past even if it was with a five year-old. Jacob and Matt seemed to hit it off naturally and it was nice for Jacob to be able to relate to a child since his opportunity to have children was cut short.

After breakfast Jacob said he had some exciting news for both of them. Over the next few days they would be looking at three different apartments and they would be able to choose whichever one they wanted. Once they had decided which one they would like, they would begin to furnish the apartment with anything they needed. Sonja and Matt were very excited to learn they would finally be having a place of their own. The new beginning that Sonja had been dreaming about looked like it was finally going to become a reality.

Today was changeover day and the second half of our tram crew would be coming in this afternoon. I still had not put much thought into what I was going to tell the guys about seeing an angel on my gen-set. So much had happened since then that it seemed almost impossible to go back and start at the beginning. But I had promised an explanation, so I had to keep my word and tell them something. How much to tell them, I wasn't sure. As we all got together in the later afternoon to prepare for our evening tram runs, of course the question came up, "So, when are you going to tell us about the angel you saw sitting on your gen-set?"

"Well, Kevin," I said, "you're the foreman. When would be a good time for all of us to get together so that I only have to tell this story once?"

"How about tomorrow morning after breakfast? We have about an hour or so for all of us to be together, so let's do it then."

"That sounds good to me," I said as we all headed out to do our tram runs. I thought to myself that at least I had fourteen hours to figure out what I wanted to say to the guys.

After the evening tram runs were over and I had eaten a quick supper, I headed straight over to Matthew's room. We had lots of things we needed to talk about and maybe our conversation tonight would help me decide what to tell the guys the next morning.

As I exited the building, I noticed Matthew and Dave waving to me from their crew truck. I walked over and jumped in and asked "So what's up...and where are we going?"

"I know where to go," Matthew said with resolve in his voice. "Let's go down to Pit 13. There's lots of room to walk and talk and who knows, maybe we will even see a few lambs on the way," he said with a chuckle.

We drove down the solitary road that lead down to Pit 13 and Matthew made comments along the way:

"This is the place where I saw the angel with the sword in my dream... This is where I saw the lamb and this is where the rest of the lambs attacked me."

As we approached Pit 13, Matthew said, "This is the place where the barricade was across the road and my feet were stuck in the sinking ground... and this is where I saw the nuclear explosion and then saw my father coming out of the pit riding on the back of that devilish beast."

"Speaking of your father," I said, "This is the first question that I need an answer to, and I need you to be honest with me. Is your father Donald King, the owner of the newly-established company called Apollyon Global?"

Matthew hesitated and then looked to Dave for confirmation about whether or not he should answer the question. After Dave gave him an affirmative nod, Matthew simply said,

"Yes, the Donald King of Apollyon Global is my father."

"Wow," I said out loud. "Since you guys have decided to be honest with me, I think I need to know more about both of your histories. Will you tell me?"

For the next two hours, Matthew and David gave me a history lesson that sounded like it came out of a fairy tale book. All the events that Matt and Dave told me came directly from the firsthand accounts of Miriam and Matt's mother, Sonja.

Other information about Donald King came from MOSSAD, the Israeli intelligence agency, some facts and some suspicions. One of the sobering facts that presented itself during our conversation was that the David I was talking to right now was the same David that had exhumed the two bodies buried in the desert, photographed them, and taken blood and hair samples. With the blood and hair samples and the DNA harvested, it was confirmed that the man lying beside Miriam in the shallow grave was actually Matthew's grandfather. Even more bizarre than that, was the suspicion of Israeli intelligence that Matthew's grandfather was actually the son of Adolf Hitler himself.

My mind was reeling as the two guys told story after story of amazing events that they had been directly involved in.

One of Matt's stories about his growing up years caught my attention because I had made a trip to Israel in November of 1996. I remembered that date vividly because I had gone to visit the Holocaust Museum just outside of Jerusalem and it was also my first born son's birthday that day. I found it almost surreal that I was standing in front of a cattle car that had hauled Jewish families to the various concentration camps and then to their deaths. As I stood there at 11 am in the morning on the 11th day of the 11th month, I let my mind wander to some of the secrets this cattle car would disclose, could it speak. Lost as I was in my own world of thought, I did not notice that a young boy had walked up and was standing beside me looking at the cattle car.

"I come here a lot," the young boy said, pulling me out of my reverie.

"And why is that?"

"Well," he said, "I feel sorry for the people who had to ride in these cars and go to the concentration camps."

"I agree with you whole-heartedly,"

The young boy continued speaking, saying, "Others should have helped them and taken them into their own countries so they wouldn't have to die."

Again I agreed with him and then added, "But unfortunately that didn't happen very often." I remember distinctly the young boy saying,

"It's my 11th birthday today and this afternoon I will have a party when I go home. I wonder if there were any other 11 year-olds on this train on their birthdays."

His words hit me straight in the heart!

"It's my son's 6th birthday today also, and I won't even be there to give him a gift."

"It's OK," he said. "He knows that you love him and that you will be home soon. Where is home for you?" he asked.

"I'm from Canada," I responded as I reached my hand into my pocket. "Here is something for you on your birthday," as I handed him a Canadian quarter coin. "Let this be a reminder of our visit and maybe someday both you and my son can celebrate your birthdays together." With that I said Happy Birthday to him, shook his hand, and said good bye, never to see him again. Since that day I have often thought and prayed for that eleven year old boy standing in front of the cattle car.

As I finished my little story, I looked up at the guys and noticed that Matt's cheeks were moist with tears. He simply stared into my face, finding it difficult to speak. I wasn't sure what was going on in his mind until he unbuttoned his shirt and pulled out a 25 cent Canadian coin that had been hanging around his neck for the past fifteen years, since he was eleven.

CHAPTER TWENTY-EIGHT

TELLING THE STORY

We sat there at Pit 13 and let the stories and events of the past couple of hours begin to sink in. I was awestruck by the things we had just talked about. It hardly seemed possible that the lives of three people from around the globe could be so connected. And for what purpose? What did all of this mean? It did seem like there was a purpose, but what was it?

Matthew's stories of his growing up years seemed like they came straight out of a high adventure movie that was playing out in real life. They were being hounded and pursued by the most powerful man in the world which happened to be Matthew's father.

They had been on the run for the past ten years, having to change their names and identities repeatedly in order to try and stay ahead of the relentless pursuit of Donald King and his network of terror. Up to this point I was the only one that they had shared their true identities and names with. To everyone else in camp they were known as Timothy Hayes and Adrian Platt, friends hailing from the province of Ontario. All of their badges and ID's reflected their false identities in the hopes of staying out of the reach of Matthew's father.

Matthew had relayed parts of his story to me, and he also mentioned that his father and his gang of thugs would eventually catch up with them here at work. Matthew said that his father would call out to him in his dreams, and once that started happening he wouldn't be that far behind in person. Those dreams had begun once again on his two weeks off at home.

Up to this point the Israeli government had provided them

with false papers, ID's, and passports. David and Matthew were getting very tired of all the running and hiding they had been doing over the past ten years. This was the first time that they had lived and worked in one place for over a year, and they hated the thought of having to pack up and move once again.

Matthew also told me stories about his mother Sonja, what she had gone through and was still going through. He told me that when he was eight years old, his mother married Jacob and they were totally happy living in Israel and raising Matthew.

But when Matthew turned fifteen years old, everything changed for the family because Donald had finally discovered where they were. From that point on until Matthew was eighteen, the family moved six times in order to stay ahead of Donald King.

A week after Matthew's eighteenth birthday it was decided that it would probably be best if Jacob, Sonja and Matthew went their separate ways. It was almost unbearable for Jacob and Sonja to say goodbye to their one and only son, Matthew.

He had become the joy of their lives and it was going to be a very hard transition not having Matt around every day and maybe only seeing him once or twice a year. On the fateful day of November 18, 2003, Jacob and Sonja boarded the jumbo jet leaving for Sydney, Australia, and Matthew and David boarded the El Al flight #411 and headed for Toronto, Canada.

The day had finally arrived to tell my story to the tram crew describing what I had seen on the top of my gen-set. After talking with Matthew and David last night, I really didn't know what I should tell them.

So much had happened since the day that Raymond and I had landed on our rear ends in front of my gen-set. An angel had appeared in my room and spoken to me, an ancient scroll was given to me and several paranormal events had occurred to Matthew, Dave and myself. And to top it all off, my two friends were now being hunted by the most powerful man in the world. Where do you begin to tell a story like that? How will anything I have to say make any sense to anyone without any proof?

My morning runs and breakfast went by quickly and before I knew it we were at the laydown trailer and everyone seemed anxious to hear what I had to say.

"Well," Kevin said to me, "you have the floor, and as you know, we are all very interested in what you have to say."

I had already decided to keep this story as simple as possible. It would not be right for me to implicate Matthew and Dave for their own safety's sake. Their lives were literally at stake and I could not reveal their true identities even though they seemed to be the major players in the story.

"Well, where do I start? Anyways, a few turnarounds ago I started noticing something strange going on with my tractor. People driving by in their vehicles would point towards my tractor and kind of swerve to get out of my way. Then one day a fellow came up to me while I was parked at a tram stop and asked me what the light was on top of my gen set. I didn't see anything, but it made me curious as to what people were actually seeing. Then one morning Raymond came up to me and also told me that he had seen some lights dancing on the top of my gen-set.

So, Raymond, would you mind telling us from your perspective what you saw and what happened to us by my tractor a few weeks ago?"

"Sure," Raymond replied, and he began to tell his version of the story.

"Well, a couple of times as I would drive by tram #3, I would notice a light or a reflection of a light that was very bright and out of place. I wasn't sure what it was, but I mentioned it to Walter and he didn't know anything about it at that time either. Then one morning when it was still completely dark outside, I noticed the light was shining brightly once again as Walter was about to take off for his morning run. I quickly ran over to his tractor, opened his door, and asked him if he was seeing anything on his gen-set. He said he couldn't see anything, so we both went to the front and he climbed up onto the front bumper and that's when it happened. All of a sudden, something exploded from on top of the gen-set and both of us ended up on the ground in front of his tractor. That's all I remember from that morning, but over the past few weeks I still have seen the lights dancing on his gen-set from time to time."

I continued. "After the explosion of light I looked to the right beside me, and Ray was lying face down and motionless.

I was totally unsure of what had just happened to us and it seemed like I had no strength left in my body to help Ray up.

I looked up towards my gen-set, noticing that the place where the explosion had taken place and was dazzling with flame-like lights. All of a sudden, I noticed the shape of a very large man beginning to form within the light.

As my eyes began to adjust to the brilliance of the light, I could clearly see the form of a man sitting on my gen-set with his feet resting on the front bumper. He was a very large man and he was holding something in his left hand that looked to me like a rolled up piece of paper or a scroll of some kind. He also spoke words to me that I clearly remember.

These are his exact words, 'Do not be afraid. I have appeared to you for a reason which shall be revealed shortly to you and your friends. Peace be with you,' he said, 'and remember, I am always here for you.'

Then with my eyes wide open, I saw this man who I would guess to be at least ten feet tall, slowly disappear into the dark, cool morning air. After he disappeared, Ray and I peeled ourselves off the ground and checked out the tractor and gen-set. Everything seemed to be working fine so we got into our tractors and did our morning runs. I would guess that the whole encounter only took a couple of minutes because we were not late for our morning tram runs.

When I had finished speaking, I noticed the atmosphere in the trailer had turned chillingly quiet. The guys were thinking about what we had said and were in the process of deciding whether to believe us or not. Kevin was the first to speak up and break the silence.

"Wow," he said, "that's quite a story you just told us, and you guys are serious when you say that all of this actually happened to the both of you?"

"It really happened," Raymond responded, "other than the fact I didn't hear or see the man that was sitting on the gen-set. And since that day, I have seen the reflecting lights on the top of Walter's gen-set a few times when he was driving by."

More silence filled the trailer as everyone was still coming to their own conclusion as to whether to believe the story or not.

I was very happy that Raymond had confirmed details and was honest about what he had seen and experienced. At least it was not just me coming up with a story that must have sounded totally crazy to all the guys.

Cory was the next one to speak up and he said,

"Great story, guys, but I don't believe it. I'm not sure what happened to your gen-set that morning, but it sounds to me like Walter had a hallucination of some kind from the impact of the explosion. The mind can work in strange ways if it has been traumatized and stressed. And as far as the lights on your gen-set go, they must be a reflection off your mirrors or something. There is a rational explanation."

All of a sudden, the dam of people's opinions broke loose and the next fifteen minutes brought an interesting mix of thoughts and debates over the story. After everyone had given voice to their own opinions, it seemed to me that most of the guys had a little trouble believing in the man on my gen-set part. I didn't blame them for not believing, because it certainly did seem to be a pretty far-fetched account.

When a lull in the conversation presented itself, I took the opportunity to give them the only real evidence that I actually had.

"I know this is a lot to take in right now, but I'm only being honest and telling you what happened to me. I'm not trying to convince you that I'm right, but I am presenting the story the way it did happen to me. There is one more piece to this story that happened to me just four days after the gen-set incident. As I was walking back to the laydown trailer after our morning runs, I looked back over my shoulder at the seven trams all parked next to each other. My tractor #3 was located right in the center of the group of seven. As I looked back, some movement on the gen-set caught my eye.

I was twenty or thirty meters away from my tractor already, so I couldn't quite make out exactly what it was. Whatever it was started rolling across the top of my gen-set box towards the edge, but stopped short of falling off.

I wondered what it could be, so I turned completely around and started walking back towards my tractor to investigate the curious sight. When I was within a couple of meters of my tractor, all of a sudden the object started rolling again. But this time it rolled right off the edge. Lunging forward, I stretched my arm out and caught it in mid-air before it could hit the ground. 'What is this?' I thought to myself. As I opened up my hand, a flash of recognition hit me. This looked like the exact same tube or scroll type thing that the angel was holding when I saw him the last time.

"Wait a minute," Edmond said, "are you trying to tell us that you have the scroll that the man or angel was holding in his hand?"

"Well yes," I replied, "that is exactly what I am trying to say."

"And you have it right here, right now?" Rob responded.

"Yes, I do," I replied, "do you guys want to see it?"

"Of course we do," was the response from everyone.

I then placed my backpack on the table, unzipped it and carefully pulled out the rolled-up scroll and laid it on the table. Everyone was fascinated as I unrolled the scroll. When the scroll reached its full extension, everyone leaned in to get the best view possible.

"What's all that supposed to mean?" was Cory's first response.

"I can't read a word of it," Mike added.

"Yes, I know." I responded, "It's all written in an ancient form of Hebrew. But I did get it translated by a friend of mine back home who does speak Hebrew. He was fascinated by the style and the wording of the Hebrew used on the scroll. He said it was probably the form of Hebrew used when the language was first created several thousand years ago."

After a few more minutes of just observing the scroll, our time was up and we had to leave and get back to work. The guys were quiet as they wrestled with the facts that were presented to them. The jury was still out in deliberation, but I was also sure it would not be long before the verdict would present itself.

It was now the end of November 2013, and almost twenty four years had passed since Sonja and Donald King's son Matthew had disappeared in Kuwait. Donald had spent millions of dollars and countless man hours over the years trying to find his quarry. To him, it almost seemed an opposing force was working against him in the pursuit of his family.

Many times over the years he had been within days and maybe even hours of catching up with the family that had abandoned him. But this time he was certain that his prey was within grasp and nothing would stop him now from retrieving that which was rightfully his. The Israeli government and its intelligence agency had been a constant pain in Donald King's side.

But now, after all these years, by what appeared to be a stroke of luck, Donald's technical team had hacked into the back door of an Israeli intelligence program that had information on the general whereabouts and locations of his estranged family. Once inside the program he found out that Sonja had remarried and was now living in Sydney, Australia.

Donald became enraged at the thought that she had abandoned him and had been with another man all of these years. Donald's rage seemed to consume most of his waking thoughts and he couldn't wait for the moment he would literally tear this man apart limb from limb. And Matthew, his son whom he had not seen since he was five years old, was now working in the oil patch of Northern Alberta somewhere.

"Yes," Donald said to himself, "I have both of them within my sights now and it's only a matter of time before I will be standing face-to-face with them.

CHAPTER TWENTY-NINE

SAM'S WORLD

I thought the meeting with the tram crew had gone fairly well. The jury was still out. The day was coming to an end, and I was looking forward to having a nice supper in the dining room. As I dropped off the last of the workers and started my ten minute drive back to the tram laydown yard, a strange sight started to unfold before my eyes. Looking through my windshield towards the oncoming traffic, I began to notice something strange happening on the top of my gen-set. At first I thought something serious was wrong as what looked like smoke or a cloud began to swirl around it without dissipating. I continued looking through the cloud, seeing white and amber lights begin to sparkle and twirl around. It appeared like a fire was ablaze within the confines of the cloud.

"This is what Raymond and some other people must have seen," I thought to myself. Although the smoke and lights of the fire were very distinct, I could also see the road and oncoming traffic as usual. It felt very surreal to me to be driving down the road and witnessing something from another dimension happening at the same time.

I continued driving towards the laydown. The fire, the lights, and the cloud began to increase in activity and intensity. I was staring into the fire when I noticed the form of a man being created by the phenomenon. Watching the transformation before my very eyes, I realized I wasn't seeing into our normal three-dimensional world. Amidst the cloud, lights, and fire, Sam was now sitting on top of my gen-set with his feet firmly planted on the front bumper.

"But how can I see his feet and legs on the front bumper?" I thought to myself. "It's not possible." As I continued to drive and watch the traffic, I was also seeing Sam from the front, from the sides, from the back, and I was even seeing through him all at the same time. My physical senses were having trouble processing all of this, but in the midst of it all I was completely calm and was even kind of enjoying the wonder of what was happening to me at this very moment.

I rounded the last corner and the laydown yard was in sight. I was startled by what happened to me next. Without warning, Sam started to speak to me telepathically. I couldn't explain it, but his words were crystal clear, and to my surprise, I answered him without uttering words.

Sam responded by impressing words on my mind that said, "Hey, Walter, I hope everything is OK with you. Sorry about the interruption, but we need to talk. I've been given permission to speak to you face to face tonight if you want to. So how about it? Later on this evening in your room?"

"Sure, that would be great," I responded.

With that, Sam was gone. The lights, the fire, and the cloud all disappeared instantly as I pulled my tram into the laydown yard and shut it down for the night. "Wow," I thought to myself, "did all of this really just happen to me? I guess I'll know for sure if I have a visitor in my room tonight."

Since I had the very last tram run in the evening, the guys had spent the last ten or fifteen minutes deliberating their positions on the conversation and story I had told them that morning. The jury was in, and it seemed to be a split decision. Raymond believed my story 100%, Kevin and Rob seemed to believe about 75% of it. Mike, Edmond, and Cory believed only the part where something had malfunctioned on my gen-set and had created a flash and explosion that had knocked us to the ground. As for me seeing an angel on it was too much of a stretch for them to believe. Possessing the scroll was just deemed someone's idea of a practical joke downloaded off the computer.

On our crew cab drive from the laydown to the kitchen, the conversation was lively and spirited. Everyone gave their opinion of the story and commented about what might have happened to make me think that I saw and heard a man speak.

"You probably were knocked unconscious for a few seconds and dreamed or hallucinated that you saw and heard someone speak to you," Cory stated.

"That's probably it," Mike continued, "Ray didn't hear or see anything, so it probably didn't happen."

"Stuff like that just doesn't happen now a days," Edmond chimed in, "and as a matter of fact, you should maybe still go and see a doctor just in case you have a mild concussion or something."

It was Ray's turn to enter the lively debate that was moving back and forth like a high-energy ping-pong match. "Well, what about the spiritual world? Just because you can't see it or understand it doesn't mean that it doesn't exist. I've experienced some things in my life that would make your hair stand up on end and they were real. I think we should give Walter the benefit of the doubt."

"We need proof," the guys said, "why should we believe it if we cannot see it? It just does not make any sense."

As the debate went on, the kitchen finally came into sight and that seemed to end the fray of opinions that were flying around the truck.

The only person not saying anything while we were in the truck was Rob. But I could tell that he was listening and thinking and that he was still in the process of forming his final decision on the matter. Kevin had also been fairly quiet during the discussions. Since Kevin had to drive the pickup truck back to the kitchen, he would have some personal time to think and form his own opinions of what he thought about this whole matter.

The evening dragged by slowly as I waited in my room for Sam to show up. It was now already after 10 pm and I was getting tired. "I'm going to bed," I thought to myself allowing my eyes to close, quickly making the transition from consciousness to unconsciousness. Soon I was sound asleep.

I'm not sure how to describe what I experienced, but it all happened as I was sleeping soundly. I seemed to wake up in another world or dimension that had very little relationship to the world that I had lived my past fifty years in. I woke up to sights, sounds and smells that I could have never imagined even existed.

I had just entered a dream world where your five physical senses made absolutely no sense at all. I seemed to be in an atmosphere that was charged with pure, pristine, exhilarating perfection. I had no way to describe what I was experiencing because words can only convey human meanings and concepts, and there was nothing human about where I was at this moment in time.

Instantly, Sam stood before me with a big, child-like grin on his face. "Welcome to my world, Walter," he said as he stooped down over me and gave me a big bear hug. I felt tiny and insignificant in the arms of this giant. He released his hold on me and straightened himself out.

"This is incredible, where are we?"

"You should know. You've always known that this is your world as much as it is mine."

Sam was right, I had always known that someday my eternal home would be the Kingdom of Heaven, but I never thought that I would experience it while I was still physically alive. Sam almost seemed childlike in his excitement that I was actually visiting him here in his world.

"I'd like to take you all over the Kingdom and show it off to you, but I don't have permission to do that. Right now we need to talk and I need to explain some things to you. We are entering a time in earth's history where everything is coming to a climax and the separation of good and evil must occur.

Matthew King is a major player in these end time events, even though he doesn't know it yet. And for reasons that I don't understand, you have been chosen to be his friend and to help him along his way. You have been brought here this evening in a dream because it is Matthew's dream that you will interpret for him.

Also, the scroll that has been given to you will become your time table of events that will happen before the separation of good and evil occurs. When you wake up out of this dream you will remember every word and every detail that has been spoken between us. It will be burned into your subconscious and you will remember these moments for the rest of your life."

Sam then began interpreting Matthew's dream and giving me vital information to pass on. I realized that time was not relevant here.

I had no concept of how long my visit to the Kingdom was. Sometimes I felt like I had been here for an eternity already and sometimes I felt like only a few seconds had gone by. I had so many questions to ask Sam, especially now that my mind seemed liberated and supercharged in this environment. When Sam had finished his chat with me (actually, it seemed more like a download), he kindly smiled at me, looked deep into my eyes, and spoke.

"I'm so happy that you have been allowed to be with me here in this dream. It's almost time for you to go and return to your own world. But before you do I have something very exciting to tell you. I have been given permission to answer any question you have for me. Also, I am permitted to give you a sign that will prove beyond any shadow of doubt that you have been here with me in the Kingdom. So, what question can I answer for you, Walter?"

My mind quickly scanned the dozens of questions I had wanted to ask, but being here in this place seemed to make them trivial and unimportant.

"Well," I said to Sam, "I would really like to know a little about you and your history and why you are my guardian angel."

"Fair enough. I'll answer it as best as a can, but even I cannot explain everything or even begin to presume that I have it all figured out. From my first memory all I can say is that I was a created being and I was only one of an innumerable company of angels just like it says in Hebrews 12:22.

Time means nothing in the kingdom so I cannot tell you when I was created. Even so, I can tell you why I was created. All angels were created for the sole purpose of worshipping and serving God, just like it says in Hebrews 1:6. And in Hebrews 1:7 it says that we are His spirit angels and His ministers that exist in a flame of fire.

That is why you first saw the smoke and the flame on top of your gen-set before you saw me sitting there. We have also been directed by God and assigned to work for those who are the heirs of salvation and will eventually inherit the kingdom just like it says in Hebrews 1: 14. I have been assigned to work with many different people during the course of their lives over the past six thousand years. Besides worshipping God and being His spirit angels, we also get assigned to different individuals over the whole course of their lives. I have been the guardian angel of dozens of individuals over the past six millennium. I have served rich people, poor people and people of various ethnic backgrounds. I have served the great and I have served the small.

God himself chooses those I serve and who will be the heirs of salvation. Although you obviously don't know any of those people I have served over the years, there is a record of one individual who I was assigned to. I am the angel of Judges 6:11 which is the two o'clock position on the scroll that I gave you. Just as I came and sat on your gen-set, I also sat under the oak tree which was in Ophrah and appeared to Gideon in chapters 6, 7, and 8 of the book of Judges."

"What? You were Gideon's guardian angel?"

"Yes," Sam responded with a smile on his face, "it was quite an exciting period for both of us. I got to fight side by side with him and both of us became famous during that era of time.

The saying that struck fear into the hearts of Gideon's enemies was the chant that preceded the attack. Gideon's army of 300 ran towards the enemy at night blowing trumpets, smashing clay pitchers, and holding lamps in their left hands while they screamed and cried, "The sword of the Lord and of Gideon."

That day an army of 300 men defeated an army that boasted one hundred and twenty thousand. It was quite a day and quite a victory. I think of that battle often and wonder if I will ever use the sword of the Lord again. I tried to give it to Matthew in his dream, but he wouldn't take it. Maybe he will take it after you talk to him."

"What? You were the angel in Matt's dream that was holding the sword?"

"That was me, and that was the first time I got to hold the sword since the time of Gideon. It felt good having it in my hand again, but it is not mine to own. It belongs to another, I was just the messenger."

My mind seemed to be totally alive in this atmosphere of the kingdom. Sam had downloaded vast amounts of information to me and I knew that every word of it was stored in my brain. What a dream I was having! I never knew that anything like this was even possible.

Sam looked at me. He smiled and said, "It's almost time for you to head back into your own sleep world. There is one more thing that I need to share with you before you return. When you arrive home and have spoken with Matthew, I want you to give him these words and these two verses of scripture. They are found on page eleven-eleven in your Bible or as you say it, page one thousand, one hundred and eleven. It is the twenty-first chapter of Ezekiel in verses nine and eleven of that chapter.

Tell Matthew his sword is ready. It has been furbished, it has been sharpened, it is ready to be handled, and it is ready to be put into the hand of the slayer.

I know that all of the information you will be giving to Matthew is overwhelming. But he must hear it and you are the one to tell him. When you are finished your conversation with him, I would like you to say three words to him. He will understand what they mean. Tell him, 'They are coming.'

Now as far as the sign that I told you about, which will confirm the visit that we had here together, this is what will happen in two days from now.

On December 5th, 2013, a great sign will occur and the whole earth shall see it and mourn. A man of peace and reconciliation will go to his eternal home and reward. All the people of the world will mourn as this great man's life comes to an end. But the world should truly mourn for itself because of the one who is taking his place.

A world leader has already arisen who will fill the world with war, hate, and destruction while preaching peace all at the same time. As you might have guessed already, this man's name is Donald King and he comes as a destroyer of all that is good. Even the name of his former and current company tell the story of his true motives. The words Abaddon and Apollyon have the same meaning in two different languages and this is what they mean. Both words mean "The Angel Of The Bottomless Pit, The Place Of Destruction and The Destroyer."

Remember that in two days the sign shall appear and the world will mourn. Goodbye for now my friend," Sam said to me as he slowly disappeared into a flame of fire that then shot up into the sky and vanished far above me.

As I lowered my head and took one last look around this place that Sam had called the Kingdom, I was again awestruck by its incredible, intense beauty. I did not want to return to my world, but I could feel myself begin to move involuntarily, and in the twinkling of an eye I found myself sitting upright in my bed staring at the ceiling. I was back from my journey into the Kingdom with a mountain of information that had been downloaded into my brain.

As I laid my head on my pillow, I quickly glanced over at my clock which still displayed the time of 10:11 pm. Either my clock had stopped working or what had just happened to me had taken less than a minute. Either way, I was totally content and happy and I knew I would never look at life the same old way again after experiencing a few seconds in the Kingdom.

CHAPTER THIRTY

WHERE DO I GO FROM HERE?

I woke up just seconds before my alarm clock was about to go off. After pushing the off button down, I put my hands behind my head and relaxed comfortably on my pillow. I couldn't help but smile as I recounted my trip into Sam's world and the pleasure it gave me to be there.

My life would never be the same after the events of my Kingdom dream. I had crossed over and seen glimpses of what the other side was like and I had done it while I was still alive. I left feeling incredibly blessed because I knew things like that didn't happen very often while your heart was still beating and you still had breath in your lungs. I also knew I would have to find Matthew today and share the story with him because he seemed to be the one that all of this revolved around.

As the day wore on I was getting a little concerned because I couldn't seem to find out where Matthew and Dave were. I had asked a couple of their crew members who said that they both called in sick that morning and nobody was quite sure where they were. I had checked their rooms and called their names, but neither came or opened their doors.

"Strange," I thought to myself, "I wonder where they are." By suppertime that evening I still had not made any contact with them and their whereabouts continued to be a mystery to everyone. "Oh well," I thought, "I'm sure they'll show up sooner or later."

As I was walking back to my trailer, I noticed Kevin and Rob walking up the sidewalk towards me.

"Hey, what's up?"

"Do you have a few minutes so we can sit down and have a little chat?" Kevin asked.

"Sure. Let's go down to the recreation room that we have church in, it's usually empty."

"Good idea," Rob said as we made our way down the sidewalk.

I assumed Kevin and Rob had finally come to their own conclusions about the story I had told them yesterday and they were now going to let me know what they thought. As we arrived in the empty room, we closed the door behind us and made ourselves comfortable on the two leather couches that filled up part of the room.

Kevin started the conversation by saying, "Rob and I have talked about the story you told us yesterday and we would like to give you our opinions."

"Sure. I'd love to hear what you guys think about all of this."

"In some ways," Rob said, "we kind of feel the same way as Mike, Edmond, and Cory. It is quite an unbelievable story if you look at it only from a strictly logical point of view. But we also realize that everything is not always logical and factual, just like Raymond was saying yesterday. Some things are just unexplainable and we realize that's just the way it is sometimes."

"But even more than that," Kevin continued, "we believe you because we have gotten to know you over the past three years and we know you wouldn't just make something like this up and try to sell it to us. There is absolutely no advantage to you to make up a story like that."

"Well thanks for your vote of confidence. I really appreciate it. But to be honest with you, the story I told you is only the beginning of many unusual things that have happened to me over the past couple of months."

"What do you mean by that?" Rob said.

"I really can't tell you all the details because most of them involve someone else here in camp and it might put them in danger if the details got out."

"I'm not really sure I'm following you here," Kevin said. "Are you trying to say you've had more strange experiences than what you've told us about?"

"Well, yes. The angel has actually appeared to me two more times and then I also had a dream last night with him in it."

I didn't want to say too much because it would just start sounding stranger and stranger the more I revealed. And not only that, I would be here for the next few hours if I were to tell the whole thing.

"Listen, I wish I could tell you the whole thing, but I can't right now. I will tell you one thing the angel told me and one thing I'm guessing will happen in the next little while. First of all the angel said that there would be a worldwide sign given tomorrow, December 5, 2013 and I will quote what he said to me: 'On December 5, 2013, a great sign will occur and the whole earth will see it and mourn. A man of peace and reconciliation will go to his eternal home and reward. All the people of the world will mourn as this great man's life comes to an end."

He went on to say more but let's wait and see what happens tomorrow because he didn't give me the man's name, although I do have a guess as to who it might be. Here is another thing that possibly might happen around here from what the angel told me. I wouldn't be surprised to see some Apollyon Global people around here in the near future."

I finished making the statement about Apollyon Global, and I noticed Kevin's jaw drop and a look of shock filled his facial features.

"How did you know that?" Kevin asked excitedly. "I have an email on my phone right now that I got about an hour ago saying that we need to do a tram tour for a group of Apollyon Global board members, and their CEO, Donald King himself, might be on it. They also requested to have tram #3 be the one giving the tour."

When the words 'Donald King' came out of Kevin's mouth, my jaw dropped open and my mind went numb. "Is this really happening?" I thought to myself. The thought of actually seeing or even meeting Matthew's father freaked me right out.

This was all a little much for me to comprehend right now and I presumed the same was probably happening to Kevin and Rob. All I knew for sure as we left the church room that evening was that I had to find Matthew and I had to find him fast.

Half way around the world in a secure military Israeli conference room, high-level meetings with senior government officials had been going on non-stop for the past 24 hours. Israel's president and defence minister had followed up on Donald King's threat of owning and using a stolen Israeli nuclear surface-to-air missile named Armageddon.

And to the utter horror of both of these men, they found that the threat was real and the possibility of him using it was real. Many options and opinions had been debated about what course of action to take. But after 24 hours, the only conclusion that the senior officials had come to was that they were all overtired and that they needed a twelve hour break before they convened the meeting once again. As all of the officials slowly dispersed and made their way out of the room, only the Prime Minister and his Defence Minister remained and sat in stunned silence.

"How did it all come to this?" the Defence Minister asked with a look of disgust written on his face. "How could the former administration have been so ignorant and try to cover something like this up? It's all absolutely unbelievable."

"But yet here we sit having to deal with the sins of our own past stupidity," the Prime Minister responded, shaking his head. "We have to come clean on this one; we can't continue to cover this up because it just gets messier and messier at each turn in the road."

"What!" the Defence Minister responded, "I think that we have gone far beyond coming clean on this one. We are dealing with one of the most powerful men in the world who also happens to be one of the most ruthless and pathological killers in the whole world. We can't play with this man or have any kind of negotiations with him whatsoever. We need to put him and the missile in the same location and take both of them out and then deal with the consequences of that.

There is no other way," the Minister of Defense said firmly. Both men sat in silence as the scenarios of a nuclear holocaust ran through their minds. There would be no way of getting out of this spider's web easily. As both men got up to leave the room, the Prime Minister turned and looked at the empty conference room table. He then spoke into the empty room and said, "God help us all."

Neither Matthew nor David had spoken a word since their crew truck left Fort McMurray and was now pointed in the direction heading back to camp. The coded message had come in at 4 am that they had to meet their contact in a secure location just outside the city.

It was hard for both men to believe, but David had just been called back to work out of Israel by the intelligence agency that he had spent most of his life working for. A situation had arisen that demanded his immediate return to Israel where he would be briefed with more details. As for Matthew, it was explained to him that a file with the general locations of himself and his mother had been compromised, and someone had acquired that information. Who exactly had stolen the information would probably never be known. But the agency's guess was that Donald King was behind it. Donald had men working around the clock trying to break into the files of many countries in an effort to find out their secrets.

Matthew and David were closer than most brothers and the thought of them being separated was hard to come to grips with. They trusted each other explicitly and had formed a bond that few men have the privilege of experiencing. Matthew actually felt lost with just the thought of David not being around any more. They had been through so much together and now everything was about to change.

The drive back to camp was turning out to be a mental and emotional nightmare as each of the men sat in silence thinking about what their futures might look like without each other. Matthew finally broke the silence about twenty minutes into the drive. "I'm having a hard time coming to grips with the reality that you are on your way to Israel tomorrow."

"I know what you mean, I feel like I'm in a dream right now and that the rug has just been pulled out from under my feet. What could be so important back in Israel that the agency needs me to return immediately?"

"Your guess is as good as mine. And what about me?" Matt continued. "Some of the files that hold the location of my mother and I have been compromised. And on top of that I've started having those dreams again that my father is calling out to me to come to him.

I have a feeling neither of us are going to be in camp much longer. And what about the connection with Walter? What has all of that been about? What about all the strange things that have happened to us over the past couple of months? None of this makes any sense to me any more. Where is all of this going?"

Silence once again filled the cab of the truck as they pulled into camp, knowing for sure this would be David's last night in Canada. He was scheduled on the first flight out of camp the next morning and he would be in Israel before the sun came up again. David had been a major part of Matt's life for the past twenty four years and now all of that was about to change and probably change forever.

Neither Matt nor David got much sleep that night. They could not escape their turbulent thoughts. As morning finally came, they met in the dining room for their final breakfast together. Polite conversation did not seem appropriate for some reason this morning. Twenty four years of relationship was about to be severed as each of them was about to head down his own individual path and destiny. It was unnerving, it was scary, but both of them knew that it must happen. As the bus pulled up to the curb and the doors opened, David stepped up onto the first stair. Turning his head, he looked down into Matthew's eyes and with tenderness, quoted a traditional phrase to Matthew in his native tongue of Hebrew.

"Good bye, my brother," he said. "Next year in Jerusalem," he shouted with a loud voice.

"Next year in Jerusalem," Matt shouted back. And the doors closed behind him.

CHAPTER THIRTY-ONE

THE SLAYER

Dawn arrived, as always. December 5th. I pulled my tram up behind the diversified bus that was now in motion and headed for the airport. I was on my third tram run of the morning as I pulled up beside the only person waiting at the tram stop. I looked down towards the person standing there, and I couldn't believe my eyes as Matthew's face came into focus. I quickly opened my side door and called out to Matthew, "Hey, my friend, where have you been lately? I've been looking all over the place for you in the last day and a half."

"It's a long story, but let's get together tonight at around 7:30 in the church room and we will talk then."

"I'll be there at 7:30 sharp, so we'll see you then," I closed my door and continued on with my tram run. "Wow," I thought to myself, "Matthew really seemed disconnected and troubled for some reason. I wonder what's happening in his world?" I was also wondering where Dave was, as the two of them almost seemed inseparable at times.

Later on that afternoon I was on my way to the gym for my daily workout when I noticed a small group of guys standing and watching something on a television set. I stopped as I walked by and noticed that it was a live special news report coming out of South Africa. When the newscaster began to speak, the first words to come out of his mouth were,

"Nelson Mandela, a man of peace and reconciliation has gone to his eternal home and reward." I stood there in shock and awe realizing that this newscaster had just quoted the exact same words that Sam had given me two days ago.

"Nelson Mandela is the sign," I said to myself, "I should have known." I continued watching the news report as it gave a short history of his life and accomplishments, along with a report on his prison years. The man truly was amazing and had accomplished something that most people thought was not even possible to consider. The ugly word of Apartheid was being slowly erased and words like hope, freedom, and forgiveness were beginning to take root in the soil of this new and ever-changing South Africa.

I felt privileged to be part of a generation that was watching history being made right before our eyes. What a wonderful thing it is in life to see good triumph over evil and the purposeful efforts of one man change the destiny of a nation. Although I was very proud to see Nelson Mandela honored in such a wonderful way, Sam's words were forever etched on my subconscious.

His words were about an evil man that would replace this man of peace and reconciliation and bring war and destruction in the near future. Sam's words up to this point had been 100% accurate, but somehow I hoped on the inside of me that he was wrong about the man who would replace Nelson Mandela. This world needed more men like Nelson Mandela and less men like Donald King.

I arrived at the church room at exactly 7:30 pm. Matthew was already sitting on the couch when I walked through the door. As I looked into his face, I noticed that the distraught look that I had seen earlier that morning had not left him.

"What's wrong, Matt?"

"Let's go sit in the truck where we can talk more privately," Matt said as he got off the couch and we both headed out the door into the frigid night. Although we closed the truck door behind us, the diesel engine of the truck continued to run, bringing the much-needed warmth into the cab in this minus twenty degree cold snap. Without warning, Matthew burst into heart-wrenching sobs and all he could choke out was,

"He's gone, he's gone."

After a couple of minutes of letting Matthew vent his grief, I quietly said to him, "You can tell me about it if you want to."

Once Matthew composed himself, he went on to tell me the story of what had transpired over the last couple of days in his life.

As he told the story, I could sense the true bond of brotherhood that existed between these two men. It was actually something I had always wanted in my life, but had never experienced.

With the telling of Matthew's story and Dave's unexpected return to Israel, I felt an urgency within myself to tell Matthew what Sam had instructed me to tell him. I knew this might not be the best timing to spring something like this on him, but things were moving so rapidly that I felt I might not have another chance. David was already gone and Matt said that his days in camp might be numbered. But where to begin?

"Matt, I need to tell you some stuff, and I know that this is probably the worst time in your life to tell you, but I have to. Please hear what I have to say and then you can walk away from me and never have to see me again."

With that, a smile came to Matthew's lips as he replied to my request, "Please, Walter, say what you need to and don't hold anything back. I might as well have my whole world collapse within the same 24 hour period than have this go on and on and on."

I decided to throw caution to the wind. I would give him the facts and then let the chips fall where they may. I had zero control over the outcome of how Matt would respond so I was just going to go for it.

"Matt, I have now had three encounters with the same angel that was in your dream. And then three nights ago I met him in a dream of my own in a place he called the Kingdom.

The purpose for my visit to the Kingdom was to be given an interpretation of the dream you had a few weeks ago. The angel also said that the scroll and the dream are very closely connected and that you and your father each have a role to play as human history unfolds.

What this angel told me (and by the way, his name is Sam), has somehow been downloaded permanently into my brain. So what I am telling you are the exact words that came from Sam himself. Are you ready to hear what Sam has to say? And I suggest you put on your seat belt because we will be going on quite a wild ride."

Matt laughed and said, "Go for it, Walter, and give me both barrels. I'm all ears."

"Here goes, The recurring dream that you have had represents your life, your calling, and your destiny. The road that you were running on in your dream has brought you to where you are today and will take you the rest of the way in order to fulfill your destiny.

The first five years of your life were mostly filled with wonder and excitement as you were the recipient of your mother and grandmother's unconditional love. As you continue running down your life's road, you notice the sign on the side of the road that is written in the Hebrew language.

The sign signals a major change in your life and Israel and the Hebrew language are all part of that change. What the sign says has several different meanings.

The sign reads, 'The Beast's Pit #13 – 11 km ahead.' For you, these numbers represent the number of years that you have been separated from your father. The number 13 represents the number of years you lived in Israel under the care of your mother and stepfather. The 11 represents the number of years you have been living independently and have been in hiding from your father. When the numbers 13 and 11 are added up, it brings us to the twenty four years that you have been running from your father. And that time has now come to an end. You will run no more.

As you continue down the road, you encounter Sam standing in the middle of the road, holding a sword above his head. You also noticed that the words 'Dragon Slayer' were engraved into the blade of the sword.

Sam says to you, 'This is your sword. You will never find out what your calling is or fulfill your destiny unless you take your sword and learn to use it. You are the Dragon Slayer, Matthew, and we are just here to help you along your way. I am Sam, Walter's guardian angel, but I also have been commissioned to help you find your path to your own destiny. You have already rejected this sword once, and it will be offered only one more time. If you reject it again you will die and never fulfill your destiny.'"

I continued, "As you resume your run, you encounter lambs with the faces of men. These lambs represent evil people who are dressed up to look harmless and gentle. But they are wolves in sheep's clothing. They run in packs like wolves in sheep's clothing. They have tried to kill you in the past and they will try to kill you in the future if they can. You will never outrun them so that is why you must pick up your sword and learn to fight with it.

As you are being chased by the lambs, you come to a barricade that crosses the road and the sign on it reads, 'The End of the Road Has Come.'

This is Pit #13 and you have run 11 km. This will be a pivotal point in your future. The end of the road has come for you. You have been born for this moment, but your feet are still stuck in the sinking sand. For all human beings, life boils down to the moment of decision and once it is made, it cannot be undone. It will be decision time for you, Matthew, as you stand and look over the barricade into the future. Your future, the world's future, the future of unborn children will all hang in the balance of one decision.

And now, Matthew, comes the grand finale of your dream. The earth begins to shake and erupts into a massive fireball that threatens to engulf the whole world. And out of that fireball comes the dreadful seven-headed beast, or dragon, that represents the seven landmasses of the earth. The dragon's influence will be felt in every corner of the globe.

And now about the human rider of the beast with reins in his hand. The rider, as you already know, is your father. He is riding the beast that is coming up out of the earth. As your father holds the reins of the beast, he thinks he has full control of the dragon he is riding. But in reality, the beast is totally controlling him and making your father do the beast's will. The beast has a will of his own for he is a destroyer and also an angel out of the bottomless pit.

Your father wears a king's crown on his head and of course that represents his thirst for power and his quest to rule the world. Donald King is a king unto himself and is controlled by the spirit of Apollyon which gives him his power.

Kings will come and kings will go and your father looks for one to rule with him. You are his choice, Matthew. You are flesh of his flesh and bone of his bone and he does not want his genetic line broken. You represent one of the small horns that is protruding out of his crown and he represents the other.

He wants to rule the world together with you. His grandfather, Hitler, attempted the task but failed. His own father was considered weak as he refused his destiny. But, as you already know, your father is on the brink of world domination and he is calling you, the other small horn to come and join him and rule the world together. The time is short, and the day is almost at hand for the powers of the underworld to be unleashed on an unsuspecting world.

The scroll is a time clock for you, Matthew. It places times and events into perspective and marks them out both in your life and the life of your father. The beginning of the end will come at one minute past-midnight and the whole world will know if the two kings will rule the world. We are now at the 6th sign of the scroll time clock.

The first sign is you, Matthew. It was I who ministered to you outside the dining room and made sure you went to church that night and also made sure that your room was in trailer 4 room 11. Thus the scripture verse Matthew 4:11.

The second sign at the two o'clock position is me revealing myself to Walter. You have a friend in him, and you will need him in your future. Judges 6:11.

The third sign at the three o'clock position is me. I am Sam, an angel of Strength and Might, sent to give strength and might to those who need it. 2 Peter 2:11.

The fourth sign at the four o'clock position is the dream about you looking over the barricade into the future and seeing the beast coming up out of the earth. Revelation 13:11.

The fifth sign at the five o'clock position is about the one who controls the world's resources. Your father now controls the majority of the food, the oil, and the wine. And he who controls these things can control the world. 2 Chronicles 11:11.

And here we are today at the sixth sign at the six o'clock position. Apollyon Global has arrived. And they had a king over them which is the angel of the bottomless pit, whose name in the Hebrew tongue is Abaddon, but in the Greek tongue has his name Apollyon. Revelation 9:11. Make no mistake about it, Revelation 9:11 is already here.

We have now passed the sixth sign and the seventh approaches. Midnight is coming and the time is short."

As I finished telling Matthew what Sam had given me to say,

I could tell that Matthew was at the end of himself. Too much was happening too fast and I knew he probably didn't understand most of what Sam had told him. I felt for Matthew because I didn't understand most of it either.

"I'm really sorry to lay this on you, but there are still two more things I need to say. There are two verses found on page 1111 (eleven eleven) of my Bible that Sam wanted you to hear. They are found in Ezekiel Chapter 21 in verses 9 and 11. These two verses say, 'Son of man, prophesy, and say, thus says the Lord; say, a sword, a sword, is sharpened and also furbished. And he has given it to be furbished, that it may be handled; this sword is sharpened, and is furbished, to give it into the hand of the slayer.'

I'm supposed to tell you, your sword is ready. It has been furbished, it has been sharpened, it is ready to be handled, and it is ready to be put into the hand of the slayer. You are the slayer, Matthew."

Again, Matthew was silent and deep in thought as I was about to speak the last three words that Sam had given me to say.

"Sam told me to speak these three words to you after you had heard the interpretation to your dream. The three words are, 'They are coming,' and he said that you would know what that meant."

A minute or so passed with neither of us speaking. What was there to say after hearing something like that? It had been a long day, we were both tired, and our minds were beginning to shut down.

Matthew finally spoke his first words after listening to me speak for the past hour. All he said was,

"I need to go to my room, Walter. Good night."

As I closed the door to the crew cab and started walking towards trailer #7, my heart went out to Matthew. How could any man carry a burden such as the one that had just been dumped on him? From that moment on, I realized that it was going to be my responsibility to hold him up in prayer, as he would have to walk much of this road into the unknown by himself.

CHAPTER THIRTY-TWO

DONALD

Sleep did not come easily for me that night. Thoughts of Matthew, David, and Donald King filled my head as I slept fitfully. After a long night of tossing and turning, my alarm clock finally jolted me into full consciousness and out of my restless slumber.

My first conscious thoughts were of Matthew and of how he was going to survive these next few days in camp. The combination of David leaving and getting a bizarre dream interpretation on which the fate of the entire world rests on your shoulders could be a little unnerving. Then the possibility of your evil dictator father reappearing in your life after 24 years all seemed a little much for one person to handle.

If it were me, I think I would just stay in bed for a week or two with the covers over my head! My heart totally went out to Matthew and the dilemmas I knew he would be facing. On top of everything that I had told him last night, I had failed to mention that the possibility of his father showing up in camp in the next few days and going on a tram tour was very high.

That possibility also sent a chill down my spine, since the group had requested to take their tour in tram #3. Why would they request that? Did they already know that I was a friend of Matthew's? Could Donald King actually read the thoughts of others from a distance? Matthew had said that his father would call out to him in his dreams. Is that how he had located him up here in the middle of nowhere?

All of a sudden my second alarm clock's high-pitched whine went off. As I threw off my covers and hit the floor running,

I could only imagine what this day might be like for Matthew. He certainly would be in my prayers today.

Half a world away in the tiny village of Abad, in the province of Khuzestan, Iran, thirteen men sat nervously waiting for the arrival of their Supreme Commander and Chief. Money had no influence among the men in this room. The only thing that carried any weight was summed up in one word, and that word was loyalty. Loyalty to the supreme commander came before family and friends. Loyalty was the only thing that kept all thirteen of these men alive.

The side door of the conference room opened and Donald King made his grand entrance. He proceeded to walk towards his seat at the head of the table. All thirteen men rose and gave a slight bow as he approached his seat of honor.

"You may all sit down," he said with a wave of his hand. "This is the first of many great days before us. Our enemies stand at the brink of defeat, and we stand at the threshold of final victory. Plans that have been laid before the foundations of the world are about to come to pass. And we have been destined to be the rulers and the guardians of those plans. The Final Solution is within our grasp and soon the world will fall on its knees before us. My son will soon join us in the dominion of planet earth. The Jews are in the process of bowing their knees to me, and the rest of the world will need what only I can give. I am the life giver. I control the food, I control the oil, and I control what we drink. We have arrived, my brothers. Let us kneel and pledge our allegiance once again to the god who is above all gods."

With those words spoken, fourteen men slid out of their chairs and onto their knees. With outstretched hands towards the ball of light that had just entered the room, each and every man spoke their pledge of allegiance in unison.

"We belong to you, oh great god Apollyon. You are the god above all gods. We are yours and you are ours and forever we will serve you, oh Angel of Light."

As the light and presence of Apollyon began to fill every square inch of the underground conference room, the weight of that presence slowly pushed the thirteen already kneeling men further down until they lay prostrate before Apollyon with their foreheads seemingly glued to the floor. Only Donald stood with his hands outstretched as Apollyon's light slowly engulfed him and the two seemed to become one. Waves of energy filled Donald's human frame until he involuntarily began to tremble and shake as Apollyon's immortal presence saturated Donald's mortal body.

Donald could literally feel a power consuming him that seemed to have no limits or bounds. He was entering a world that he knew existed but never could quite arrive at. Now, at this very moment, everything that he had ever dreamed about seemed to be coming to pass as he stood detached from human limitations and was being filled with the dark secrets of the Universe. This kind of knowledge did not come by hearing with natural ears, but was imparted instantaneously to Donald as a computer would download files. Donald was seeing and understanding multiple streams of information coming at him, and was able to retain all of it without any effort on his part at all.

Simultaneously Donald was able to see World events, Past, Present and Future. He had access to the realms of Science, Astronomy, Alchemy, Music and a host of other human concepts and initiatives, some discovered and some yet undiscovered. He had no idea how this was all possible, but what he did know was that right now, in this moment of time, he felt more like a god than a man.

As the download of information ended, and the presence of Apollyon seemed to lift, Donald slowly opened his eyes and found himself standing alone in the now empty conference room. For a moment Donald stood disoriented, wondering where everyone had gone. He looked down and read the time and date on his wristwatch, and realized that over twelve hours had passed while he had visited another world.

It was hard to keep my mind focused on my tram runs that morning . Too many things were happening simultaneously and I felt like I had very little or no control over what was happening in my life. I was very much looking forward to getting aboard a plane on Monday and leaving this part of my life behind. But between now and then I would have to try and figure out how to get through these next few days.

When I sat at the breakfast table with Kevin and Rob that morning, the conversation of course quickly focused on the death of Nelson Mandela and the sign that he represented.

"I could hardly believe it," Rob said "when I heard the news that Nelson Mandela had passed away!" "Yes," said Kevin "when I heard about it, I immediately remembered all the words that you said that the angel had spoken to you. But you also said that what you told us was only a part of what the angel told you about Nelson Mandela being a sign. What about the rest of it? What else did the angel say? Will you tell us?"

I paused for a moment and recalled Sam's words about who was going to replace Nelson Mandela. I wasn't sure if I should say anything or not. Giving a prediction about a death, and revealing the upcoming World's evil leader were two different things altogether. Although I knew what Sam had told me would come to pass in time, I wasn't sure how Kevin and Rob would react to knowing that Donald King would become the world's evil dictator and that he was scheduled to be here in camp in a few short days. As I pondered what my response to the guys would be, the remembrance of my first encounter with Sam sitting on my Gen-Set came to mind. His words were burned into my subconscious as I brought them to mind and quoted them silently to myself.

"Don't be afraid." Sam said. "I have appeared to you for a reason which will shortly be revealed to you and your friends. Be at peace and remember, I am always here for you."

Did Sam actually want me to share everything that was happening with my friends? Was that what he meant by what he said? I thought about the implications of how all this might come across to Kevin and Rob, but I decided to go for it and at least answer the question that Kevin had just asked.

"Well," I said to Kevin "I will answer your question, but I'm sure you are not going to like what I have to say. What Sam told me has to do with the future of the world and it will probably take some time to come to pass. But anyways, here is what Sam said to me word for word and you will have to decide for yourselves whether you believe it or not. And please, I would keep this information to myself if I were you because most people will not believe it. Here is all of what Sam said to me word for word.

On December 5, 2013, a great sign will occur and the whole earth shall see it and mourn. A man of peace and reconciliation will go to his eternal home and reward. All the people of the world will mourn as this great man's life comes to an end. But the world should truly mourn for itself, because of the one who is taking this man's place. A world leader has already arisen who will fill the world with war, hate and destruction while preaching peace all at the same time. As you might have guessed already, this man's name is Donald King, and he comes as a destroyer of all that is good. Even the names of his former and current companies tell the story of his true motives. The words Abaddon and Apollyon have the same meaning in two different languages, and this is what they mean. Both words mean, The Angel of the Bottomless Pit, The Place of Destruction, and The Destroyer."

When I finished Sam's quote, silence surrounded the breakfast table as all three of us were contemplating the words and their implications. After a minute or so of unbroken silence Rob finally broke that silence with the words "Wow, that is quite a story. I'll have to think about that one for a while." With the finishing of Rob's last statement, we all got up, pushed our chairs under the table and headed for the exit. "Yes" I thought you myself, "there sure is a lot to think about isn't there." As we walked out of the dining room together, I was happy that I had told the guys about what Sam had said to me. At least now I felt like I was not carrying this burden alone.

Donald stood in the empty conference room. He pondered what had just happened to him in the past twelve hours. He had seen glimpses of the past, present and the future, and the future that he had seen included his son Matthew standing beside him as they took control of the world together. Yes, he thought to himself, in a couple of days from now, he would be standing face to face with his son, whom he had not seen in twenty-four years. In a couple of days Donald King would be standing in Northern Alberta with his son by his side. Soon there would be two Kings, ready to rule the world of men. He had seen it in his future and now his future was about to come to pass.

CHAPTER THIRTY-THREE

MATTHEW

Sleep evaded Matthew all that night. Thoughts of what Sam had told him through me completely consumed him and so unsettled his mind that he was unable to rest. He had already made a phone call to his company telling them that he was sick and would not be coming in to work that day.

Matthew knew that he was too distracted to go to work, but sitting in his room all day with these thoughts spontaneously running through his head did not appeal to him either. Even though he was exhausted from a lack of sleep, he decided he needed to get out of his room and try to clear his weary mind. The morning air of December 6, 2013 was cold and brisk, but the sun was shining and by the afternoon the temperature would probably hit the -5 degree Celsius range.

Matthew walked the perimeter road that circled the plant, feeling rejuvenated as the cold, crisp air began to clear his mind. About a kilometer into his walk he found himself at the entrance to the road leading down to Pit #13. Without giving it too much thought, he made a left turn and started down the road that he had dreamed about so many times. As he arrived at the exact spot where the huge man had offered him a sword in his dream, he slowed his pace and then came to a complete stop.

The split second his feet stopped moving, a strange feeling came over him and he felt like he had just stepped through a door into another world. Up to this point in his life and even as a child, he'd had dreams that seemed to point to future events that would soon take place.

Right here, right now, however, he was not sleeping and what was happening to him was not a dream. Standing right in front of him, shining much brighter than the snow all around him, was the same man that had offered him a sword in his previous dreams.

Matt stood frozen like a statue, not knowing what to say or do in the presence of this giant. The only conscious thought coming to his mind at this point was 'run, run, run'. On impulse, he turned to do just that. But to his surprise, his legs would not move, and when he looked down at his feet, he noticed that they were stuck in sinking sand, just like in his dream.

His eyes scanned up from his feet until he was looking directly into the face of this giant glowing man. He stood there breathless and spellbound as their eyes met and time seemed to stand still.

"Good morning Matthew" said the giant being as he extended his hand towards Matthew in order for him to shake it. Without even thinking, Matthew extended his arm and instantly found his hand lost in the grip of a firm handshake with a hand that was almost twice the size of his.

"Good morning" Matthew responded weakly as the two of them released their grips.

"First of all, it's really great to be able to meet you face to face and not just in a dream. As you've probably guessed, my name is Sam, and I'm the angel that Walter told you about yesterday. I've been really excited all morning knowing that I've been given permission to meet with you right here, right now."

Matthew just continued staring intently at the angel that stood firmly planted right in front of him, not being sure if he should do or say anything.

Finally Sam continued by saying "Let's talk and just get to know each other a little bit, and please don't be afraid to ask me questions. I will answer them the best that I can within the scope of my own knowledge and understanding."

As Sam continued talking to Matthew, a sense of unworthiness fastened itself onto him. Here in the presence of this brilliant, shining, glory-filled angel, Matthew felt small, dirty, ashamed and unworthy to even be in his presence.

When Sam finished speaking, Matthew let out a deep sigh, and with all the courage he could muster he said "Why am I feeling so insignificant and unworthy as I stand here beside you?"

"Well," Sam responded with a disarming smile on his face, "the simple answer is that you are unworthy, totally unworthy, to be in the presence of someone who comes from the Kingdom. You are a man from planet earth and I am an angel that comes from an untarnished dimension called the Kingdom of Heaven. You live in a broken, fallen world that has been in that condition since the day rebellion and selfishness was embraced and the good and righteous was rejected. Tell me honestly Matthew, in your heart of hearts, are you a good and righteous man or a rebellious and selfish man?"

The question Sam asked caught Matthew off guard, but he knew right away that if he answered the question honestly, he would have to put himself in the category of the rebellious and selfish.

Sam continued, "You are the son of your father Matthew, and your father was the son of his father, and so on and so on. There is not even one good and righteous father out there anywhere through the millennia of time. All have been rebellious and selfish and mankind continues to reap the rewards of that selfishness and rebellion."

While Matthew was still mulling over the answer that Sam had given him, Sam asked another question that took him by surprise. "Tell me about your father Matthew. Is he a good and righteous man, or is he a rebellious and selfish man?"

Without hesitation, negative emotion filled Matthew's body, and with anger resonating in his voice he spewed out the words "My father is an evil and unrighteous man! I hate him and I always will!"

With eyes full of compassion Sam turned to Matthew and simply said "You are the son of your father, and will do the same things, unless the line is broken."

"What are you talking about?!" Matthew asked angrily. "I am nothing like my father and never will be! He is a monster and I am ashamed to be called his son!"

Once again Sam simply and gently said "Matthew, you are the son of your father and you will do the same things, unless the line is broken."

Overwhelming emotion came over Matthew as the cry of his heart made its way from the pit of his stomach forming words that seemed to just roll out of him. "I don't want to be like him!" he sobbed. "Help me Sam, I don't want to be like him. I don't want to be like him. I hate him!"

"The line must be broken, redemption must come." Sam said as he knelt down to embrace Matthew, whose face was stained with tears and whose body shook uncontrollably. At this point in his life, Matthew just needed a father to hug him and tell him that everything was going to be all right.

Once Matthew regained control of his emotions, Sam stood up and gave him a moment to compose himself and collect his thoughts.

"I know that all of this is very hard for you to understand right now, but please just believe me when I say that you were born for this moment and only you can determine if you will fulfill your own destiny right here, right now. I have been chosen to offer you this sword one more time. You rejected it in your dream once already, and you ran. You can reject it again and run or you can accept it from my hand and begin a journey that only you can fulfill."

When Sam spoke those words, a brilliant shining sword materialized in his right hand. He bowed to one knee in front of Matthew, holding out the sword that now rested in the palms of his two massive hands. "This is the sword of the Lord, Matthew, and the Lord Himself offers it to you and to you alone. Now is your moment of decision. It will change your life forever, one way or the other."

As Matthew looked at the gleaming sword in front of him, he noticed his feet were not stuck in the sinking sand any more. He could now freely run, or he could voluntarily pick up the sword of the Dragon Slayer. Although he had no idea what his life might look like if he picked up the sword, for some strange reason, he felt drawn to it, and he no longer felt unworthy as he had only moments ago.

Something had changed inside of him. Something had shifted. He didn't know what it was, but one thing he did know for sure – that he would run no more. His days of running were now over and whatever his future held, he would not run from his father for even one more day.

As Matthew looked into Sam's eyes, he felt as if he was gazing into another world called eternity. He had never experienced anything like this in his entire life, but he liked what he saw, and he liked how it felt.

Without hesitation, he reached for the sword and took a hold of the handle. It fit his hand perfectly. With the sword in his hand, he felt complete somehow. There had always been a missing part somewhere deep inside of him, but now with this sword in his hand, for the first time in his life he felt totally alive and whole. What was this power that he felt as he gripped the sword? Was this all real he wondered, as he turned the sword from side to side and just enjoyed exploring this new-found freedom? What was happening to him? Whatever it was, he embraced it wholly, and as he looked confidently at Sam, he said to him, "I choose the sword and I choose the destiny that the sword brings."

With a smile on his face and his arms raised towards the heavens, Sam spoke these simple words and then vanished into thin air... "It has now begun."

Matthew watched Sam disappear right before his eyes, and the obvious question replayed itself in his mind "What had just begun? What was Sam talking about?"

The sword Sam had given him was still firmly gripped in his right hand, and the fact that it was still there seemed to mesmerize him. He continued to examine every square inch of it as he turned it from side to side remembering the words that Sam had spoken to him about the sword. Sam had said "Your sword is ready, it has been furbished, it has been sharpened, it is ready to be handled and it is ready to be put into the hand of the slayer. You are the slayer, Matthew."

Matthew continued to handle the newly polished and sharpened sword, and on impulse he tested the sharpness of the blade with the side of his thumb to find out for himself how keen it really was. With very little pressure being applied against the edge of the blade, Matthew instantly noticed that the white fallen snow around his feet now had three drops of blood mixed in with it. The sword had drawn its first blood and that blood was his own. His curiosity now being satisfied that the sword was sharp, and extremely sharp at that, he lifted it up over his head towards the sky. It glistened and reflected the sun's rays.

"Thanks Sam" he said out loud, and then repeated the final words that Sam had spoken before he disappeared: "It has now begun!"

Then he lowered his now empty right hand. Sam was gone, the sword was gone, but the blood that had dripped from his hand was not gone, and his sense of completeness and worthiness was not gone. Something had changed inside of him. Something was new and he was not the same person he was an hour ago – and for that he was grateful.

CHAPTER THIRTY-FOUR

DAVID

While the plane touched down in Tel Aviv, Israel, David's mind was attempting to shift gears toward the professional side of his life, which he knew awaited him the moment he would put his feet on Israeli soil. The trip from Toronto, Canada had been long, but healing to him in some ways. During the flight he had the time to quietly stop and reflect on all the different things that had happened to him and Matthew over the past few months. He had participated in a series of events that he, at one time, would have never even dreamed was possible. And now, here he was on the other side of the world, not even knowing the reasons why he was here. It would be good to see his family and friends back here in Israel again, but very difficult not knowing the next time or if he would ever see Matthew again. He pushed those thoughts from his mind and stood up to retrieve his overhead luggage. Taking a deep breath, he put on his professional face and exited the plane into the unknown.

Once through airport security, David was met by two men from his intelligence agency who he had never met before. Few words were exchanged as all three of them got into a waiting car and headed to a location in the heart of Tel Aviv. David knew better than to ask a lot of trivial questions that the two men sitting beside him would not be able to answer anyways. He would just have to have patience because he knew that in the process of time, the reasons for him having to leave Canada would become clear.

Once the car and its occupants got waved through a security check point, it turned left and headed down into the underground parking lot of some kind of government facility.

As the three men exited the car and headed towards the nearest elevator doors, David noticed the high level of security and the multiple cameras that were spread throughout the parking lot. The three men arrived in front of the elevator doors. A red light flashed on the monitor screen beside them that required both retina scans and fingerprint confirmation from each of them. Once this information had been processed and their identities confirmed, the light turned green and the outer doors of the elevator opened.

Inside the doors was another set of doors that opened once the two men entered their clearance codes into the computer. David marvelled at the security upgrades that had taken place in his own country over the past eleven years. Living on the run with Matthew had taken him away from this high tech world and all of its complications.

Stepping into the elevator with the doors closing behind them, an automated female voice filled the compartment saying "This elevator has been activated." To David's surprise, he felt the motion of the elevator going down instead of up. It took several seconds to reach its destination so he guessed that they must now be several floors below ground level. "It must be a bunker of some kind" he thought to himself as the doors slowly opened in front of him.

Walking through a maze of people who were at the helm of countless computer and video screens, they finally came to a door at the end of a short hallway labelled "Military Intelligence." David was intrigued by what he was seeing all around him, because even with his security clearances, he did not even know that a place like this existed.

One of David's escorts opened the door, motioning for David to enter. The door was then closed behind him. David stood motionless as he scanned the room with at least a dozen people in it. He did not recognize anyone, and was unsure of what to do next.

"Welcome, David" said the man at the head of the table. "Please come and take a seat over here, as I'm sure you're very curious as to why you are here." David sat down, feeling very uncomfortable, as the eyes of all those in the room were focused on him.

"To begin with," the man said "we will not give introductions here today because this will probably be the only time we will ever meet. Let me just say that certain situations have arisen within our country that require our attention. We all work in different facets of our national government, and we answer only to the Prime Minister himself and his closest advisors. We would like you to answer some questions for us so that we can get a clear picture of what is happening, or what could happen in the near future with our national security."

David's mind was starting to run wild. "What could these people possibly want with him, and what information could he give that had any bearing on National Security?" He had been out of the country for years and most recently had been assigned to an oil sands camp in the middle of nowhere in northern Alberta. None of this made any sense to him, but he knew for sure he was about to find out why he had been summoned.

"Let's get started," the man at the head table said, as he slid a piece of paper across the table right in front of David. David focused on the paper that now lay before him and his eyes got wide and his jaw dropped.

"What is this?" the man repeated. David's eyes remained frozen on a copy of the scroll that lay directly in front of him. As he raised his head to meet the gaze of all those seated in the room, he knew that he was going to be here for a long, long time.

Meanwhile, more talks between the Israeli Prime Minister and his senior officials had come to an impasse. The threat Donald King posed, and the possibility of a nuclear holocaust had put the country on high alert.

This lined right up with Donald's agenda. His goal was to instill fear and force Israel's hand to act in some way. Whichever way they chose, Donald would ultimately win, and soon have complete control of the whole world. Since a clear course of action had not been agreed upon by the senior officials, it was decided that the meetings should be postponed until the information that David was providing could be collected and examined thoroughly. Another long day for the Prime Minister had come to an end. His dishevelled look and bloodshot eyes told the story of how his day had gone.

How was David going to tell a story to these high-level government officials that he barely believed himself? Although he knew the things that had happened to him were real, still, they were unexplainable especially to someone who had not experienced them. David felt like he was in a trap and there was no way he was going to get out of this without appearing to be crazy. Just as he was about to start speaking, he was inspired by a thought encouraging him to "Just tell the truth, exactly how it happened." As he began to speak, he followed through on that thought.

When he finished his story, all the man at the head table said was "Very interesting." He then said, "I have another question for you, David. Are you aware that Donald King was just issued a Canadian Visa and will enter Canada tomorrow? He will be in the same camp from which you just came."

"What?!" said David, not sure that he had heard correctly. "Does Matthew know? You have to warn him! You have to get him out of there!" David said with an urgency denoting the seriousness of the situation.

"We have one more question for you, David, and this one is the most important one of all. We know that you are like a big brother to Matthew and that you have known him and been with him almost constantly for the past twenty-four years. The question is, can he be trusted implicitly? And to the best of your knowledge, would he remain loyal to the wishes of the Israeli government?"

David responded to the first question in the absolute affirmative. The second question related to some unknown factors that David was not sure about. Although David felt Matthew was totally trustworthy in the general sense, he did not know if he would go along with everything the Israeli government would want him to do. Matthew had grown up to be a man of principle and his convictions ran deep. Although he had grown up almost exclusively in Israel until his late teen years, he did not always agree with the political or moral issues of the Israeli government. Matthew had a mind and a will of his own and he stood strong on the convictions that were the basis of his belief system.

The group was satisfied with David's description of Matthew's character and values. The whole process had taken almost four hours and David was still hungry and tired from the long flight from Canada.

The man at the head of the table stood, thanking David for cooperating and then went on to say that a room and food was prepared for him down the hall and that he would have to stay in the facility for at least twenty-four hours. The group David had spoken to was going to meet with the Israeli Prime Minister and his staff within the next twelve hours. David would have to remain close just in case his presence was required and more questions needed to be answered.

David almost felt like he was being held against his will, but he knew that this had always been part of his job. You did what you were told, collected your paycheck, and didn't ask too many questions, out loud anyways. Although David was content with the food and the place to stay, he could not get his mind off the fact that Donald King was on his way to Northern Alberta and would probably be standing face to face with his son in just a matter of hours.

Had the twenty-four years he had spent protecting and running with Matthew been in vain? Was everything going to come undone, and would Donald King finally get his hands on Matthew? Many questions ran through David's mind for which he had no answers. One thing he knew for sure was that he needed to try and get over this severe case of jet lag, because in Israel you never knew what tomorrow might bring.

The meeting had come to its conclusion and the Israeli Prime Minister breathed a sigh of relief. After being briefed by the group that had interviewed David, it was decided by himself and his group of advisors to put the whole Donald King threat on hold for the time being at least. There was too much information coming to light that required time to process and the need for definite plans to be drawn up. They would not be pressured by Donald King into reacting before they were ready with all the details in place. Only the Prime Minister and his Minister of Defence remained in the conference room.

David had been awakened after ten hours of sleep and was then led to the conference room without any fore-warning as to who he was about to meet. As David entered through a side door, he was shocked when he realized he was now standing face to face with the two most powerful men in the State of Israel.

"Welcome David" the Prime Minister said as both men reached out their hands and shook David's. "I wish we didn't have to meet for the first time under these conditions, but circumstances have forced it to be so. Please sit down."

The defence minister then gave David some background on Donald King's threat of a nuclear holocaust and the blackmail scenario that he was using to gain world peace. David could hardly believe what he was hearing and it reminded him of Matt's dream where his father was riding a seven headed dragon that was coming out of a nuclear explosion.

As the Defence Minister finished briefing David on how all of these things might play out, he stopped, redirected the conversation, and said "But we, as the government, have decided on another plan, and we need your help to see it through."

"Of course sir" David responded with no hesitation. "I will help in any way that I possibly can."

"Thank you" said the Defence Minister. "We knew that we could count on you. Here is the decision we have made, based on our latest intelligence and also the information you have provided.

First of all, we are not going to extract Matthew from his present situation in Northern Alberta. His father is en route there and we are going to let whatever plans Donald has to play out regarding Matthew. If Donald takes him, Matthew could be a valuable source of information as to Donald's upcoming world dictatorship plans and possibly his nuclear holocaust aspirations. We realize that it is a risky venture, but when weighed against a nuclear holocaust, we feel we need to take that chance.

We would also like to test one of our country's most recent innovations. Our scientists have discovered a way to track and locate any person with our upgraded satellite capabilities. The program is called Soluble Anatomy Monitoring.

In layman's terms it is quite simple. A soluble solution has been engineered that, when taken orally, gets trapped as it passes through the kidneys and creates a homing beacon. We can track that signal with our satellites when the person is outdoors anywhere in the world. The signal lasts only for about seven days and the more water that the person consumes, the weaker the signal becomes. The solution is safe to be taken internally and totally undetectable by any means that we know of. We would like Matthew to drink this solution before he meets with his father, and then we would like to monitor him and find out where he is taken.

We feel that Abad might be the site of his headquarters or possibly even the location of the stolen Surface to Air nuclear missile. We need some feet on the ground out there in Iran right away and we believe that you are the man.

If our suspicions prove correct, and Matthew does end up in Abad, that is the place where you are to extract him and the information that he will possess. We need to know where that missile is, and we need to know as soon as possible. As we speak, we have a plane on the tarmac, fueled and ready to go. We have a man on board just waiting for our signal to take off and head back to Canada, and then northern Alberta.

We need to arrive in your camp before Donald does, explain the situation to Matthew and get him to drink the solution so we can monitor him. We may have some security concerns about getting into the camp, since we have not been able to contact Matthew in the past twenty-four hours. "

"Come, David" the Prime Minister said. "Let's go into the Intelligence Chamber and talk to the professionals. We need a plan to get through camp security, get this information and the tracking solution to Matthew. Time is of the essence. We need to get this plane up and off the ground, and make it to Northern Alberta before Donald does."

CHAPTER THIRTY-FIVE

SAM

Today was Saturday, December 7, 2013. I had not seen or spoken to Matthew since Thursday evening, when I told him about all the things that Sam had asked me to share with him. Actually, I wasn't even sure if he wanted to see me again, after I had dumped all of Sam's words on him. He had been very distraught the last time I had seen him, and all I had been able to do since then was to pray for him. "I would not want to be in his shoes right now" I thought to myself.

One thing that still bothered me was the fact that I had forgotten to tell Matthew about the tram tour that was happening tomorrow with the Apollyon Global people on board. Just last night Kevin had confirmed with me that the tour was a go, and was slated for Sunday December 8th at 10:00 am.

Kevin also confirmed that Donald King would be on board with his team, and I was to pick them up at the baseball diamond, which also served as a helicopter pad. They would be coming in on a black Apollyon Global helicopter at 9:45 am and would be leaving from the same place at 11:45 am.

The thought of actually seeing or maybe even having to speak with Donald King was freaking me right out. To everyone else in camp, the arrival of Donald King was almost like turning the day into a national holiday. Everyone wanted to catch a glimpse of the man who would broker world peace and was the inspiration for many world leaders. A short, but informal welcome was planned for him, and then he would spend the next hour and a half touring one of the facilities of which he was considering becoming a major shareholder. It would be my job to transport the group around the site for an hour and a half, and then take them back to the ball diamond.

As my day wore on, I could hear the buzz of people talking about the big day tomorrow with the arrival of Donald King. Even though I had not been able to tell Matthew about his father showing up, I was sure he had heard about it already, just like the rest of the camp had.

As the day was coming to an end, the guys and I were chatting about tomorrow's events around the supper table. The mood and conversation was very buoyant and everyone on the tram crew was excited, except me. I did not really want to be the one doing this tour, but I had to because the Apollyon group had requested Tram #3 and its operator. Kevin and Rob understood my reluctance, but encouraged me by saying that everything would be just fine. I knew they were probably right, but I certainly was not looking forward to going where my work duties would take me tomorrow.

Walking back towards my trailer, I decided to keep going, and stop in and see if Matt was in his room. After knocking three times, I figured that he was not in his room, or that he was not wanting to answer. I hated the thought of not seeing Matt again after our last get together. I just wanted to make sure that he was okay. So much had happened to both of us over the past couple of months, that I could not even imagine not seeing him again. As I walked back to my bunkhouse, I whispered a short prayer into the cold evening air and said "God, please get Matthew through the day tomorrow and keep him safe."

I lay on my bed that evening, with several different questions rolling around in my mind… questions like "I wonder where Matthew is?" and "How he is going to deal with all of this? I wonder how David is doing back in Israel. Will I ever see either of them again?" What a roller coaster ride the three of us had been on. "Would the ride be over tomorrow? " Tomorrow was the day to find that out, and it was coming way too fast for me.

As I moved in and out of slumber that evening, I began to hear a voice that I recognized, calling out to me by name. "Walter" the voice said softly. Then again it said "Walter, wake up." Then the third time, instead of hearing a voice, I felt someone grip my leg and start to pull. Instantly I was awake, staring into the mischievous face of Sam.

"What are you doing here?" I said without thinking.

"What am I doing here," Sam said. "the question should be 'Why are you always summoning me and asking me questions?'" Sam laughed out loud as he looked at me struggling to sit up.

"You had better not laugh so loud." I warned him, "or you'll wake up the guys sleeping next door." Sam just laughed louder and said in response "They won't hear me, but they will hear you, and think that you are talking to yourself."

As Sam settled down from his bout of laughter, he just sat there on the end of my bed with a big grin on his face. "So tomorrow is a big day for you, Walter. What do you think about it all? Has it gotten you feeling a little bit uptight?"

"You sure have that right." I said to Sam. "I have no desire to meet or even see Matthew's dad, never mind take him on a tram tour. I'm already looking forward to tomorrow being over, and then heading home the next day. On top of that, I forgot to tell Matthew that his father was going to be here, and I can't seem to find him anywhere. Do you have any idea where Matt is these days?"

Sam looked at me with that same disarming smile on his face. He simply said to me, "I've come here for a reason this evening, but I will also answer the questions you asked me in your thoughts. First of all, I'm not exactly sure where Matthew is at this exact moment, but I know that he is still here in camp. Be assured that Matthew is just fine, and he is well aware that his father will be arriving here tomorrow. Actually, Matthew is more than just fine, he is doing better now than he has been up to this point in his entire life. But I will let him tell you his own story when the time is right. As for David, he is also exactly where he needs to be right now, and who's to know, maybe your paths will cross again someday. You were also wondering if all of this would be over with Donald King's arrival tomorrow? I will tell you the exact same thing as I told Matthew. Nothing is over, Walter, it has now begun."

"What!?" I exclaimed excitedly. "You talked to Matthew yourself? What did you tell him? And what has now begun?"

Sam responded quickly to my new questions by simply putting his finger in front of his lips and softly saying,

"Shhhh. Everything is just fine, and you will find the answers to all of your questions. I have not come here tonight to answer those questions, but I have come for a purpose. The scroll clock is moving. Time never stands still.

I have come here to give you some insight into the last six signs of the scroll clock. As you know already, the first six signs have been fulfilled, or are in the process of being fulfilled. The next six signs are about to take place in the earth and the twelfth sign will be unmistakable. All the world will know, and all the world will see what is in the heart of man. But let's begin with the seventh sign that is already underway around the world.

The seventh sign says 'That they should believe a lie' II Thessalonians 2:11. Rightly did the prophet Isaiah say in his writings when he wrote 'Woe unto them that call evil good, and good evil; that put darkness for light, and light for darkness; that put bitter for sweet, and sweet for bitter!' in Isaiah 5:20.

These are the lies that Donald King heralds around the whole earth. He speaks of the good and the peace he will bring to the world, but he is evil, and evil only breeds evil. He is darkness, but he proclaims that he is the light, and that he will show the world a better way. But evil cannot be light, and he cannot show the world a better way. He speaks of the goodness and the sweetness that will come when he brings equality to all that live in the world. But in reality, only bitterness will come. Make no mistake about it, Donald King is evil, Donald King brings darkness, Donald King is the gall of bitterness. But the world will believe his lie and follow him, as the blind lead the blind.

The eighth sign says 'The wicked works a deceitful work' Proverbs 11:18. Rightly did the prophet Jeremiah say 'For among my people are found wicked men: they lay in wait as he that sets snares; they set a trap, they catch men. As a cage is full of birds, so are their houses full of deceit; that is why they have become great and rich.' Jeremiah 5:26-27. In the coming days and months, the deceitful seeds of the wicked will come to pass. The events that will take place throughout the world have been carefully planned, just like a trap that is about to spring on an unsuspecting world.

Once the deceitfulness of the wicked has reached maturity, great violence will raise its head on a global scale. So the ninth sign will come.

The ninth sign says 'Violence is risen up into a rod of wickedness.' Ezekiel 7:11. Rightly did Moses say in Genesis 6:11 that 'The earth also was corrupt before God, and the earth was filled with violence.' This is exactly what will come to pass in the coming days and months. The earth shall be filled with violence in an unprecedented manner. Terror, anarchy and rebellion will reign, and will fill the earth's highways, cities and lands. Violence and the wickedness in man's heart will be unleashed, and the Kingdoms of this world will begin to fall.

The tenth sign 'A drought upon the land, and upon the mountains, and upon the corn, and upon the new wine, and upon the oil, and upon that which the ground brings forth.' Haggai 1:11. Rightly did the prophet Jeremiah say 'A drought is upon her waters, and they shall be dried up; for it is a land of graven images, and they are mad upon their idols.' Jeremiah 50:38. And so it shall be in the days to come, the fresh waters will lose their flow, and a great drought and decrease will come upon everything that the earth produces. Hunger and thirst will drive men to demand that Donald King become their god and savior and give them the resources they need to survive.

The eleventh sign 'And the King shall do according to his will, and he shall exalt himself, and magnify himself above every god.' Daniel 11:36. And Donald King will exalt himself and do according to his own will and the will of Apollyon. He will magnify himself above every god and the peoples of the earth will worship him willingly. He will have great power for a short time, but his days will be numbered, and his time will come to an end.

The twelfth sign 'The Beginning of the End' 'And at that time shall Michael stand up, the great prince which stands for the children of your people; and there shall be a time of trouble, such as never was since there was a nation, even to that same time; and at that time your people shall be delivered, everyone that shall be found written in the book.' Daniel 12:1 The midnight hour for the earth is coming. This last and final sign will signal the beginning of the end, and it will be unmistakable. Midnight will arrive when the first modern nuclear missile detonates on the earth. Seventy years will have been accomplished from the time man unleashed hell on the earth on August 6, 1945. From that moment on, there begins a time of trouble such as never was since there was a nation, even to that same time; from the moment destruction comes, the earth will be living on borrowed time."

As Sam finished speaking about the twelfth sign, and the events that would signal the midnight hour, I realized that I was holding my breath as he spoke. When I finally let the breath out of my lungs, I think I was still in shock, as the words he had spoken kept rolling through my mind. I had always thought that it was inevitable that someday, something like this would transpire. But with Sam speaking the words, it now seemed imminent.

"I have to go now." Sam said softly, as he put his hand on my shoulder and squeezed it gently. "I don't know if, or when, I will ever see you again in person, now that my scroll assignment is complete. It has been a great honor and privilege for me to be able to get to know you in human time and space. We do not get this privilege very often, and I certainly have enjoyed it."

Sam stood, and his head and shoulders disappeared through my ceiling.

A sense of loss immediately swept over me. "Would I ever see Sam again? Was this our last and final goodbye?"

"I don't want you to leave." I called out to Sam. But as Sam's feet began to rise off the floor, and his body began to levitate upwards through my ceiling, I called out after him and said "Goodbye Sam, and thanks for everything."

As I sat there, staring at my ceiling, Sam's calming voice returned with his final words "Goodbye Walter." he said. "And remember, whether you see me or not, I am always here for you, because I'll always be your Tram Angel."

CHAPTER THIRTY-SIX

ANTICIPATION

Making its final approach into the Fort McMurray airport, Donald's private jet was right on time for its 9 am landing. Once on the ground, the Apollyon Global Group would have a few minutes to meet with the Mayor and council of the city, and then would enter their fueled and ready helicopter for the short flight out to camp.

As the plane began its final descent, Donald's private assistant smiled and leaned over to speak to Donald in hushed tones.

"We finally have them in our possession, after all these years. Your ex-wife and her husband have been found and abducted. They are now on one of our jets on their way back to Iran," he said with a sinister smirk on his face.

Donald leaned forward in his chair, looked into the eyes of his assistant and said, "Wonderful. It's about time. But there is one thing I want to make clear to you, and everyone else. Never again call her my ex-wife, and him, her husband. From this moment on they shall be referred to as the whore and her pimp; and everyone shall address them as that. I look forward to the moment where I see them both face to face and curse that pimp who stole my family. I look forward to watching the skin rot off his body as his whore watches, day after miserable day, until the last breath of air finally leaves his stinking body."

I did not look forward for my tram runs to end that morning. I would finish driving at 8 am, have breakfast, and then get my tram ready for the tour that started at 9:45 am.

About halfway through our breakfast, Kevin's phone rang, and he excused himself from the table to answer it. In a few minutes he returned with a serious look on his face and said, "Hurry up and finish your breakfast Walter. You need to make a quick trip out to the security gate, and then still make it back in time for your tram tour."

He quickly explained to me that my friend Adrian (David), who was still in Israel, had just phoned and said that it was imperative that I go out and talk with a friend of his on the outside of the security gate. Kevin then said that Adrian (David) was trying to get a hold of Timothy (Matthew) or myself, but both of our phones had been turned off for the past few days. That did not surprise me, in my case, because the only time I ever turned my phone on, was when I would call my wife back home.

As for Matthew's phone being off, I had no idea. Kevin then told me to go to my room, get my phone, and head out to the security gate. He said that Adrian (David) would call back on my phone in fifteen minutes while I was en route to the gate.

After quickly retrieving my phone, I jumped into a company truck and headed for the security gate. I had only been driving for a few minutes, when my phone rang, and a familiar voice started to speak on the other end of the line. It was good to hear David's voice once again, and it didn't take him long to get to the reason for his call.

Sitting, parked on the side of the road, I could hardly believe what David was telling me. He gave me a quick overview of what had happened to him over the past few days, and also of the plans that the Israeli government had for Matthew. I could hardly believe what I was hearing, as the conversation began to wind down. When David finished giving me all the details of the proposed plan, I began to speak, although I was continuing to process all the information that he had just given me.

"Listen," I said to David. "I understand how important all of this is, but there are a few problems associated with the plan. First, I have not seen Matt in three days and I have no idea where he is.

I also don't know if I can get the Soluble Anatomy Monitoring solution through security. And even if I do find Matthew in the next hour, and a have a chance to talk to him, there is no guarantee that he will drink it."

David seemed to understand my concerns, and at the end of the conversation he simply said "All we can do is try, and we'll have to leave the results up to God."

With the phone call ended, I was on the road again, heading for the security gate. I was amazed at the change I could sense in David's life. A couple of months ago he would have scoffed at the idea of God having any part in our daily lives, but now it was obvious that a change of some kind was happening.

Both Sonja and Jacob sat quietly next to each other on the Apollyon Global jet that was now, no doubt, on its way back to Iran. Sonja's mind was reeling at the events of the past few hours. One moment they were on their way to a shopping mall in a suburb of Sidney, Australia, and the next, they were prisoners of her former husband, Donald King.

It had been twenty-four years since she had found herself in a similar position of being abducted. The first abduction had eventually led to freedom, but this one would be like going through the very gates of Hell itself. The only consolation she had at this point was the fact that her son Matthew was safe and free, and at least that thought gave some hope. Sonja did not want to let her mind wander to what Donald King might have in store for her and her husband, Jacob.

The last twenty-four years had been wonderful for Sonja and Jacob. Jacob had been the love of her life, and she sometimes wondered how she had been so fortunate to be able to share her life with such a good man. She also knew the fury and the hatred of her former husband and shuddered at the thought of the two men meeting.

As she lay her head on Jacob's strong shoulder, she whispered something into his ear that put a smile on his face.

"Jacob, I love you more than you could ever imagine."

He turned and smiled, then gave her a kiss on the cheek, simply replying "Yes, I know."

To my pleasant surprise, the security gate issue did not materialize at all. After going through the gate, and talking with the Israeli intelligence person for a couple of minutes, he handed me the tracking solution that had been placed in a Canadian container that had once held apple juice.

The instructions he had given were simple and all I had to do was find Matt and encourage him to drink it. Getting back through the security gate had just been a simple matter of showing my badge, and I was waved through. Now came the more challenging part of finding Matthew. Since I only had a very limited amount of time before I had to go and start my tour, I wondered where I should start my search.

Should I check his room first, or perhaps the dining room? Pondering where he might be, a strong impression came to me while I made my way down the gravel road that led me back to camp. I would check the room that we used for our church services on Sunday nights. I now had a destination in mind as I glanced down at my wristwatch. I had fifteen minutes to find him before I had to go back to the laydown and get into my tram.

I pulled the truck up in front the recreation centre we used for our church services and ran up the four stairs that led into the building. Once inside, I scanned the three rooms with great anticipation, but soon found that every room was empty, and that I was the sole occupant of the building. As I exited the church room, I noticed a folded piece of paper stuck on the bulletin board with my name highlighted on it. I quickly took it down, unfolded it and began to read. It was a handwritten note from Matthew that, I'm sure, he meant for me to find that evening when I was to conduct the church service.

"Hi Walter," the note read. "It looks like today will be my last day in camp. I wasn't sure if I would see you today or not, so I thought I would write you this note. So much has happened to me over these last few months, but especially in these last three days. I cannot even begin to explain it here on paper. I was hoping we would get a chance to talk, but it looks like that might not happen. I just wanted to thank you for being a friend to me over these last couple of months. I never dreamed my life could be so radically changed in such a short period of time. I also wanted to tell you that I met Sam the other day, and since then my world has been turned upside down. I can't explain it, and don't understand it yet, but I have hope, and a peace that has changed me from the inside out.

Right now there are only two things in my life that I know for sure. The first one is that I have picked up the sword that Sam offered me, and the second is that I will never be on the run from my father again. I will accept my destiny no matter where it takes me or what price I may have to pay in order to follow it. I am happy, I am content, and I know I am doing the right thing. I'm not sure exactly what our futures hold, but I want us to remain friends. Say hi to Sam for me if you see him. It was amazing to be able to meet him.

Goodbye, Walter. Let's try and stay in touch.

Matthew."

When I finished reading the note that Matthew had left, two things stood out that gave me pause. Something profound had happened to Matthew in his encounter with Sam, and by what he had said in his note, it sounded like this really might be his last day in camp. He was going to face his father once and for all, and it sounded like today would be that day.

As I carefully folded the note, and put it in my pocket, I quickly got back in the truck and headed for the laydown. It was now my turn to do a task I really did not want to do. Maybe I would meet Matt's father before he did.

After calling me, David was whisked away to one of Israel's secure locations that housed the technology for the Soluble Anatomy Monitoring program. He would be given a crash course on how the program operated. It was still in its experimental stages, but all the tests had proven positive up to this point. David would also be in charge of the reconnaissance mission, if it ever got to the point of extracting Matthew.

David did not relish the idea of going back into Iran, but he would happily do so, if it meant getting Matthew out and exposing the plans of Donald King. All the events of the last few days had put David in a position of being in the center of an ongoing, national security event. So, with the affirmation of the Israeli Prime Minister, and the Minister of Defence, David was promoted in rank and given a security clearance that gave him access to many of the country's national and international programs.

David wasn't sure if he wanted this promotion, but it would come in handy if he ever needed high level intelligence to help get his friend Matthew out.

As I got back to the tram laydown, Kevin and Rob were already there going through the trams and making sure everything was in order. A security team that Donald had sent ahead, was also going through the tram cars with some kind of electronic equipment. The security team was there to make sure everything was safe and would go according to protocol with the tram and also with the driver. They asked me several questions and even gave me a 'pat down' before they let me into my tractor. All of this attention did not help my case of nerves as I could literally feel my heart beating inside of my chest.

When I was about to leave, Kevin and Rob came up to my tractor with smirks on their faces. "Well this is it," Kevin said "Your big day has finally arrived" as both of them tried to hide their amusement.

"Thanks guys. I'd trade a day's pay if either one of you got up here and did this tour for me."

Rob laughed and said "Why are you so worried? You've got a four hundred pound angel sitting up there in front of you, and I don't think he would trust us driving your tram!"

I laughed with them as I put my tractor in gear and headed out towards the ball diamond. Although what Rob had said was funny, it also dawned on me that it was very true. I did have Sam riding with me, even though I couldn't see him.

With that positive thought in mind, I manoeuvred my tram through the plant as I had done thousands of times. Even though I had full confidence in my driving skills, somehow today everything felt different. Today I would be driving a tour for one the most evil and powerful men in the world, and that gave me an almost sick feeling in the pit of my stomach.

When I had pulled my tram up to the side of the ball diamond, I noticed a fairly large crowd had already gathered. It was cold and crisp outside, but no one seemed to mind the wait. We had seven minutes before the scheduled landing time arrived, but as I looked into the distant skies, I noticed a small black dot that was growing larger in size with every moment.

242

CHAPTER THIRTY-SEVEN

IT HAS NOW BEGUN

The crowd looked at the helicopter that was hovering above the ball diamond. Since my eyes were also glued to the helicopter, I failed to notice the person who was standing beside the door of my tractor. When the helicopter touched down, and the engine's R.P.M.s started to abate, I heard a knocking on my tram door.

"Matthew!" I shouted as I reached for the handle and swung my door open. "I can hardly believe it's you! I've been looking for you everywhere for the last three days!"

"It's a long story" Matthew responded, "but it sure is good to see you Walter."

He stepped up the ladder and I sensed a real peace surrounding him. Even his facial features seemed to be relaxed and unusually calm.

"I'd love to hear your story Matt, but right now I have some very important things to tell you that just cannot wait."

After a quick explanation of the phone call that I had received from David, I told him of the request of the Israeli government wanting him to drink the Soluble Anatomy Monitoring solution. After hearing what I had to say, and holding the bottled solution in his hand, he quietly said, "I'm not sure if I want to do this."

"It's up to you, Matt," I said, "nobody is going to force you to take it, and I can't tell you what the right thing to do is either."

"I wish Sam were here to ask." Matthew said. "I can't wait to tell you about my encounter with Sam. It was absolutely amazing!"

Simultaneously, we both turned towards the helicopter, and noticed that the official welcome was almost over, and the group of Apollyon Global executives were looking longingly to get out of the cold and into a nice warm tram.

At the head of the delegation stood Donald King, who was now shaking hands with the representatives of the oil company. Our time for talking was running out.

"I guess it's almost time for me to go." Matthew said as he looked towards the group of people that were slowly making their way towards the tram. "Walter," Matt continued, "what did you say was the name of the program of this solution that I'm supposed to drink?"

"It's called Soluble Anatomy Monitoring, and it is the newest innovation to track people anywhere in the world without detection."

"And what is the acronym for it?" Matthew asked, with a smile on his face.

"Well let's see," I responded, "I guess it would be SAM!" I said as the light went on and a smile also crossed my face.

"Well then, here's to Sam!" Matthew said, as he lifted the bottle and drank down every last drop.

Just as Matthew disappeared into the crowd, I could feel the movement of people boarding my tram and sitting down in their seats. This was it, the moment I had dreaded, had now begun.

When my tram pulled away from the ball diamond, people were still waving and trying to catch the last glimpse of Donald King and his entourage. My route and its stops had all been predetermined, so it was just a simple matter of driving and stopping when required. The group had official tour guides who would give them the details of what they would be seeing.

During the halfway point of the tour, the schedule stated that the group would exit the trams and walk through one of the cogeneration facilities. As that was now in the process of taking place, I noticed that Donald King did not get off the tram with the rest of the group. As the tram stood stationary on the side of the road, I watched one of the tram doors open and Donald King start to make his way towards my tractor.

Instantly my pulse and heart rate skyrocketed as he began to climb the ladder of my tractor, and motion for me open the door. There I was, trapped in my own tractor, looking into the face of the man who would one day soon rule the world.

"Well, well, well." He said to me as his cold black eyes seemed to penetrate my very soul. "I was right about you and your pet that you have sitting up there on your gen-set box. I have seen both of you in my dreams and visions and I don't like what I saw. You are my enemy and I would kill you right now, but that would be a little messy, and I do need someone to drive us back to the helicopter.

I've seen that you also know my son and have been trying to influence him against me. You have no idea what you've gotten yourself into by listening to your pet. You should never listen to your animals, they will always give you bad advice. And as for my son Matthew, he is now mine, for he is the son of my blood. I am his father, and the same things that I do, he will do also. Make no mistake about it, your little angel games will only get you killed and nothing can change the destiny that Matthew has before him."

I sat motionless in the tram with my eyes wide open. I felt the literal presence of evil filling the entire tractor cab. I felt like I was suffocating even with the door wide open. What was happening to me? How was all of this possible? Just as I thought I was going to pass out, the group started to make their way back from the cogeneration facility and into the trams.

With a twisted grin, and a mocking voice, Donald looked me directly in the eyes and said "I have a special parting gift for you. Something that you can remember me by. Here it is!"

He pointed his finger directly into my face. "I now curse you!" he said "Cursed be the very skin on your bones!"

With his words came a wind that blew directly into the tractor cab and made me feel nauseous from the inside out. But as Donald climbed down the ladder and found his way out, the evil presence that he carried seemed to follow him out of my tractor. Almost instantly I was feeling better as I put my tractor in gear and somehow managed to get through the rest of the tram tour.

I could hardly wait to get this group of people out of my trams once and for all. I had never dreamed or even imagined that anything like this could ever happen to me. I was visibly shaken by the experience and still was not feeling one hundred percent.

As I watched the group of Apollyon Global people make their way back to the helicopter, I noticed a familiar face standing among the group of men that had searched me and my tram. There stood Matthew! His father Donald walked up to him, gave him a hug and then escorted him into the waiting helicopter.

I watched the helicopter take off and disappear into the horizon, and I said a quick prayer for Matthew.

I then remembered the words that Sam had spoken to both Matthew and myself, "It has now begun." Sam had said.

Proof

Made in the USA
Charleston, SC
10 November 2015